Ember

Death Collectors

JESSICA SORENSEN

For information:

http://jessicasorensensblog.blogspot.com/

Cover Design: Mae I Design

http://www.maeidesign.com/

Cover Model: Maria Amanda Shaub

Photographer: Mike Thomassen

Ember — Book 1

ISBN 9781939045003

Once a blooming red rose, full of streaming life in its veins

Now a wilting black petal rupturing with death and pain

—Ember

Prologue

"Emmy, can you hand me that Allen wrench?" My dad sticks his hand out from beneath the Challenger.

I push the jar of screws and coins out of the way and grab the wrench out of the toolbox. I skip around the fender lying on the ground, and set it in my dad's hand. "Is it fixed yet?"

His legs wiggle as he scoots further under the car. "Patience, Emmy. These things take time."

"Like how long? An hour?" I ask impatiently. "Dad, I want you to drive it really fast. And I want to be in there too."

My dad laughs. "Alright, we can do that."

"You promise?" I say. "You cross your heart?"

He laughs again and drops the wrench onto the concrete. "Yeah, cross my heart and hoped to die."

My eyes wander to the corner of the garage as I return to the jars of screws and coins. I pluck out the pennies one by one and arrange them in groups on the concrete. The metal clinks with each coin dropped. I hum along with the song on the radio, a song about death and the acceptance of it. I wonder if it might be talking about my friend in the corner of the garage, the one who always watches and follows me wherever I go. He wears a funny cape like a superhero only there's a hood over his head. His face is always hidden, but I bet his skin is made of rainbows and light.

He breathes a warning about the coins and the map I'm supposed to be creating. "Didn't I do it right?" I poke at a penny. "It looks right to me."

My dad sticks his head out from under the car. Grease stains his face and there's a layer of metal shavings in his black hair. "Emmy, who are you talking to?"

I hum along with the song playing from the car stereo. "No one," I lie, because I'm not allowed to talk about my imaginary friend with anyone—those are his rules. I even crossed my heart and hope to die, stick a needle in my eye. And the last thing I want to do is stick a needle in my eye.

My dad shoves out from under the car and wipes his greasy hands on the front of his torn jeans. "Hey, Emmy, you wanna go get something to eat?" He peers over my shoulder at the map of the cemetery I've created.

Each coin represents were a body is buried. "Playing a game," I reply.

His breath hitches. "Stop that!" He scatters the pieces with his boot and picks me up in his arms. He grips me forcefully as he carries me to the trunk of the car and sits me down with my legs dangling over the edge.

"Who told you to do that with the coins?" The anger in his eyes is frightening.

"I don't know." I try to squirm from my dad's arms. "Daddy, you're hurting me."

His eyes enlarge as he glances at his hands, like he didn't realize he was holding my arms. "Emmy, this is really important." He loosens his grip. "Who told you to do that?"

My eyes stray to my friend in the corner. "I'm not supposed to tell you."

"Ember Rose Edwards." He only uses my full name when he means business. "You tell me right now or else I won't let you ride in the car with me. Do you understand?"

I cross my arms. "Fine. My imaginary friend told me to do it."

My friend glares at me and I'm scared he's going to leave me. *Please don't leave me. Please don't leave me.*

My dad follows my line of gaze and a spark of his death surfaces through his touch—*darkness*. I shiver as he turns back to me with a stern look on his face.

"Emmy, you need to ignore him, okay?" he says, his grey eyes softening. "You can't have imaginary friends—

people will think you're crazy. And we can't have people thinking that."

"But I don't want him to go away."

"Well, he has to. It's time for him to go away. Do you understand? No imaginary friends. *Ever*."

"Fine... go away, friend." Tears sting the corners of my eyes as my friend dissipates into air. "It's not fair."

"Life isn't fair," my dad says as he helps me down off the trunk. "And the sooner you realize that, the easier life will be."

I sulk back over to the jar and begin picking up the mess, chucking the pennies and screws into it.

"And Emmy." My dad scoots back under the car. "If he ever comes back, you need to tell him to go away."

"Alright." I frown, dropping pennies into the jar. Once my dad is under the car, I dare a peek at the empty corner, secretly hoping my friend will be back. But he's not and my heart aches. He's the only person I've ever met who understands death like I do.

Chapter 1

Nine years later.....

I love the cemetery. It's quiet and peaceful—it's the only place where I get a break from death. I loathe crowded places, crammed with voices and life. It hurts to be around life. People don't understand how close death is, right over their shoulders, around the block, at the end of a street. It's everywhere. And I'm the only one who knows where it's hiding. I see death every day. But a cemetery is already dead.

The moon beams vibrantly tonight; it's only a sliver away from being full. Dry leaves fall from the oak tree and the air smells crisp with autumn. Headstones entomb the ground and a light mist dews the grass. I lean against a tree trunk with my notebook propped open on my knee and a pen in my hand. I scribble words that are important to me.

The cemetery is my sense of comfort, my sanctuary in a world of darkness, the one piece of light I have in my life.

I remove the tip of the pen from the page and read over my words. I sound obsessed with death, like Edgar Allan Poe or Emily Dickinson. But death is a huge part of who I am. With a simple touch I know when someone will die. Whether they'll go painfully. If their life will be stolen.

I set the notebook on the grass and tuck the pen inside the spine. I pull my hood over my head, cross my arms, and stare out at the desolate street. One of the streetlights flickers and a dog barks from behind the front gate of a redbrick home. It's late. I glance at my watch. *Really* late. I grab my notebook and start across the cemetery. The ground is damp and my clunky, black boots sink in the dirt. I eye the headstones; big, small, intricate, plain. I wonder if the details of a headstone define the life of the person resting beneath it. If it's big and fancy, does it mean they were loved by many? Or were they lonely, but had money? Do small and plain ones declare that they lived a lonely life? Or were they just not materialistic?

I'm probably the only one crazy enough to be walking around thinking these thoughts.

The wind howls like a dust storm. Leaves whirlwind around my head. I tuck my chin down, fighting through the dust toward the front gate. Pieces of my black hair curtain my pale face and grey eyes, and stick against my plump lips. My clunky boot catches on the corner of a grave and I face-plant onto the grass. My notebook flies from my hand and my head smacks the corner of a headstone.

"Ow," I mumble, clutching my head. I smear dirt off my cheek. My gaze travels upward to a statuesque carving of a hooded figure. Its head is tucked down and in its hand is a scythe.

"The Grim Reaper, huh?" I rise to my feet, stretching out my long legs, and tilt my head up. "I bet you know what it's like, don't you? To be surrounded by death all the time? I bet you understand me."

The wind violently picks up and carries my notebook away. Shielding my eyes from the dust, I chase after it. It dances through the leaves and glides across the grass, finally resting against a soaring angelic statue in the crook of the cemetery. I hurry after it. A black raven swoops down from one of the trees and circles in front of me.

"Why are you always following me?" I whisper to the raven. "Is it because you know what I am—a symbol of death like you?"

"Damn it, I am so sick and tired of doing all your dirty work. It's such crap." A voice cuts through the cemetery.

I hastily take cover behind the angel statue and the raven perches on the head, ruffling its wings. No one hangs out in cemeteries late at night, except for weirdos and people like me. (And as far as I know, I'm the only girl of my kind.)

A shovel cuts into the dirt. "I'm always the one who's gotta dig these things up."

I peek through the cracks between the angel's wings. A thin guy, with frail arms and a pointy nose, stands in a hole, shoveling dirt. My journal is inches from the discarded dirt pile. One more scoop and my life thoughts will be buried.

"If I were you, Gregory, I'd watch my tone." A tall figure hops from the roof of a small marble mausoleum. His hair is as pale as the moon and his eyes are like ash. His long legs stretch as he strides toward the hole. "I can easily find someone else to dig up the grave."

Gregory mutters under his breath and scoops up a shovel full of dirt.

The taller one cups his ear. "What's that? Speak up, I can't hear you."

"Nothing," Gregory mumbles and continues digging.

The other guy's smile catches in the moonlight. His face is beautiful, but burdened with sadness, as if he carries the world's sorrows on his shoulders. I long to reach out and trace my fingers along his lips, his jawline, and erase his pain.

The pages of my journal flutter in the breeze and he picks it up. I cringe with embarrassment, but then realize that he's a guy who hangs out in a cemetery, digging up graves, so my penned words of death shouldn't bother him. He flips through the pages and then pauses on one. He studies the page, and then his eyes skim the cemetery. I crouch down and hold my breath. Silence blankets the night, except for the shovel scratching the dirt.

"Where'd this come from?" he asks Gregory.

I peek through the feet of the angel statue.

Gregory takes the notebook and turns it over. "I'm not sure…" He hands it back. "It says Ember Rose Edwards on the back."

The tall figure runs his long fingers along my name. "Ember…" His haunting voice envelops me and beckons me to move out from behind the statue. I start to step out.

"Hold it right there." A light shines over my shoulders.

I tense and the shovel stops cutting into the dirt. The night grows quiet, filled with only the hoot of an owl.

"Now slowly turn around," a deep voice instructs. Static cuts through a stereo. "I'm with the suspect now."

Damn it. They're going to think I was digging up the grave. This is not my first time getting into trouble, so they won't go easy on me.

"I said slowly turn around and keep your hands where I can see them," the cop orders.

I shut my eyes and slowly elevate my hands to my sides.

"Good, now turn around slowly," he says.

I sprint off across the graveyard.

"She's on the move," he yells and the speaker statics.

My clunky boots rip against the grass as I hop and maneuver around the gravestones. The cop pursues me, his footsteps loud and the keys on his belt jingling. I speed up as the brick fence pierces my view. Springing onto my toes, I leap for the top. My stomach slams against the edge and I quickly pull my legs up. The cop grabs my boot and yanks on my leg.

"Don't even think about it, you little punk." He starts to haul me back to the ground by the leg.

I wiggle my foot, trying to slip it out of my boot. His hands move higher up my leg, just below my knee. My fingertips scrape the brick as they dig down to hold onto the edge.

The cop's fingers wrap around my other leg. "Just let—"

The cop abruptly releases my legs. My knee crashes into the fence. I scramble to the top and glance behind me. The cop lies unconscious on the grass. The tall, dark stranger stands over him, watching me. The dusky shadows of the trees dance across his face and his untamed eyes smolder like cinders.

"Ember." His ghostly voice encircles around me like smoke.

I inch forward until the tips of my boots align with the ledge of the fence and my hand powerlessly reaches for him. I can't fight the urge to be near him—I'm hypnotized by his beauty and the haunting sound of his voice.

"Come here," he purrs softly, extending his arms for me.

My other hand rises to my side and I bend my knees, beginning to jump off the ledge, desperate to touch him.

"Don't move." Sirens screech from the gate and red and blue lights flash across the cemetery. I flinch and quickly crouch down. A police car slams to a dirt-grinding stop on the other side of the cemetery. Two cops barrel out of it and dash through the gate, hollering over their radios. I glance down. The tall stranger is gone, but a single black raven feather floats in the air. I catch it and my gaze sweeps the cemetery possessed with shadows and dark corners. The cop on the ground stirs and I spin around, leap onto the sidewalk, and sprint down the street toward my home, never looking back.

Chapter 2

"Wakey, wakey, sleeping beauty." My best friend Raven singsongs as she fluffs my hair.

"I am not a dog, you crazy woman," I mutter, still half asleep. "Now leave me alone."

She blows in my ear, careful not to touch me with her death omen, even though I've seen it before. "Ember, come on. Wake up."

"You are such a weirdo," I murmur sleepily.

"*I'm* the weirdo," she teases. "You're the one who sees death."

I roll my eyes open to the brightness of the sunlight spilling through my room. "Way to tell the world."

Her sapphire eyes glimmer against her glittery pink eye shadow as she gestures at my black and red walls, sketched with mythical drawings and depressing poetry. A thin black curtain veils the closet doorway with photos of dead poets and authors tacked along the frame.

Raven hops off my bed and runs her fingers along a penciled drawing of a female angel with black-feathered wings spanning across the wall. The angel's black dress flows to the floor and her eyes are shut. There is despair in the way she carries her head and how her arms curl around herself.

"Do you remember when I drew this for you?" Raven asks.

I climb out of bed and rummage through the dresser drawer for some clothes. The feather from last night sits on my dresser, ruffled and bent in the middle. "Yeah, what were we… like thirteen or something. It was right after I moved back and accidentally told you I could see death."

"I thought it would protect you from death." She laughs bitterly. "I was too little to realize that nothing can save you from it, not even an angel."

Painted on the opposite wall is a bone-faced creature in a long black cloak, holding an hourglass in its emaciated hand. A raven shedding its wings is suspended on the shoulder.

"You know he swears it's not a Grim Reaper." Raven observes the drawing closely. "But it sure as hell looks like one. If I didn't know better I'd swear your brother put it there on purpose, because he knows about your little death thing and wants to drive you mad."

"He doesn't know about it," I remind her. "No one does but you."

She squints up at the Reaper's hand. "And what's with the hourglass?"

I shrug. "It's one of the symbols of the Reaper, like, 'your time is in my hands.'"

She traces the hourglass with her finger. "Well, your brother could have at least put sand in it then, so it wasn't like your time had expired."

"I'm sure he wasn't thinking that far into it," I assure her. "Besides, he only did it to impress you. He wanted to show you that you two share an artistic side."

She chews on her bottom lip. "You know I would never date him, right? I've had one too many manic depressives in my life." She pulls a guilty face. "Sorry, Em. I didn't mean it to come out like that."

"It's okay. I know my brother has problems. And I know you've been through too much to want to deal with it." I pause. "How's your mom doing?"

She shrugs, staring at the drawing. "Fine, I guess. I haven't gone to visit her in a while."

Raven's mom is in a drug treatment facility. She suffers from depression and self-medicates. Her illness has been going on for years. A couple of months ago, Raven came home from school and found her mom on the living room floor with a lit cigarette in her hand. She wasn't breathing and barely registered a pulse. Raven called an ambulance and the paramedics resuscitated her. Raven chewed me out for not telling her it was coming. I realized that day that there were many negatives to my gift. I didn't tell Raven her mom was going to die, because I knew she wasn't going to die that day. I refuse to tell Raven when anyone in her family will die—including herself—because no one needs that burden on their shoulders.

Raven was mad at me for two weeks and wouldn't talk to me at school. It was the loneliest two weeks of my life. Raven is my one and only friend. When I get older, I'll probably end up a spinster with ten cats and maybe a bird. Raven will pay me visits every so often with her children and make sure I stay sane.

"What is that?" She stands on her tiptoes, leaning in my face. With her pink fingernail, she chips away a flake of mud off my cheek. "Why do you have dirt on your face?" She turns my hand. "And your fingers are rubbed raw."

I pull my hand away. "Last night, while I was in the cemetery—"

"I thought you stopped going there so much," she interrupts with disapproval written all over her face. Raven has

never understood my need to be alone—my need for the quiet.

I grab a purple and black T-shirt with torn sides and a pair of black jeans out of the dresser. "I haven't been sleeping very well and it's relaxing, being there."

She twists a strand of her shoulder-length, bubblegum pink hair around her finger. "I don't understand you sometimes. I told you to come to my house whenever you want. You don't need to go hang out in a graveyard—it's creepy."

I don't have the heart to tell her that her house is one of the worst places, chock full of death, even after her mother went away. Her brother, Todd, has an early death. He will get lung cancer from the two packs of cigarettes a day he's been smoking since he was thirteen.

"The cops busted me," I admit, knowing she'll find it humorous.

Her lips quirk. "Oh yeah, did you run?"

I nodded. "Yup. Really, really fast."

Her smile broadens. "Did they chase you?"

I nod again. "I'm pretty sure he stumbled and landed on his face, too," I exaggerate, knowing she'll love it— Raven's all about the drama.

A laugh sputters from her lips. "Okay, I'm kind of jealous. I wish I could have been there to see it."

"It was pretty funny," I admit. "Except for…"

"Except for what?" She presses. "Come on, Em, tell me please. Don't do your secret-keeping thing."

I sink down on the bed and ball the clothes up on my lap. "There were these guys there, digging up a grave."

Her forehead scrunches and she sits down beside me. "Ew, like grave robbers?"

"I'm not sure what they were doing, but it was kind of creepy."

"Did they take anything from the grave?"

"I have no idea. I was too busy running from the cops…" It dawns on me. "Shit. I think one of the grave robber guys might have my notebook."

"The one you're always writing your deepest darkest secrets in?" she asks.

I nod. "And it has my name on it."

Tapping her finger on her chin, she muses over something. "Was he hot?"

I fiddle with a loose string on my pajama pants. "Are you seriously asking if the grave robber was hot?"

"Grave robbers are people too," she says with attitude. "And just because they like to dig up graves, doesn't mean they can't be hot.'"

Hot? More like intense and frightening. Shaking my head, I stand up. "You are a weirdo. I'm going to go get dressed."

She eyeballs me with suspicion. "Quit trying to change the subject, Emmy."

I head for the closet. "You know I hate it when you call me that." It's the nickname my dad gave me and I hate being reminded of him.

"You know you always do this," she calls out. "You always run away from guys. If you keep it up, you're going to end up a lonely old spinster."

"Which is just what I want." I pause at the curtain. "I'm going to go out on a limb here and guess we're going to a party."

Her mood suddenly lifts and she grins impishly. "What gave it away?"

I eye her outfit and count down on my fingers. "Four things: leather shorts, pink high heels, knee high socks, and a sparkling top."

She sticks out her hip and pops up her foot, striking a pose. "Come on, admit it, I look hot."

"You look like a—"

She tosses a pillow at me. "Watch that dirty mouth of yours, Death Girl."

Laughing, I duck through the curtain into my closet. Immediately, my lips sink to a frown. Parties equal lots of people. And lots of people mean lots of death omens. But I have to go with Raven to protect her from herself because she tends to get reckless.

"So whose party are we going to tonight?" I slip my plaid pajama bottoms off and tug on my jeans.

"Remy's," Raven replies, and I can hear her delving through my jewelry drawer.

Pulling a face, I slip on my shirt. "Doesn't she live all the way up by the lake?"

She pokes her head inside the closet. "Don't be such a party pooper. Just for once can't you let loose and have some fun?" She moves back as I step into my room.

"I'm not being a party pooper." I collect my car keys from the dresser, clip on my maroon pendant necklace, and set the feather in the jewelry drawer. "I just hate driving my car all the way up there. It gets such crappy gas mileage. And there's just so many people at Remy's parties."

She pouts out her lip and bats her eyelashes at me. "Pretty please, Em. Just for once can't we go have fun like two normal teenage girls?"

I force a smile. "We always go to parties."

She pokes my arm playfully. "But you never have fun, so just for the night, can't you try?"

I sigh and nod. "All right, I'll try. But it's kind of hard to have fun when people look at you like you might kill them."

"No one still blames you for your dad's death. The cops even said there was no way it could be you—that's why they dropped the charges."

"Actually, they didn't say that. They just didn't have enough evidence to push the investigation further."

"Yeah, but no one thinks you really killed him," she reassures me.

"Everyone in this town does," I disagree. "They think that's why I disappeared for a week—that I was on the run from the cops."

"Well, maybe if you'd tell someone where you were…" She waits, but my lips stayed sealed—and they will stay sealed until the day I die. She rolls her eyes and crooks her pinkie finger in front of her. "No one thinks you're a killer. Now swear on it that you'll have fun."

"Fine," I grimace and hook my pinkie to hers. "I swear I'll try to have fun."

She tightens her pinkie. "Not try—will."

"I promise I will have fun," I sulk.

She jumps up and down, clapping her hands excitedly. I fasten my studded bracelet to my wrist and we head out the door.

"And remember what happens if you go back on your word," she says, skipping down the stairs.

"Yeah, yeah, the bad karma will catch up with me," I say, lacing my boot up as I hop down the last step. Raven is very big on karma. But karma has had me by the throat since I was four when I accidently took my grandmother's life.

"Dude, why do you look like you're about to commit murder?" My brother, Ian, leans against the kitchen doorway, singeing a stray thread on his hoodie with a lighter. His scraggily brown hair is hidden beneath a grey beanie and, as usual, he has paint all over his hands.

I shake my head and steal the lighter from his hands. "Why do you insist on being such a pyro?"

He lunges for the lighter, but I dodge around him and dash into the kitchen where the carpet switches to tile. I smash the lighter against the floor.

"What the heck is wrong with you?" Ian shouts, picking up the broken pieces.

Ian is nineteen, two years older than me. But more often than not, people think he's the younger one. Ian is the same height as me—five-foot-eight—and he's kind of scrawny. At sixteen, he declared himself a struggling artist, which meant he would forever live here, raiding the refrigerator and hanging out in the attic—his "studio."

He snatches hold of my hand. "Why do you have to be such a bitch sometimes?"

I tense. *Fire everywhere, the roof of our house roaring in flames. Ian lies on the floor, dying—he wants to be there.* I jerk away and inhale sharply through my nose. I've seen his death before, and each time is equally as painful. In a beautiful world full of roses and sunshine, I would be able to change his self-inflicting death. But as far as I know, death omens are irrevocable. Death is as permanent as the ink that stains the pages of my journal.

He rubs the black and yellow paint off his cheeks. "Look Em, I'm sorry, okay." He glances at Raven, worried about her reaction. "I just haven't been sleeping that great lately."

"It's okay. And I'm sorry I broke your lighter." I pick up the rest of the pieces of the lighter and toss them into the trash. "Are you taking your medication still?"

He rubs the back of his neck tensely. "I am, but I'm not sure I need to anymore. It's been two years since Alyssa… And I'm feeling pretty good these days."

The fact that he can't talk about her death proves he's not ready to get off his medication. Ian never forgave himself for the disappearance of Alyssa, his high school girlfriend, which ultimately led to her body being discovered in the lake.

After her body was found, Ian spent his entire senior year drunk and stoned. He even tried to kill himself once. He denies it to this day, saying he accidentally swallowed too many pills, but I know the truth—I read his goodbye note.

When I discovered him on the bathroom floor, unconscious and barely breathing, I knew he wasn't going to die, but it stilled scared the shit out of me. He loved Alyssa so much and the guilt of her loss consumes his life and poisons his head with dark thoughts he may never get rid of.

His arms open for a hug, but I evade around him. "Raven and I are headed out. Let mom know I'll be home late… if she shows up."

He goes to the cupboard and takes out a box of cereal. "Even if she comes home, she'll be too drunk to notice."

"I know." I collect the dirty dishes off the table and put them in the sink. "But I thought I'd let you know just in case by some small miracle she comes home sober and notices I'm not here."

He waves at us as we head for the front door. "Yeah, yeah, will do."

Raven blows him a flirty kiss. "Thanks, Hun."

Ian raises his eyebrows questioningly. "Hun?"

I jerk the door open. "I thought you said you would never go out with him?"

She shrugs and whisks out the front door. "I won't, but I never said I wouldn't flirt with him."

I wave goodbye to Ian. "See you later and if you need anything, call me."

"Oh yeah, I almost forgot." He backs into the kitchen and, seconds later, returns with my journal. "This was on the front porch this morning."

Astonished, I take my journal, brushing the dirt off the black leather cover. "Do you know how it got there?"

"I thought you dropped it or something." He shrugs. "I didn't see anyone come in this morning, except for you."

I swallow hard and flip through the pages. It looks normal, except for the last page.

Blinded by the opaque veil of mortality, her eyes are always sealed, like a tomb

She wants to know—wants to feel that fire, the brightness of the moon

So she searches for light, only to realize it's in her, like an ember equipped to ignite.

The handwriting is flawless, as if each curve of the pen meant something. I touch the page delicately like it's something precious.

Raven peeks over my shoulder. "I thought you lost that?"

"I guess I was wrong." I shut the journal. "Wait for me in the car?"

She nods, but shimmies toward Ian. "So I have a beef to pick with you."

I leave them to their flirting, go upstairs to my room, and stare at the poem. It's beautiful, but who wrote it? The guy from the cemetery? I tear the page out and tack it up beside my bed. I read over the words again before heading out the door.

Will I ever see the mysterious stranger again? And what will happen if I do?

Chapter 3

Raven and I have been best friends since we were in diapers. Our parents were friends in high school and they moved next door to each other after they married. Our moms were pregnant together—twice—and our dads worked at the local auto shop. It was the picture perfect scene, until two years after Raven and I were born. Then the perfection withered like a famished rose.

My parents started fighting a lot. At first it wasn't bad, but then it started happening every night. My mom said my dad didn't want to spend time with us—that he was too caught up in his job and hanging out at the bar. And she was right—my dad was drunk all the time. Finally, he moved out and Ian and I barely saw him.

Raven's dad bailed on her family a few years later. Just up and left. *Poof.* Not too long after, our moms developed drug habits. And our brothers live in their own world. Actually, Raven's brother Todd isn't too bad, just a little unconventional. But I don't know what I'd do if I lost Raven. She's my stability.

Remy's party is more lively than usual. A mob of teenagers are jam-packed in the tiny living room, swaying to "(Don't Fear) The Reaper" by Blue Oyster Cult. Beer bottles and cigarette butts litter the hardwood floor and the air reeks of sweat and beer. Death is everywhere.

I hang out in the emptiest corner of the house, near the stairway. By accident, I ran into three people and their death omens still tint my skin like small bruises. Sipping my punch and watching people dance, my thoughts keep drifting to the guy from the graveyard. What is he doing right now? In my head, he's sitting in his Victorian home, scribbling beautiful words in his notebook. His house is secluded from the world by a dark forest, constantly haunted by fog. I'm sure this isn't accurate, but that's the beauty of an imagination.

"Ember!" Raven shouts over the music. She dances through the crowd, her bubblegum pink wig popping out in the sea of bodies. Sweat trickles down her skin. "What are you doing? You promised to have fun." She points an accusing finger at me and blinks her blurry eyes. "In fact you swore on it."

I take the plastic cup from her hand. "I know and I'm trying, I promise." I swish the drink around and the stench of Jack is intoxicating. "No more drinks, okay?"

She pouts out her bottom lip. "Come on, Em. You promised."

I fake an excited dance move. "I'm having a blast, I swear. Now go. Dance. Have some fun for the both of us."

Annoyance burns in her eyes. "Are you just being a pain because you're here, or is your little death thing putting you in a bad mood?"

My gaze swiftly sweeps the room and I hiss, "Lower your voice. Someone might hear you."

She waves her hands animatedly. She's completely wasted and her split personality is coming out. "Oh, big news over here! Little Emmy can see death! Does anyone care?!"

I pour her drink into the garbage can. "No more drinks for you."

She snarls, about to spit foul words. But a lanky guy, sporting dark jeans and a black T-shirt, interrupts us. "Death is everywhere, my friends. And it will all eventually catch up to us, so what's the point of running from it. Instead, we should live life to the fullest." His green eyes are outlined with black eyeliner and crossbones tattoo his wrists. He drapes his arm around Raven's shoulder and drunkenly staggers forward, inadvertently bumping his knee into mine.

A heavy mass takes over my body. *Black water. Trees. Rain pouring down from the dark sky. Glass everywhere.*

Blood... they can't breathe... they can't breathe! Feathers fall to the ground. I gasp, nearly choking on how much it resembles my father's crime scene where his car was found.

"Does that scare you?" His eyes scrutinize me, noting the gothic tone of my clothes. "By the looks of you, I wouldn't think it would. But hey, maybe you're just a pos- er."

"You know, you shouldn't judge people by their looks." I let my hair screen my face and I close my eyes. I don't want to look at him. His life is approaching the end, the last rose petal about to wilt from the fading stem. I tuck my hair behind my ear and sigh. "You got a 'DD'?"

"What the hell's a 'DD'?" he slurs, stumbling, and spills his drink on the floor.

I rub the sides of my temples. *Idiot.* "Do everyone, in- cluding yourself, a favor and don't drive home tonight. Okay?"

The guy lets out a sardonic laugh. "What is that, like an omen or something?" He holds up his hands. "Ooo, scary..." He pauses and the recollection clicks. "Hey, wait a minute. Aren't you that girl who killed her dad?"

I swallow hard. "No, I think you're thinking of someone else."

His glazed over eyes squint at my face. "No, I'm pretty sure it was you. Didn't you like, call the police and confess, then like run..." He blunders over his feet and grabs my arm for support. Again, I'm blasted with the burden of his impending death. "Wait... what was I saying again?"

I slip my arm free and scoot back from the drunken idiot. "You were saying that you need to quit drinking."

"Are you feeling okay, Em?" Raven asks, her voice laced with concern. "You look a little pale."

"I always look pale," I say. "And I have a *headache*." Our code for *I'm having a death episode*.

"Oh, I get it." She coils a strand of her hair around her finger and flutters her eyelashes as she conjures up a plan. "Oh! Okay, I got it."

Goth boy looks back and forth between us. "Got what? Wait a minute? Are you two fighting over little old me?" He grins and I roll my eyes. "Don't worry, ladies, there's plenty of Laden love to go around."

Raven's hand falls from Laden's chest and she pulls a face, no longer interested in him. But she puts on her game face. "Hey, why don't you and I go dance." She laces her fingers with his, and leans in to give me a quick kiss on the cheek and I wince. "I'm sorry for acting crazy." She sways her hips as she leads Laden toward the dance floor. Before she vanishes into the crowd, she peeks over her shoulder and mouths: I'll get his keys.

I lean against the wall, let my head fall back, and shut my eyes. "Breathe, Ember, breathe. You can't stop death— it's endless."

"God, it's like mating season in here," a deep male voice whispers.

The softness of his breath tickles my ear. I shudder and stumble forward, tripping over my feet, and stepping on the toe of his shoes. Actually, boots; black ones with little silver skulls on the buckles. I like his boots. My eyes slowly travel upward; dark jeans, a plaid shirt over a black T-shirt, and a skull necklace hooks around his neck. There's a sequence of leather bands on his wrists and a metal loop threads his eyebrow. His inky black hair dangles in his eyes and hangs shaggily down over his ears.

His slate grey eyes tantalize my skin as he takes me in. "Sorry, I didn't mean to frighten you."

The sound of his voice causes soft vibrations over my skin. "Sorry about your shoes." I retreat backward, putting space between us. The last thing I want is to find out when this gorgeous guy dies. "Crowded rooms just make me a little uneasy."

He laughs softly and tosses his cup into the trash. "I know what you mean. All this," he motions at the people grinding against one another, "is an excuse for the opposite sex to rub up on one another."

"That's a pretty good observation." I almost smile.

He presses his lips together and leans over my shoulder. I stiffen, worried he'll touch me and this magical moment will end. But he's careful, leaving a sliver of space between his lips and my ear. "Take those two for instance. I think they've got their own mating ritual going on. Although, I think it might be a one-sided mating ritual."

I turn and follow his gaze. Raven is dancing with Laden. She has one hand on his hip and the other on his back pocket. Laden moves all over the place like he's trying to break dance and disco at the same time. Raven captures my gaze and rolls her eyes.

"I think you're right." I turn and meet the beautiful stranger's eyes. "It looks like she's bored."

He leans away. "Is she a friend of yours?"

"Her name's Raven." I wonder if he likes her. Most guys do, which has never bothered me. Raven's bold and flirty—everything I'm not.

"Like the poem?" He cocks his pierced eyebrow.

"You know Edgar Allan Poe?" I ask, not expecting much because *The Raven* is one of Edgar Allan Poe's more legendary poems.

"A little bit." He stares at me like he's trying to unravel a maze. "And what's your name?"

38

"Ember." I inch forward, holding my breath as a girl wobbles by, waving her finger, chewing out the air.

"Ember… I like it." He inches closer. "'And each separate dying ember wrought its ghost upon the floor,'" he quotes a line from Poe's The Raven.

"I thought you said you knew a little?" I ask, impressed.

He shrugs and stuffs his hands in his pockets. "What can I say? I'm fascinated with the idea… love, death, and the insanity it brings."

Growing uncomfortable with his mention of death, I scan the crowd for Raven. "Trust me, death isn't that fascinating." I'm slightly nervous I can't find Raven. I turn back to the mysterious stranger. "It was nice talking to you, but I need to…" I glance around. "Where did she go?" I check up the stairway and then browse the crowd. The top of Raven's pink head is bobbing up and down in the middle. A band is setting up their instruments at the front of the room—things are about to get hectic. Inhaling, I tuck in my shoulders and weave around the edge of the room, careful not to come into contact with anyone.

"Raven!" I holler over the music. The pink wig descends further into the crowd. I press my back against the wall and edge my way toward her.

Remy, a short girl with black hair and choppy bangs, stands up on a chair. "Alright guys! Are you ready?" She motions her heavily tattooed arms at the band. "Give it up for Breaking Up Mayhem!"

The guitarist flares at the guitar strings and the singer shouts. "Is everyone ready?!"

Okay, time to bail, before things get out of—

The band begins to play a raging song and everyone goes wild. The house rocks and bottles rattle against the hardwood floor. Elbows and shoulders smack into me. Death courses through my veins.

"I can't breathe." I rush toward the door. *Blood. Pain. The silence of a heart... the shadow of trees... the blackened lake. Bones breaking. Someone can't breathe. It hurts... there's so much blood. A last breath is strangled away. A red "X" stains it all. An empty hourglass. Murder.* My body twitches. I seek the faces of the people nearby, but I can't tell who the death omen belongs to. I trail my fingers along bodies. *Hospital bed. Old age. Broken heart. Sacrifice.* I can't endure it any longer. I knock people out of my way as I run for the front door.

"Hey, watch it!" someone shouts.

I burst through the door. Two guys are drinking beer on the front porch. I shove them out of the way, ignoring their death omens, and sprint across the trashed front yard. I stop in the middle of the lawn, panting and dripping with sweat. The moon is a bright orb, the stars cut the sky like diamonds, and the forest and mountains shield the illegal party.

I hunch over, brace my hands on my knees, and slow my breathing. "Get it together, Ember," I whisper to myself. "Death is death, in any shape or form. You can't stop it." I pull myself together and head back to the log cabin, ready to find Raven and tell her it's time to leave. Cars are lined bumper to bumper, blocking the driveway. A rusted black Cadillac drives slowly, the wheels half on the grass and half on the gravel. Through the tinted windows, a bubblegum haired girl winks her sapphire blue eye at me.

"Raven... What are you doing?" I wave at her and hurry toward the car. She knows better than to get into a car with some random guy, especially one I just had a death omen about. "Get out of the car!"

She blows me a kiss, and tips her head back laughing as the car speeds off, kicking up dirt and gravel.

"Damn it!" I chase the car down the driveway and into the trees, following it all the way to the highway, where it vanishes into the night. Out of breath, I stare down the desolate road and tug my fingers through my hair. "Shit." I pull out my cell phone. "No signal." I run back down the driveway to my car, a beat-up 1970s Dodge Challenger, wedged between a truck and a massive SUV. The car belonged to my dad. We were working on fixing it up, but then he disappeared. It's been three years since it happened, but it still hurts to think about him. Especially because I don't know if he's dead or alive.

I pat my pockets for the keys. "Where are my keys?" Trying not to panic, I retrace my steps as far as the front porch. "Come on. Come on. Where are they?"

"You lose somethin', sweetheart?" a guy with greasy hair and a thick neck says. He looks like a wannabe Danny Zuko, with his sideburns and leather jacket. Except he has this strange black "X" tattoo crossing his eye.

I back down the stairs. "Nope, I'm good."

He chugs the last of his drink, crushes his cup, and chucks it over the railing into the bushes. There's something in his eyes that I don't like. "You sure?" he asks. "Because I could help you with whatever."

"No thanks." I keep walking backwards, for my car, too uneasy to take my eyes off him. "I got everything I need."

"Hey, aren't you that girl that killed her dad?" he asks as he skulks down the porch stairs.

My eyes never waver from him, even as someone passes close by and nearly bumps into me. "I think you're thinking of someone else because my dad's not dead."

"You know, I saw someone messin' around with your car," he hollers out. I stop, curious even though the guy's a total creeper. "That Challenger over there—that's yours, right?"

I nod. "Um… yeah…"

He advances toward me, lengthy strides that put him close quickly. "There was some guy that came around here just a few minutes ago. He got in it, messed around, and then left."

So maybe my keys were stolen, not lost. "Thanks. I'll make sure nothing's missing."

A shady look masks his face. "I could give you a ride home, just in case." His hand snaps out and he grasps my elbow with his painted black fingernails. They press deep into my skin and send a revolting sensation through my blood, thick like oil. I gag on the bitter taste. *Blood stains his hands. He stumbles through the night, to the edge of the rooftop. A dark cape flaps behind him. He smiles and leaps.*

He releases my arm and a smirk creeps across his lips. "Tell me, Ember, have you ever danced with death or been paid a visit by the Reaper?"

"Back the hell off." I reel for my car and hop into the front seat. The guy retreats for the house. My heart settles, but his words linger in my mind. Does he know about my curse?

"I'm sorry," I apologize to the car, then grab a screwdriver from under the seat and pry off the panel. I yank out the correct wires, twist them together and pump on the gas pedal. The engine revs to life and "The Kill" by 30 Seconds to Mars blasts through the speakers. I carefully set the wires back in and slam the car door shut.

My dad and I used to steal cars. When I was young, I'd sit in the backseat while he worked his hotwiring magic. However, when I reached my early teens, he taught me how to do it. I was his protégé. At twelve years old, I couldn't see the bigger picture; that the situation was messed up and a small sign that my dad would eventually lose his mind.

I crank the steering wheel to the side and ramp onto the grass. The greasy haired guy eyes me from the porch as I cut across the front lawn and peel out down the driveway.

The trees blur by as I zoom down the road that threads between the lake and the mountain. When the tires reach the asphalt, I throttle the gas pedal to the floor, hoping Laden and Raven will remain on the highway and hopefully I can catch up with them.

By accident, I saw Raven's death once. I'm usually very carefully not to touch people, especially ones that are close to me. I don't want to know how it ends for them, how I'll lose them, how I'll hate myself for not saving them. But when Raven and I were younger, we were playing in Raven's tree house. Raven had tripped and landed near the edge, almost falling off. By instinct, I reached to grab her. Once my fingers touched her arm, I wanted to erase everything. What I saw. Our friendship. Raven will die young, in a very painful and terrifying way. It will happen by the water, during a rainstorm, just like Laden's death. Only her life will be stolen.

Clouds blanket the sky, the moon and stars are fading, and the air smells fresh like before a rainstorm. I try not to panic and speed up. I don't look at how fast I'm going, but I'm not scared. My death will come when it's time, just like everyone else's. It will happen on a dark night, a faint light will sparkle, and I'll be alone. I don't know when, though. And I'm thankful for that. If anyone knew when they'd die, the fear and obsession to change it would own them and they'd have no life to save.

Headlights reflect in my mirror and a car rides up on my tail. "Back off, asshole," I mutter, adjusting my mirror.

The car edges closer until it's only inches away from crashing into mine. A sharp corner approaches, so I tap the brakes. Nothing happens. I stomp on the brake, but the car accelerates faster down the hill. The corner emerges. I try to down shift, but the engine grumbles. Sucking in a deep breath, I crank the steering wheel to the right. The car spins and the tires screech. The front of my car crashes into the railing and the sound is deafening, like a train roaring up the railroad tracks.

There's a split second where my car hovers over the edge, like it might not fall. A raven dives down and lands on the hood. But the tailgater slams into the rear end. My head smashes against the windshield, the car flips, and rolls down the hill. My seatbelt locks and I'm jerked back to the seat. My body is stabbed, beaten, broken. Then the car hits the lake. Suddenly it becomes clear: I'm going to die today.

Death feels natural, like breathing. The water pierces my skin and floods the cab of the car. I unclip my seatbelt and float to the roof, pressing my head to the ceiling. It's dark and the water is up to my neck. I let my legs float upward and I kick the side window with the heel of my boot until my calf muscles ache. I run my fingers along the door and grasp the handle. Then I wait for the water to completely fill the cab.

My dad was big on survival. He taught me things like how to escape a car when it's submerged in water. If the water's low enough, the door will open. But once it reaches a certain point, the pressure of the water inside has to equalize with the pressure of the water on the outside. Which means I have to wait for the car to completely fill up the cab, without drowning first.

I remain calm as the water rises and rises. I slant my head back and take a deep breath before the water suffocates me completely. Immediately, I flip the handle, but it snaps off. Bubbles escape my mouth as I bang on the door. The black water encases the cab and I swim for the other door, but I smack into the roof, which is concaved, forming a wall. I twirl around and bang my fist on the windshield. It's dark. Cold. The car sinks further into the lake.

Ember

My eyes stay open as bubbles gurgle from my mouth. I can't see. I can't breathe. Death is no longer peaceful. The air slips away, my heart dies, and my necklace floats off my neck. The water stills. *Am I dead?* The metal of the car crunches as it buckles beneath the weight of the water.

"Ember," someone whispers. "Hang on."

I glance from left to right. Darkness and I'm alone, just like my death omen. A faint light swims through the water to the window, and glitters the inside of the car. I reach out to touch it.

"Ember," the voice growls. "Don't touch it."

The light flashes, and then shifts into a black mass.

"Emmy," it whispers and a black cape drapes over me. "Come with me."

No, not again. My body ignites with flames. I scream as a tunnel opens up and swallows me.

Chapter 4

My first death omen happened when I was four. My grandma Nelly came to live with us, back when things were somewhat normal and hadn't completely gone to shit yet. Grandma Nelly was old and suffered from dementia. By the time she moved in with us, she was fairly gone—forgetting things, wandering off in the middle of the night. My grandpa had passed away several years before and there was no one to take care of her. Eventually she started to suffer from hallucinations. She forgot who everyone was. The night she died, she snuck into my room and sat down on the bed next to me. I'll never forget that night—it changed my life forever.

She took off her necklace and placed in my hand. "Here, Emmy, this is yours now."

The oval pendant filled up the palm of my hand. "Grandma, what are you doing?"

"Do you feel that, Ember?" Her eyes lit up with anticipation as she took my hand and placed it over her heart.

Her heart beat rapidly beneath my palm. I sat up, confused. "Feel what, Grandma? Your heart?"

She shook her head excitedly. "No, Emmy, my life. Do you feel it leaving?"

"No," I answered and glanced at the door. "Are you okay, Grandma? Maybe I should go wake up Mama."

"No, no," she whispered. "You need to listen closer, Emmy. You'll hear it—my life slipping away. You need to take it, okay?"

There was something momentous in her eyes, so I shut my own and listened to the flutter of her heart, the whisper of her breath, the lull of her blood as it danced through her veins. There was warmth, then coldness. A light flickered inside me and for a moment, I felt powerful. When I opened my eyes, she was lying on the bed. Her eyes were shut and she looked peaceful. I let her lay there for a while before waking up my mother and telling her Grandma was gone.

My mom asked what happened, so I told her. She looked at me like it was my fault. And maybe it was. I had felt her life leave her body and my own life grow. After the funeral, my mom sent me to live with my dad, the mechanic/car thief. He did his best raising me until he vanished. Then it was back to live with my mom and my brother.

"Open your eyes," a deep voice asserts. "Come on, not yet. Open your eyes, goddamn it." The whisper alters to a desperate plea. "Please, Ember... Please wake up... You have to be one of them—I know you are."

Soft lips touch mine and a jolt of life slams my heart, like a defibrillator charged it to life.

"Take it, please..." the voice begs. "You have to take it."

Something soulful and poetic whispers for my mind to bring my body back to life. Then the life of another connects to every part of me and lifts my body to life. My heart expands and sends the blood flowing through my body again. A hand presses firmly against my heart and my lungs swell. My eyelids open and water rushes up my throat. I hack up dirty water until oxygen flows through my lungs again. I think I spot my body floating up above me in the trees, but everything's blurry, like an unfocused camera lens. I rub my eyes, gradually sit up, and the body evaporates into the night sky.

"Are you okay?" my rescuer asks, coughing.

I dry my eyes with my fingertips. "I think so... How did you..." *What the hell was that?*

The moon reflects behind the hazy clouds and rain sprinkles from the sky. The gorgeous guy from the party kneels on the rocky shoreline next to me. His black hair is damp and beads of water drip down his pale skin. The silver skull on his necklace glints in the moonlight and his long, black eyelashes flutter against the rain. His beauty is breathtaking and I almost forget where I am.

"Did you… did you jump in and save me?" I cough with my hand over my mouth.

He watches me in a way no one has ever done before, like I'm something valuable. "Yes… I thought I lost you for a second, though."

I eye the cut forehead and the dark half-circles under his eyes that weren't there at the party. "Are you okay?"

He nods, his eyes doing a slow sweep of my body. "I'm fine. It's you I'm worried about."

"What happened?" I smooth back my drenched hair. *Did I just die?*

"I'm not sure," he says, befuddled. "I was driving home from the party and saw the guard rail crushed to pieces. It wasn't that way when I drove up, so I thought I'd check. I saw your car sinking into the lake, so I ran down and jumped in."

"That was very brave of you." I hack up water; my lungs feel bruised.

"I think we need to call an ambulance and get you checked out." He stands up and brushes the dirt and pebbles off his jeans. "That was a pretty bad crash and you weren't breathing when I pulled you out."

Metal fragments of the Challenger spot the rocks on the hill. Bits and pieces of what happened rush back to me. "I think the brakes went out and then I think someone ran into me."

His eyes widen. "And then they just left you."

I shrug. "They probably thought I was dead."

He swallows hard and then clears his throat. "You have to report this. It's basically like a hit and run—this is partly their fault."

"No, it's not. My brakes going out caused it." I delicately touch the side of my throbbing head. "Although, I'm not sure how they went out. And I just checked the brake pads and lines."

Did someone cut them? Like the owner of the car who ran into me? Or the creeper with the *X* tattoo on his eye? But who would want to hurt me? A lot of people, come to think of it.

He arches an eyebrow, shooting me a peculiar look. "You change your own brake pads?"

"My dad was a mechanic," I explain. "And he liked to teach me while he worked on cars."

"*Was* a mechanic?"

"He died a few years ago."

"Sorry, I know how hard that is. I lost my dad too.'" He extends his hand to help me to my feet. "My cell's in my car. Do you think you can walk? Or can I carry you?"

I love the idea of him carrying me, but he would have to touch me, so I pass on his offer. "I think I'm okay walking..." I tense as his fingers graze my knuckles, slide down the back of my hand, and thread through my fingers. No one has ever touched me like this before without death suffocating me. There's no blood, no pain, no expiration date. It's exhilarating and terrifying, like street racing.

His eyes stay on me as he pulls me to my feet. Once I'm standing, he slips an arm around my lower back. The rain pours down on us as we hike up the hill. My legs feel heavy as weights and my skin is scratched and bruised. I touch a tender spot on the hollow of my neck and then panic.

"Oh my God." I turn back to the lake. "I lost my necklace."

He moves in front of me and puts his hands on my shoulders. "I'm sorry. Was it important to you?"

"My grandma gave it to me before she died." I watch the lake ripple from over his shoulder, picturing the necklace floating to the top. But my imagination isn't powerful enough to return it and I force my attention to the hill.

"So you never told me your name," I say as we hike up the loose gravel.

He hand tightens on my waist as we maneuver over a steep lip of the hill. "Asher… Asher Morgan."

"Did you just move to Hollows Grove?" We break off the hill and onto the highway. The rain lets up, but the ground is mush, mud, and puddles. My clothes are soaked and weighted with dirt. "I've never seen you around school before."

"Monday will be my first day." He turns down the road, with his arm still around me, and walks a line near the guard rail. "My mom and I just moved from New York."

"Why on earth would you want to move here?" I glance back at the dark, empty road.

He chuckles softly. "For the beautiful scenery."

I frown at the pine trees bordering the road. "I guess that could be a plus for some people, but I'm sure it's not really why you moved here, is it?"

"You don't like it here?" he inquires, evading the question.

"No… I don't mind the low population, but a lot of people do. My best friend Raven hates it here." I stop as the past hour catches up with my traumatized mind. "Oh no." I slip from Asher's hold and take off down the road, stumbling like a drunken person.

He captures my arm and turns me to face him. "You can't go running off like that—you might have a concussion or something else and your shock's just numbing the pain. Honestly, I don't even know how you made it out alive."

Neither do I. It happened just like the omen said. "I have to find my friend Raven—that girl with the pink hair. She drove off with this guy who I... who was drinking. That's what I was doing—trying to chase her down. And I couldn't get a signal on my phone." I pat my empty pockets. "How far is your car?"

"It's just up the road, at the turnoff. I didn't want to leave it parked in the street and cause another accident." He embraces my hand and we walk to the turnoff, where a black 1960s GTO, with red racing stripes, is parked. The door is open and the headlights and engine are running. He hops into the driver's seat and checks the bars on his cell phone.

"No signal," he mutters.

I tap my foot anxiously, glancing around the forest. *Rav, where are you?*

"Let me take you to the hospital so you can get checked out," he says. "I'm sure your friends made it home by now, and if not, you can call her once we get a signal. And you should call the police"

"No thanks. I'm feeling pretty okay now." Hospitals are overflowing with death. "And no police."

"I think you should go. You might feel fine now, but you could just be in shock." He eyes my head. "And you got a pretty wicked cut on your head."

I walk around the front of the car for the passenger door. "Can you please take me home? I'll get my mom to take me, after I tell her about the car." I pause as another memory resurfaces. "Did you see anyone else driving around, like maybe right in front of you?"

He ducks his head and climbs out of the car. "I haven't seen anyone else on the road."

I grip the door handle as a spout of dizziness crashes through me. "Dammit. I was hoping you might have seen who hit me."

He treads through the mud around the front of the car. "Do you remember anything at all about what the car looked like?"

I shake my head and crack the door open. "I only saw the headlights."

"Here, let me get that." He reaches around and opens the car door for me.

"Thanks," I say, picturing Asher in a fedora and pin-striped suit, like it's the 1940s and guys were gentlemen.

I slide into the car and he slams the door shut. The inside of his car is nice. Reupholstered leather seats, a crack-free dashboard—this is what my dad wanted to do to the

Challenger. But now it's gone, resting at the bottom of a lake, along with my death, which I can no longer see, feel, or taste.

I sigh heavily. What does it mean if my death has vanished?

Asher buckles his seatbelt. "What's wrong?"

"It's nothing." I fasten my seatbelt. "I was just thinking about my car."

He thrusts the shifter into drive. "Is your mom going to freak out about it?"

I frown sadly. "No, she won't even notice, unless I tell her. It was actually my dad's car."

"I'm sorry, Ember." He gently squeezes my hand. Again, I tense from the contact, but relax as tranquility lulls my uneasiness.

"It's okay." I stare out the window at the profiles of the trees. "It was old and falling apart anyway, which is why the brakes probably went out." But deep down, I wonder if it had anything to do with the creeper at the party or the guy he supposedly saw in my car.

"What kind of car was it?" He cranks up the heat and the warm air feels nice against my damp clothes.

I wrap my arms around myself. "A 1970 Dodge Challenger."

He lets out a slow whistle. "Damn, that sucks."

I shrug again, watching the road as we curve through the mountains and around the lake. "It was just a car. I'll live."

"So were you close with your dad?" His voice edges cautiously.

I pick at the black fingernail polish on my thumbnail. "Yeah, we were pretty close. I moved in with him when I was four and lived with him until he vanished."

"How did he die?" he asks and adds, "You don't have to tell me if you don't want to."

"I'm not sure," I say quietly. "The cops never found his body, but they found his car parked up in the mountains and his... blood was everywhere."

His grey eyes expand. "That has to be hard for you—not knowing what really happened to him?"

I nod, leaving out the details of the hourglass painted in blood on the windshield, the massive *X* staining the grass in front of the car, and the black feathers everywhere. "It is and I really don't like to talk about it."

He offers a sympathetic look. "I get it. Even though my mom loves to talk about my dad, it still hurts sometimes."

"How did he die?" I ask. "If you don't mind me asking."

We arrive at the rim of the mountains and breach through the trees and out into the valley. The town is silent, everyone tucked away safely in their beds. Porch and streetlights dot the fields and houses like fireflies.

The speed limit drops and he slows down the car. "He was killed on the... job."

It seems like he's holding back details. "Where did he work?"

He swallows hard and his knuckles whiten. He picks up his cell phone and checks the screen. "I've got a signal now if you want to call your friend."

I don't press the subject. If anyone can understand the need for secrecy it's me. I give him the directions to my house and then dial Raven's number. After a few rings, it sends me to voicemail.

"Hey Rav, I was just wondering if you were okay, since you bailed out on me with Goth Boy. I've had a crazy night and lost my cell phone. But I'll call you as soon as I get home." I hang up and hand Asher the phone.

"So I have to ask. How did you two end up being friends?" Asher asks. "You seem like opposites."

"We are, but she's my best friend," I reply. "My only friend, really."

His dark eyebrows knit. "Your only friend? That's pretty hard to believe."

My tone drips with sarcasm. "Really?"

He turns down my street and then smiles. "Why does that surprise you? You're easy to talk to, beautiful, and know a thing or two about classic cars."

I press back a grin. "So I don't get points docked for making you jump into a lake to rescue me?" I eye his crinkled clothes flaked with dried dirt. "And ruining your clothes."

He parks in front of my house, a narrow two-story townhome in desperate need of a paint job. "Are you kidding me? You let me fulfill my life dream of being a hero." He grins at me.

"Yeah, yeah, we'll see." I open the door, stifling a smile. "I'm sure when you start school on Monday you'll forget about little old me."

"Little old who?" he teases.

"See, you've already forgotten," I joke back and start to close the door.

"Wait." He leans over the console. I duck my head back into the cab. "First off, make sure to tell your mom what happened and then have her take you to the hospital. If you don't want to call the police, then fine, but at least get checked to make sure you're okay."

"I will," I lie. My mom doesn't need any more stress added to her life, and since I know she won't notice the car's missing, there's no point in telling her what happened.

"And second, no one could ever forget about you. Trust me." His eyes sparkle with a look that makes my skin warm.

Having no idea how to react, I shut the door. I walk up the driveway as he drives off. "Yeah, we'll see if you feel the same way on Monday," I say, but a smile breaks through my lips. He said I was beautiful. No one has ever said that to me before.

***

"Yo, where the hell have you been?" Ian hollers from the living room sofa. He's eating a bowl of Fruit Loops and watching a movie starring people who have thick French accents.

"I told you before I left that I was going to a party." I slip my jacket off and toss it on the banister.

He glances over his shoulder and his mouth falls open. "Why does it look like you went swimming in a lake with your clothes on?"

"Haven't you heard? It's what all the cool kids are doing." I lug up the stairs.

"Since when have you been cool?" He yells as I reach my bedroom door.

I don't answer and close the door. I flip on the lamp and slip off my waterlogged boots. I groan with each movement. My legs and arms are heavy and my head is pounding. "Those were my favorite pair of boots." I trudge toward the closet to put them away, hoping they'll dry out and won't be ruined.

Sobbing drifts from the back of the closet and I freeze. "Hello?" I pull back the curtain. "Who's in there?"

Raven runs out and throws her arms around my neck. "Oh my God! Where were you?"

Rain, water, blood. She can't breathe. I pat her back, but I'm irritated. "Where was I? I think I should be the one asking where the hell were you. You just left me there. And you left with a guy who I had a death omen about."

"I know." Her tears soak the shoulder of my shirt. "I'm sorry, Em. I just thought... Well, I don't know what I was thinking. It's hard to remember anything."

I draw away and frown at her. "Raven, you didn't drink from a cup someone offered you, did you?"

She bites on her lip guiltily. "I needed another drink and you dumped mine in the trash. So I drank one that this really cute guy offered me. Well, except for this weird *X* tattoo across his eye."

"Raven." I take a frustrated breath. "I love you and everything, but sometimes you're an idiot. How many times have we talked about drinking from cups from people we don't know? Especially ones like what you just described. Because I think I met that guy and he wasn't cute—he was a creep. But you were too drunk to notice it."

"I know," she wails. "And I'm so sorry."

I feel kind of bad. "I know, but you have to be careful."

She wipes away the mascara dripping down her cheeks with the back of her hand. "Do you think I was slipped something?"

"I'm not sure." I guide her to the bed and she curls up in a ball like a scared child. "Do you remember what happened with Laden?"

She shakes her head quickly and hugs a pillow to her chest. "Everything's all blurry." Her eye twitches—her lying tick. "But Em, I think I saw death tonight."

My muscles tense and my lips burst with a hundred questions. But her cries alter into hysterical sobs. I sigh, deciding not to press until morning when she's gotten some rest and sobered up. I grab some pajamas and head to the bathroom to shower.

"Em… why does it look like you went swimming? And what did you do to your head?"

"It's a long story." I sigh. "I'll explain in the morning after you've got some rest."

She shuts her eyes. "Leave the light on, okay?"

***

After a hot shower and fresh set of clothes, I stare at myself in the mirror with my hand over my heart. I died tonight.

My heart stopped beating, and then revived, all because of Asher. But how did he save my life? It felt like when my grandma died, and her life entered me.

I tiptoe back into my room. Raven is passed out on her stomach taking up the bed. I cover her up with a blanket and notice bruises on her wrists and elbows. Her shirt is torn and there's a small scratch across her shoulder blade in the shape of an *X*.

"What happened to you tonight?" I whisper, placing a finger lightly on the spot. She winces and rolls over.

My brain is growling and my skull feels cracked. I grab a blanket, snatch a black marker from my dresser, and hide out in the closet. I situate on the floor, near the wall that displays the rest of my ramblings, and press the marker to the wall. It's like my hand is possessed.

Like a feather in a dust storm, with no direction

The Raven flies through life, helpless and omitted

Until night declares and the wind expires.

Then it flies to the land of stones and etchings

And becomes an Ember, breaking away.

I decide my poetry might be off tonight so I set the marker down, but my hand takes on its own life, forcing the tip to the wall again. I scratch down *X* after *X* until they nearly cover the wall, pushing so hard it peels through the paint. Then, in the center, I sketch an hourglass.

Ember

The marker falls from my hand and I scoot away from the wall. I blink and blink again, but the drawing stays. Is this aftermath of the accident? Or am I starting to lose my mind, just like my dad?

I fall back on the floor, exhausted. Seconds later, I drift asleep.

Chapter 5

A week before my dad's disappearance, he was acting strange. One day when I came home from school, I found him in the garage with his head tucked under the hood of the car and the engine running. I hurried and pushed the garage open and he coughed as the door rolled open.

"Sorry, Emmy," he said. "I didn't realize it was shut."

I walked down the steps and peered under the hood. "Dad, are you okay…" The inside of the hood was covered in little red X's. "What are those?"

"I'm not sure… I don't remember how they got there." He slammed the hood and I had to jerk back to avoid my fingers getting squished. "But you don't need to worry about me, Emmy. I got everything under control. What I need for you to do is find that necklace Grandma gave you."

"The maroon stone one?"

He perked up. "Yeah, do you know where it is?"

I shook my head. "I'm not sure where I put it… but I'll start checking in the boxes in the basement, if you want."

He nodded and a flicker of yellow lit in his grey eyes. "Could you do that for me, Emmy? Please?" he asked and I nodded. Then he glances over his shoulder at the wall. "Do you see anything behind me?"

I shook my head. "There's nothing there but the wall and the toolbox."

He hopped into the passenger seat of his car, and took out a small knife from the glove box. "Good. Now go find the necklace."

Through the open garage door, a raven flew in and landed in the beams, shaking its feathers to the ground. My dad went ballistic.

"You get out of here, you little demon!" He threw a screwdriver at the raven, but missed. The raven cawed, tormenting him. "Get out!" As it flew away, he relaxed. "Emmy, if there's one thing you need to know about life, it's to never trust anyone or anything. Life is a freaking mind game and you and I are the pawns."

It was the first time I worried he might be losing his mind. After that, he rapidly went downhill, especially when I couldn't find the necklace.

***

I wake up on the closet floor with my cheek pressed to the marker, a feather on my forehead, and the strange drawing on the wall.

"What on earth?" Sitting up, I rub my eyes and blink at the sunlight glistening through the curtain. I pick up the feather and notice smudges of red paint on my hands. "What did I do last night?" I remember crashing into a lake, Asher saving me, and Raven crying. Then nothing. It's like I'm hung-over, but I didn't have a drop of alcohol last night.

Raven's not in bed and the room is cleaned up. It's her way of saying sorry. The neighbor across the street watches me from their front porch as I flick the feather out the open window. I start to pull the window shut, but pause. Someone is looking up at me from the sidewalk. His hands are inserted in the pockets of his black jeans and black eyeliner contours his eyes. His skin is as pale as a ghost and his hair as black as a raven.

"Laden?" I squint.

His gaze holds mine and a hostile smile cambers on his lips.

"What a creeper." I pull the window shut and back away.

I change into a pair of black plaid shorts and my favorite Alkaline Trio T-shirt. I scrub the red off my hands and the marker off my face. I dab some black eyeliner around my grey eyes, tousle my fingers through my long, black hair, and I'm good to go. The aches and pains from the accident have subsided, except for a minor headache and a tiny cut on my forehead, which has shrank in size.

Raven and Ian are downstairs at the kitchen table. Raven's denim skirt barely covers the top of her legs and she has her favorite pink shirt on, one that shows a lot of cleavage. Ian has a knitted beanie pulled over his messy brown hair and the jeans he's wearing are spotted with various colors of paint.

Raven bats her eyelashes at him and skims her fingernails up Ian's arm. "God, that's so cool."

"It's so fabulous," he says in his deep voice he only uses to impress girls. "You should totally come check it out."

"Oh, I bet it is." Raven licks her lips and smiles, like everything is fine. She glances up at me and her smile brightens. "Em, darling, I've been waiting for you to wake up." She hops up from the chair and links her arm through mine, scorching me with her omen. "See ya later, Ian." She winks at him.

"Later, beautiful," he says and then targets his attention to me. "Hey, Em, have you talked to mom lately?"

"No," I say as Raven tugs me toward the front door. I wiggle my arm free and breathe in the death-free air. "Why? Is something wrong?"

"I'm not sure." He wanders into the foyer. "She's been acting kind of weird. And not her normal weird… I caught her talking to herself, but it was almost like she was talking to someone that wasn't there."

"Are you worried she's not taking her meds again?" I gather my leather jacket from the coat rack. The fabric is crisp and still smells like murky lake water and fresh rain.

"I'm not sure." He glimpses at Raven and lowers his voice. "I was running low on mine, so I went to get some from her bottle, and it was full."

"Why didn't you just go get a refill?" I slip on my jacket and dust off the dried dirt. "You guys don't even have the same prescription."

"It's all the same to me," he says with a shrug. "Besides, that's not the point. The prescription was from like a month ago."

Raven's cell phone rings. She unlocks the door and walks onto the front lawn to answer it.

"Well, we need to talk to her," I tell him. "You know what she's like when she's not on them and the last thing she needs to go through again is another meltdown."

"I know," he agrees gloomily. "Why don't you make sure you're home tonight and I'll make something and we can sit down and talk to her?"

"*You'll* make something?"

"Well, I'll pick up something."

"Alright, I'll be here then." I step outside and shut the door.

Raven's still on the phone, bobbing her head up and down. "Yeah, uh-huh." She mouths to me, *Where's your car?*

"That's part of the long story," I utter.

Her face contorts. "Huh… No, not you," she says into the phone.

She carries on with her conversation while I stand on the curb by the spot where Asher dropped me off last night. The shock has worn off and I add up bits and pieces of the accident. Finally, I come to a mind-boggling conclusion: I should be dead. It happened exactly like my death omen said, but my heart is alive and my lungs breathe beneath my ribs.

"So what happened to your car?" Raven strolls up to the curb and tucks the cell phone into the pocket of her denim skirt. "And why are you staring at the curb like it's the most wonderful thing in the world."

I jerk my eyes away. "What happened to *you* last night?"

She bites at her bottom lip. "Well, things kind of got out of hand and I think I might have overacted."

"Overacted?" I question. "About what?"

"Um… Laden being a jerk. I mean, he totally tried to put the moves on me, which is fine—I'm used to it. But I really wasn't in the mood."

"I think I might have seen him standing in front of the house this morning." I point over my shoulder at the spot.

Her body goes rigid. "What was he doing?"

"Staring at me like a weirdo." My tone is light. "What exactly did you do to him last night? Break his heart into pieces?"

She shakes her head, gazing off into empty space. "I didn't do anything to him. He was the one who tried to push me too far."

"So that's why you were crying?" I ask, watching crisp autumn leaves blow down the street. "Because he pushed you too far?"

"Pushed too far…" She pulls her hair into a bun and secures it with an elastic off her wrist. "Look Em, I know I freaked out on you last night, but I swear it isn't what you're thinking. No one slipped me a roofie and I wasn't as drunk as you thought."

We jump back from the curb as the sprinklers turn on. "Then what was that talk about seeing death?"

"What are you talking about?" she asks as we run to the edge of the driveway, out of the reach of the sprinkler. Our shoes and the bottoms of our legs are wet.

I lower my voice. "You said you saw death last night."

She takes a pack of gum out of her pocket and pops a piece into her mouth. "I did?"

"Yup. And you were more than just upset—you were freaking out."

She pops a bubble. "Hmm.... Maybe I wasn't as sober as I thought. Or maybe your gift was confusing my head." She chews on her gum slowly, considering. "Well, I don't know why I was talking about death, but I was upset because this really hot guy totally wasn't that into me, so I wandered off with Laden because he was interested."

"I've never seen you that upset, except for once." Right after she found her mom. "Guys are disposable to you. How could you be so upset because one blew you off?"

"Okay, first off, he didn't blow me off." She flares up her hands and sways her head with attitude. "He was just distracted. And besides, that's not the only reason I was upset. Laden left me on the side of the road like a total douchebag."

I gape at her. "How did you get home?"

"I walked," she explains nonchalantly. "We were just on the bridge, so it wasn't that big of a deal."

"It seemed like a big deal last night," I point out.

She sighs and sits down on the curb. I plop down beside her and we stretch our legs out into the road as the sun shines down on us. "Remember when we used to sit here and wait for my dad to come home?"

I give her a small smile and lean back on my hands. "He always used to bring something for us, like a candy or Play-Doh."

She laughs at the memory and her eyes crinkle at the corners. "God, he always seemed like such a great dad, but he turned out to be a total jerk, bailing on his kids like that."

"It wasn't your fault he left." I stare at the jack-o'-lanterns on the porch of the house across the street, remembering when Raven's dad helped us make one that looked like a cat. It was one of our rare perfect moments, full of weightless laughter, pumpkin seeds, and the gentle autumn air.

"I know. It was my mom and her stupid drug habit." She pauses, her jaw taut. "How did we end up with such crappy parents?" Her eyes widen. "Oh crap, I didn't mean that. Your dad was a good guy. He just had some bad habits."

"Like stealing cars," I mutter, gazing up at the clear sky.

"I said I was sorry… Look, I'm still pissed off about that guy last night and I don't even know why I'm saying this stuff."

"It's fine." I flick a gnat off my knee. "But I have to know something."

She rubs some lip gloss over her lips. "What's up?"

I know what she wants me to say—what will make her feel better. "How hot was the guy?"

Her eyes light up and she squeals. "Oh my God, he was *so* hot. Seriously, Em, like hotter than any of the losers at our school."

"And how old is he?"

"He's a junior, like us. He actually just moved here from New York."

A lump rises in my throat. "Oh yeah? New York, huh. That's pretty awesome."

"It's not pretty awesome. It's amazing." Her voice effervesces. "And he's got these really beautiful dark eyes and his sexy eyebrow ring."

"Sounds like your type." Jealousy burns under my skin. "But I mean, you said he wasn't into you, right?"

She narrows her eyes at me. "Not yet, but he will be. And you're going to help me." She pulls me up by the arm and I wince. "His first day of school is tomorrow so I have to look fabulous." Her eyebrows furrow as she stares at the empty driveway of my house. "You never told me where your car was."

"I wrecked it last night," I say with no desire to explain it to her. "On my way home."

"Oh no, Emmy, I'm so sorry." She gives me a big hug.

"It's okay." I give her a soft pat, desperate for her to let me go. "It was just a car... Raven, can you let me go please."

"Oh, sorry." She frees me from her arms. "Is the car fixable?"

"Not unless we can get it out of the lake." My tone is sunny, but my heart is dark. *It's just a car.*

"Wait a minute. You drove it into the lake." She swats my arm and I flinch. "Why didn't you tell me last night when I made that comment about your clothes?"

"You were upset." I scuff the toe of my boot against the rocks in the driveway. "I didn't want to make it worse."

"I'm sorry." She frowns. "I'm a terrible friend."

"You're not a terrible friend," I reply. "You were just distracted by your own problems."

We wander down the sidewalk toward her townhouse right next door. The street is quiet and the air is gentle against my skin. Crisp leaves flurry from the branches of the trees and cover the lawns with pink and orange. It's late October and the lawns are ornamented with Halloween decoration: giant witches, fake tombstones, skeletons.

"Em, how did you get out of the lake?" She pauses to readjust a loose strap on her sandal. "Alive?"

"All those survival tips my dad always crammed into my head finally came in handy."

"You got out by yourself? How? And how are you walking around completely okay?"

"I guess I'm just really lucky." I don't know why I lie. It's like there's this part of me that doesn't want her to know.

"Lucky? More like a freaking walking miracle." She steps in front of me and looks me in the eyes. "I can't believe I wasn't there for you. I'm so sorry." She pauses and then shifts the subject. "Come on. You and I are going shopping because you need some cheering up and I need a sexy new outfit for school tomorrow."

I follow her up the driveway and wait by her Corolla while she runs inside the house and gets the keys. That's the thing I love about Raven. She hardly asks questions. She didn't ask how I got home. What I was going to do about my dad's car. Why I didn't go to the hospital. But as much as I love not being grilled, I wonder if there is something wrong with our friendship, if she should have asked those questions. I once read a quote by William Shakespeare about friendship: "A friend should bear his friend's infirmities." If I told Raven the wrong thing—something she didn't want to hear—would our friendship end?

"Okay, so we have to stop and put some gas in because it's low." She swings the keys around her finger.

"I think I might stay home," I tell her. "I'm feeling kind of sick."

She points a finger at me. "No way. You have to come be my fashion advisor." She eyes my clothes over. "Or at least keep me company."

I surrender and get in the car. "Can we at least stop and pick up a new cell phone? Mine is somewhere at the bottom of the lake."

"Sure." She backs down the driveway, but slams on the brakes as a U-Haul drives up the road, followed by a red Jeep Wrangler. The U-Haul parks in the driveway of the house across the street and two doors down, and the Jeep parks out front. It's one of the larger houses on the street, two stories with an upper deck and rose bushes blooming in the yard.

"It looks like someone is finally moving into Old Man Carey's home," she says with inquiring eyes.

A man and woman climb out of the U-Haul. The woman is wearing a black pencil skirt, a white cashmere sweater, a pair of stilettos, and her blonde hair is done up in a high bun. The man looks very businesslike, in a collar shirt and slacks, and blonde hair slicked to the side.

"Oh my God, they so don't fit in." Raven laughs and backs down the driveway. "Which instantly makes me like them."

We're pulling onto the street when the long legs of the driver stretch out of the Jeep. His blonde hair shines in the sun and his ash eyes glow with intensity. Dark jeans hang on his hips, fancy leather shoes cover his feet, and a tight-fitting Henley shows off his rock-solid abs.

"That's the guy from the cemetery," I say aloud.

"What guy from the cemetery?" Raven watches him like he's something delicious as he struts across the lawn. She fans herself. "Good God, he's hot."

"We should get going." I shift the car into drive for her. "I promised Ian I'd be back by dinnertime."

We're parked in the middle of the street and it's obvious we're staring at the new neighbors. The guy from the cemetery stops in the middle of the yard and watches us with an amused glint in his eyes.

"Oh! You mean he's the grave robber." Raven slams her hand on the steering wheel animatedly. "We *so* have to go over there."

"Don't even think about," I hiss, but she's already turning the steering wheel. "You just said it yourself—he's a grave robber."

Her eyes sparkle mischievously. I slouch in the chair as she drives toward his house.

"What's your problem?" she asks. "Don't you want to find out who he is? And why he was digging up a grave in the middle of the night. I mean maybe you misunderstood what was going on and now he could explain it to you."

I shake my head and shield my face with my hand. "Why? So you can date him?"

"Or maybe you could?" She parks in front of the Jeep and turns down the radio. "You really need to get over this fear of men, Em."

"It's not a fear of men, but a general fear of people. And can we just go? Please," I beg. "We're not going to make it back in time if we don't get going."

"You are so weird sometimes." She rolls down the window and waves him over. "Lighten up."

He swaggers over with a predator's smile. Each movement states self-assurance and cockiness. He bends down and rests his arms on the door.

"Hi there," Raven purrs in a seductive tone. "We noticed someone is finally moving into Old Man Carey's house and we thought we'd come over and introduce ourselves."

"Old Man Carey's?" He cocks his head, amused, but beneath the surface, pain emits. "I assume you're talking about my grandfather."

"Oh, he was your grandfather." Raven presses her hand to her heart. "I was so sorry to hear that he died."

"You knew him?" The stranger asks warily.

"Oh yeah, I used to bring him soup all the time when he was sick." She traces her fingernails up his arm. "I was very heartbroken when he died."

"I bet you were." His dark eyes focus on me and my adrenaline surges. "Did you get your notebook back, Ember?"

I'm shocked. I thought he would deny he knew me, considering the circumstances under which we met.

"I did." I straighten up in the seat. "Thank you for dropping it off at my house."

"I could tell it was important to you." His gaze penetrates under my skin. "Did you get my message?"

"You mean the poem," I correct. "Yeah, I got it."

"But did you *get* it get it?" His voice floats out hauntingly like the night I first saw him.

"I'm not sure." There is a need to touch him, a fire in my veins burning to connect with him. It's intense, like standing at the edge of a cliff preparing to base jump, but I'm not sure if the parachute will open.

"Read it closer." His eyes smolder. "I think you'll get it eventually."

Raven clears her throat. "Um, sorry to break up your little moment, but we gotta get going."

I forgot she was there. "Yeah, we should get going."

He pats the car door and backs away. "Perhaps I'll see you around later tonight." He winks at me. "At the cemetery maybe."

My stomach flutters with fear and exhilaration. "Yeah, maybe."

Raven rolls the car forward and he starts to walk away.

"Wait," I shout and he pauses. "You never told me your name."

Raven cocks a reprimanding eyebrow at me. "Don't you mean us?"

"Cameron." He flashes me a sexy grin. "Cameron Logan." He waves and turns back to his house.

Raven rolls up her window and turns the car around. "Okay, what the heck was that about?"

I bite on my thumbnail to hide my smile. "What was what about?" I ask innocently.

"You never talk to guys like that." She floors the car to the end of our street and then speeds onto the highway. "And how did he know your name? And where you live?"

"They were on my journal." I shrug.

"Still, it's really creepy." She flips down the visor. "And what poem were you guys talking about?"

I roll down the window and let the breeze cool off my overly warm skin. "The one he wrote in my journal."

"You mean that creepy one on the wall?" She frowns. "The one that sounds like it was written by a serial killer?"

"That's what you say about all poems," I remind her. "And his was just deep."

"Whatever, Em. In my opinion the guy was a total creep."

"Why? Because he knew my name and writes poetry?"

She rolls her eyes and laughs. "I'm not jealous of you."

I flip through the radio stations. "I never said you were."

She swats my hand away from the stereo and cranks up some song by Katy Perry. She sings along at the top of her lungs, waving her hands and bobbing her head. I rest my head back and watch the trees drift by. I'm almost asleep when she slows down the car.

I open my eyes and start to unbuckle my seatbelt. But we're stopped in a line of cars, not at the store. "Where are we?" I rub my tired eyes.

"Stuck in traffic." She impatiently drums her fingers on the steering wheel.

"Wait, what… traffic?" I sit up. The town is too small for traffic. But there is a row of cars running each way over the bridge and down the road. Police cars barricade the street and policemen are sectioning off the middle of the bridge with tape and trying to detour everyone to the side.

"What's going on?" I mumble, rolling the window all the way down to get a better look.

"Somebody probably did something stupid," she replies in a bored tone as she inspects her fingernails for chips.

The line of cars crawls forward. Raven presses on the gas and drives by slowly. In the middle of the taped off section, an X is spray-painted across the asphalt. Smashed into the cement barrier of the bridge is a rusted black Cadillac. The windows are broken, the hood is smashed in, and there is blood dripping from the back tire. And there are black feathers on the ground and on the hood.

"Isn't that Laden's?" I squint at the car. "Oh my God, it is."

"Hmm… I guess he must have got into some trouble last night." She smiles at the thought.

"This couldn't have happened last night," I say. "I just saw Laden this morning."

"How can you be sure of what you saw?" She questions with a sparkle in her eye.

I eye her over questionably. "Is there something you're not telling me?"

"There's a lot of things I'm not telling you." She grins and blasts the stereo.

I turn back to the scene. There's an hourglass painted on the back of the window in red and feathers all over the hood and the ground. It's the exact scene of when the police found my dad's car, just a different location. And I worry that, like with my dad's disappearance, I'll become the prime suspect.

Chapter 6

When night falls, I don't visit the cemetery. The news announced that Laden is considered a missing person and that there is evidence of foul play. My mom ended up skipping out on dinner and so Raven took her place at the table. She acted like a lunatic, like she was high on the news of Laden's disappearance.

While Raven and I were shopping, I tried to press her about the details of last night, but she shifted the conversation to clothes every time. I end up going to bed early. But late during the night, I'm woken up by the sound of my mom's voice.

"Ian," she yells up the stairs in a drunken slur. "I need your help."

Ian is locked away in the attic, with his "muse," a mysterious person that sneaks in every night so he can paint them. I climbed out of bed and pad to the top of the stairway.

"Mom, Ian's in the attic," I say tiredly. "What do you need?"

She frowns up at me, disappointed. "I need help getting up the stairs."

I sigh and trot to the bottom. Her brown hair is disheveled and her eyes are bloodshot. She used to be pretty, but her lifestyle has aged her. She tugs down the hem of her dress and drapes her arm around my neck. She smells like tequila and cigarettes. Her death omen smothers me, like it always does: *lying in a bed of pills and bottles, dying in her own flames.* Holding my breath, I help her to her room, lie her down on the bed, and pull off her high heels.

She blinks at me through her blurry eyes. "You look so much like him," she mutters. "You have his eyes and everything."

She's referring to my father. "Shhh… get some rest."

"I wonder if you'll turn out like him," she says, rolling onto her side. "I bet you will… a killer…you did kill your grandma."

Her words stabbed at my heart, but it's not the first time she's uttered them. "Mom, Dad didn't kill anyone."

"Yes he did… yes he did." She drifts off to sleep.

I force back the tears and rush out of her room. I don't cry, but I can't fall back asleep. So I read Cameron's poem, over and over again until the words blur together and make no sense at all. Just like my life.

***

I'm running late the next morning. There are bags under my bloodshot eyes and I look pallid. I quickly get dressed in torn jeans, grey combat boots, and a black vest over a striped T-shirt. Raven texts me as I'm barreling down the stairs, pulling my hair into a ponytail.

Raven: Need 2 get ur own ride 2day.

I halt at the bottom of the stairs and text back.

Me: Why? Is something wrong?

It takes her a second to answer.

Raven: I got things 2 do 2day. Can't b late.

Me: Just hold on. I'm almost out the door.

Raven: Already gone.

Raven: FYI the news said Laden disappeared the night of the party

Me: … that makes no sense. I saw him outside the house.

Raven: whateva u say. U would know how he died though. U saw it remember. It's why I had 2 hang out with him

Me: He's not necessarily dead yet, only missing.

Raven: If you say so. But anyway gotta go. C u at skool ;)

I throw my phone into my bag. I consider hitting Ian up for a ride, but then I'd have to explain what happened to dad's car. And I'm not ready for that yet. The only other alternative is to ride the overly crowed bus that is brimming with unavoidable death omens.

"What's up with you?" Ian asks, munching on a Pop-Tart in the kitchen doorway.

"Nothing." I snatch my house keys off the table. "I'm just tired."

"Did mom say anything to you last night?" he asks. "Like maybe why she hasn't been taking her meds."

"Does she ever talk about anything?" I snap.

Ian holds up his hands. "*Sorry*. I was just asking a question. But I guess I'll keep my mouth shut."

I open my mouth to apologize, but he turns back into the kitchen. I grab my jacket off the banister and step outside. I slip on my jacket and stare at the end of the street. Walk or ride the bus?

Cameron's Jeep pulls up to the curb. He rolls down his window and crooks his finger at me. I hesitate.

"I promise I don't bite." He dazzles me with an exquisite smile.

On their own accord, my feet trot down the steps and across the grass. I stop inches away from his door.

"Hop in." He nods at the passenger seat. "I'll give you a ride."

I adjust the handle of my bag. "Who said I need a ride?"

"I noticed your friend leaving this morning without you." He slides his sunglasses down the brim of his nose and gives me a look that makes me feel naked. "And then you walked out of your house, looking as if you were making the hardest decision of your life. So I'm guessing you don't have a car, and you're debating between walking and riding the bus."

"I was going to walk." I adjust the handle of my bag. "It's really not that big of a deal."

He shakes his head and laughs. "Hop in, Ember. I don't mind giving you a ride. Trust me."

I glance at the corner of the street where a line of people wait for the bus. "Fine. Thanks." I walk around the front and hop into the passenger seat. The inside of the car smells like vanilla mixed with a hint of earthy cologne. Cameron waits for me to buckle my seatbelt, then pushes up his sunglasses, and drives down the road. He's wearing dark blue jeans and a black button-down shirt with the sleeves rolled to the elbows. His hand rests on the shifter and his fingers tap to the music murmuring through the stereo. The compulsion to reach over and entwine my fingers with his nearly devours me.

"So are you always this quiet?" he asks after minutes of silence drones by.

I turn my head away from the window. "I just don't see the point of talking unless there's something to say."

He widens his eyes. "Okay, sorry for asking."

I fidget with my leather bracelet. "Sorry. I didn't mean for that to come out so bitchy. I'm just having a rough morning."

He nods and proceeds with caution. "But I'm pretty sure you and I do have something to say, so the question is do you want to say it or should I."

"I wasn't expecting you to put it out there," I say, shocked. "But okay."

"The first thing you should know about me is that I hate secrets. They are pointless and request too much energy from an individual, unless the revelation of the secret brings pain to someone." His lips move like they are a poet's pen on a sheet of paper.

"Okay, so why were you digging up a grave in the cemetery the other night?" I lay it all on the table.

His grin enhances with amusement. "To see if they really do put dead bodies in coffins."

I'm unsure how to respond. "I'm pretty sure they do."

"See, that's why I think you and I can get along," he re-marks cleverly. "Most people would have jumped out of the car with that response."

I tuck my bangs out of my eyes. "Most people wouldn't have gotten in the car in the first place."

"Excellent point." He flips on the blinker and turns onto the school road. "I was doing my parents' dirty work. My grandfather—or Old Man Carey as your weird friend calls him—owned a jewel that had a lot of sentimental value to my family. It's been passed down from generation to gen-eration. But no one can find where my grandfather put it, so they sent me to check in his coffin, just in case he requested to be buried with it and never told anyone except his friend who handled my grandfather's funeral arrangements."

For some reason, his story reminds me of a 1980s Tom Hanks movie I watched once—*The Burbs*. "Did you find it?"

"Again, you're not fazed." He grins, pleased and enter-tained. "No, I didn't find it."

"Did you think to ask your grandfather's friend, before you went rummaging around in his coffin?" I question. "It might have been an easier place to start."

"Hmm…" He rubs his chin thoughtfully. "I never thought of that." He laughs and smiles. "Of course I did, but it turns out my grandfather's friend has already passed away himself, only days after the funeral ended."

"That's weird." I'm torn whether I believe him. "So who was that man doing the actual digging?"

His smile falters and his face reddens with anger. "You saw him?"

I nod slowly. "Yeah…"

His anger alarms me. "He's my uncle."

"You don't like him?" I ask.

He fiddles with the keychain and sadness hues eyes. "He's… tolerable." He turns into the crowded school parking lot and everyone stares. The town is lowly populated and a new vehicle is *big news*. I can almost see the invisible stream of gossip move from car to car. "Wow, it's like being a movie star," he comments as he parks in an empty spot.

A smile lurks at my lips. "Oh, it's going to get a lot worse for you. Trust me. The new guy in school—it will be the headline of the newspaper. Well, maybe it won't be quite that big. I think there might be someone else starting today too."

He takes the keys out of the ignition. "Do you know who it is?"

"Yeah, I met him at a party Saturday night." I unbuckle the seatbelt. "His name's Asher Morgan."

A dark shadow possesses his expression. "And you've already met him?"

"Yeah…" My eyebrows scrunch. "At the party, like I said."

He stares at the dashboard, jingling the keys with anxious energy. Then he opens the door and climbs out of the car. I hop out and meet him around the back.

"You said you don't keep secrets," I say as we head for the front doors of the school. "But it kind of seems like you are."

"No, I said secrets were pointless unless they hurt someone." He picks up the pace and waves over his shoulder. "See you around, Ember."

The whole female student body watches him swagger up the sidewalk with hungry eyes. I roll my own and shift directions for the side entrance. By afternoon, he'll probably be dating Mackenzie Baker and be swooned over by the entire cheerleading squad.

The side exit is the mellow area of the school. It enters through the art hallway, unlike the front entrance, which goes directly to the quad and is always abundant with people. I dig through my bag, pull out my cell phone, and text Raven.

Me: U at skool yet?

I wander down the hall lined with fake spider webs and orange and black confetti, with my head tucked down, waiting for an answer.

Me: Hey, r u ok?

Again, no response. I put my phone back in my bag and decide to check in Mr. Morgan's art room. Sometimes Raven goes there before and after school to work on projects, mainly so she can use the school's supplies.

I poke my head inside, but the only person there is a guy painting in the far corner. I begin to back out.

"Ember," the guy calls out.

"Asher?" I step into the classroom. "What are you doing in here?"

He stifles a smile and raises the paintbrush in his hand. "Painting."

"But isn't this your first day?"

"Mr. Morgan is my dad's brother."

"So you have connections?"

His smile illuminates his slate eyes. "I guess you could say that."

I grow flustered with the impulse to walk across the room, run my hands up his lean arms, and tangle my fingers through his hair.

"Well, I'll see you around." I wave and step back to depart the room.

"Aren't you curious if I'm any good?" He sets the paintbrush down and motions me over.

I set my bag on a table and weave through the desks. His eyes never leave me. By the time I reach him, my skin is scorching. He has a black hoodie pulled over his At the Drive-In T-shirt. His faded jeans are stained with little droplets of black paint, the same look Ian often sports. He brushes his black hair out of his eyes and I notice a small scar along his brow line, right beneath his eyebrow piercing.

He gestures at the canvas. "So what do you think?"

It's the most beautiful painting I've ever seen. Flawless strokes of black paint brush the shape of a male angel. His head is tucked down and his dark hair blows in the wind. His feet are traced with a black circle, like he's bound to the lonely spot. He's crying and the agony and torment in his expression is so real, I want to reach out and comfort him.

"It's beautiful," I breathe. "I can feel his pain and anguish. It's like it's killing him, being trapped to that single spot."

"You understand it like a true artist," he observes, with a trace of ache in his eyes. "Do you paint?"

I shake my head, fixated with the painting. "No, my brother does. And Raven. I'm more of an artist with words."

"So you're a writer," he says.

I turn to face him. He's standing closer than I thought. Out of habit, I step back, and the heel of my boot collides with the easel. "I want to be one someday."

He sweeps a strand of my hair back and tucks it behind my ear, a reminder that I don't have to fear his touch; that his contact only brings solace, not sorrow.

"Do you know some believe that the eyes are the window to the soul?" he asks softly.

I arch my eyebrows. "You know that's a pick-up line, right?"

His intense expression is breathtaking as he cups my cheek and grazes his thumb along my cheekbone. The feel of his skin against mine brings a comfort I've never experienced before.

"It is now, but a long time ago people used to believe that a person's eyes gave insight to one's soul. It showed what they were really feeling and their vulnerability." He slowly traces his finger below my eyes. "You have beautiful eyes, but there's so much sadness in them."

I swallow the lump in my throat and focus on his lips. Dear God Almighty, he has such luscious lips.

"Ember," he whispers like he's known me forever, temporarily unhitching the chains that bind me to every single person's death. It's strange, but exhilarating. "I want to kiss you." His voice drops to a husky whisper. "Please tell me I can kiss you."

I've never been kissed before—I've never been able to get close to anyone like this without feeling smothered by death.

He closes his eyes. I inhale as his lips inch nearer. My heart dances vigorously in my chest.

"Asher, what are you doing?"

Our eyes snap open and we back away from each other. Mr. Morgan, the art teacher, is standing by his desk. He's in his mid-forties, with chestnut brown hair and hazel eyes. He wears a lot of cargo pants and polo shirts, smeared with charcoal, paint, clay—any art supply, really.

"Oh, hi there, Ember." He sets a stack of artwork down on his corner desk. "Have you seen Raven this morning? She usually comes in here, but I haven't seen her."

"I think she might be a little late this morning," I explain.

"Oh, I see." His gaze flicks to Asher and something in his eyes makes me want to leave.

I wave goodbye to Asher. "See you around, I guess."

He picks up the paintbrush distractedly. "Yeah, sure."

Raven and I usually sit around and talk before class, but she still hasn't texted me back. So I collect my books from my locker and head to class a little early. I have English first period with Mr. Mackerlie. He's writing on the whiteboard when I walk into the classroom and doesn't notice me.

My bag lands on the floor loudly and he turns with the marker in his hand. "Oh, Ember, I didn't see you come in." He clicks the lid on the marker and sets it in the tray.

Today's assignment is on the board. We are studying William Shakespeare's *Romeo and Juliet*. I read the book when I was fifteen after Raven made me watch the movie—the newer version starring Leonardo DiCaprio and Claire Danes—so I already know how the story goes: love, rivalry, violence, and tragedy.

Mr. Mackerlie shifts through papers on his desk. The bell rings and people start wandering into the classroom. Mr. Mackerlie walks back to my desk with a smile on his face.

"I really enjoyed the poem you wrote for last week's assignment, Ember." He taps a finger on the paper in his hand, stained with my undying penmanship.

"Thanks," I reply uncomfortably. I never meant to turn in that particular poem.

"If you don't mind, I'd like to read it aloud to the class," he says. I shake my head in protest, but Mackenzie Baker taps him on the shoulder, sidetracking him.

Her eyes skim me like I am a ghost. "Mr. Mackerlie, I just brought in the new guy." She points over her shoulder at Cameron, who winks at me.

I called that one.

Mackenzie has strawberry blonde hair, green eyes, and wears clothes that barely pass the dress code. She's kind of like Raven in a way, only maybe a little less forward. In fact, the only reason they're not friends is because Mackenzie is rich and looks down on us low-lifes who live in the rundown townhomes on the far side of town.

"He needs his books and stuff," she states. "And a place to sit."

"Oh, yes, you must be Cameron Logan," Mr. Mackerlie says and he glances back at me. "Don't worry, I'll say it's anonymous."

I throw up my hands exasperatedly. Is he joking? The poem is titled *Ember*.

"You look a little upset." Cameron slides onto my desk, trying to act nonchalant, but sorrow haunts his eyes.

"I'm fine." I take a pen and notebook out of my bag. "I'm just having a rough morning."

"Did you find your friend?" he asks. "The one with the pink hair?"

I shake my head. "No, I stopped by the art room this morning, because she likes to go there a lot, but the only person there was the other new kid." I bite at the end of my pen pensively, remembering what *almost* happened in the art room.

"You ran into Asher this morning?" He studies my face closely, as if he's looking for cracks that will reveal some hidden secret.

I pull the pen out of my mouth. "You seem like you know him."

"Only from word of mouth." Placing his hands on the desk, he leans in, smelling of mint hued with a woodsy aroma. "I'm finding out you were right about the whole new-guy-popularity thing."

"I told you they'd eat you up," I remark.

"No, you told me they'd be star-struck by me." He smirks. "The only one who looks like they could eat me up is you."

I fight my instinct to look away. "No, I don't, Cameron."

From a desk in the front row, Mackenzie crosses her legs and crooks her finger at Cameron. "Come here, Cam. You can sit by me."

Cameron leans away and touches his chest. "My fans are calling me." He saunters up to Mackenzie, whispers something in her ear, and she giggles, patting his chest.

I roll my eyes. He fits the part.

After the bell rings, and Mr. Mackerlie takes roll, he stands in the front of the room with my poem in his hand. "Listen up, everyone," Mr. Mackerlie says. "I wanted to share with everyone something that I think is an excellent poem that was turned in for last week's assignment. But I'm going to keep it anonymous." His gaze flicks to me for only a second, but it's enough that eyes wander in my direction.

"The poem is called *Ember*." Every looks at me and Mr. Mackerlie clears his throat. "The ember dies slowly in a mound of ash. Darkness and mourning, it longs to burn fire. But the smoke and sorrow let it die. The need for a spark asserts fiercely. But a spark won't surrender. So the ember continues to smother. Into ash, into dust, into nothing. And that's how it will stay forever."

Please let this Ember die now.

Everyone is staring at me like I'm the lunatic they always thought I was, ever since my dad's disappearance.

But I refuse to cower, so I sit up straight and wait for Mr. Mackerlie to move on.

Some jock coughs, "Psycho killer."

Giggles flutter the room and Cameron raises his hand.

"Yes," Mr. Mackerlie says. "Is it Cameron?"

Cameron nods. "Personally, I think it was an amazing poem about pain and survival."

Mr. Mackerlie browses over the poem again. "Well, that's a good interpretation, but I think perhaps it's more about the natural process of death."

Cameron taps his fingers on the desk. "Death might be a theme, but I don't think that's what it's completely about. I think it's more relative to the pain someone feels about death and their need to survive through the pain, even though they think they can't. Perhaps they've even lost someone close to them and they are trying to break free from the continual heartache and torment."

Everyone goes silent. I swear I could kiss those pretty boy lips of his. He turns around and gives me a look that says, *You know you're in love with me now.*

"Well, that's very deep, Cameron." Mr. Mackerlie looks about as befuddled as the rest of the class. "Were you in AP English at your old high school?"

Cameron clicks his pen. "I was, but it seems the English department is limited here."

"We are a small town," Mr. Mackerlie replies, shuffling through some papers in his hands. "Where did you live before here?"

"New York." Cameron jots down something in a notebook.

"Oh, the Big Apple." Mr. Mackerlie selects a paper from the stack and places the rest on his desk.

"That would be the one." Cameron sounds bored.

"Well, it's great to have you here," Mr. Mackerlie welcomes him and moves on to Shakespeare. Cameron doesn't glance at me during class. However, I can't take my eyes off him. He is both fascinating and frightening. Who is this guy that digs up graves in the cemetery? Who speaks up for me in class and writes the most beautiful words? Who is from New York, just like Asher?

***

My next class is about as uneventful as watching paint dry. But during third period, while Mr. Peabody is scribbling math equations on the board, the intercom clicks on.

"Mr. Peabody." The secretary's voice statics through the room. "Can you please send Ember Edwards down to the main office?"

"Go ahead, Ember." Mr. Peabody turns back to the board.

The entire class looks at me. I sigh, grab my bag and book, and head to the office. The secretary is talking to a slender woman with blonde hair, a sharp nose, and glasses framing her narrow face. Her hair is tight in a bun and she sports a pinstriped pantsuit. I drop down in a chair and wait.

"Yes, I know, but I don't see why you have to do it here," the secretary, Mrs. Finnelly, tells the woman.

The woman leans on the counter. "Can you just check again?"

Mrs. Finnelly sighs and types something on her keyboard. She rolls her chair back to the corner filing cabinet and takes out a thin manila folder. "Here you go, Beth, but I don't see how her file is going to help… Oh, Ember, I didn't see you walk in." She looks nervous.

Beth turns around and her blue eyes promptly darken with abhorrence. "Ember Edwards, I'm detective Crammer."

My lips twitch. "Why am I here?"

"I think you already know the answer to that." She motions to the counselor's office door. "But why don't we go in here so we can talk more privately."

105

I follow her into the councilor's office, which is packed with plants and family photos. There's a bag hanging on a coat rack in the far corner and the air smells like pumpkin and spice. Detective Crammer takes a seat in the office chair and I sit down in front of the desk.

She opens the file with my name printed on it. "You excel in English… but your math grades look a little weak." She takes off her glasses and tosses them on the desk. "Well, I'll get straight to the point since we only have the office for a few minutes." She rolls forward in the chair, and overlaps her hands on top of the desk. "As I'm sure you've heard, Laden Miller disappeared last night. Now, the last place he was seen was a party you were at. Is that correct?"

"Yeah," I answer. "But a lot of people were."

"Just a simple yes or no will suffice," she says snidely. "Now, as I'm sure you've also heard, Laden Miller's car was found down at the bridge in a very similar situation as how your father's car was left after his disappearance three years ago. You were the only one ever investigated for his disappearance—the police never had any more leads."

I brazenly cross my arms. "The charges against me were dropped."

She pulls out a small notepad from the pocket of her jacket. "I pulled up your father's case and it said that they got a call right before your dad disappeared. The call was from you and you said he was going to be murdered."

"No, I said he was going to die. There's a huge difference."

"Huge difference or not, it's highly suspicious. And then you ran away right after."

I opt for silence, knowing from experience that fewer words mean fewer opportunities to twist what I say around.

Her eyes narrow and then she jots something in notepad. "It's such a strange case. Raven feathers, an hourglass, the bright red *X* on the road. And of course there's the blood."

"They're all symbols of death," I say. "I told the police this last time."

Her eyebrows furrow as she reads over her notes. "Hmm… no one ever made a note of that."

I shrug indifferently. "Well, it's true. Except for the *X*, they all represent death. You can Google it if you want. It's pretty common knowledge."

"Did you do that before or after your dad disappeared?"

"After."

She reddens with frustration. "You know, I find it highly suspicious that you were at a party Laden Miller attended and then he disappeared. And there were witnesses that said they saw you peeling off in your car right after Laden drove away with another girl."

Witnesses? "My mom has a strict curfew," I lie, but not very well.

She sifts through the notepad. "Actually, if I read the note in the file right, your mother's a pretty inactive parent. In fact, she gave up her custody of you and sent you to live with your father when you were four."

"Well, she still likes me home at a certain time." I make an effort not to fidget, or she'll use it against me.

Her eyes scrutinize me. "Where were you between the hours of two to four a.m. on Saturday?"

Crashing into a lake, drawing crazy notes on my wall, blacking out. Shit! "I was with Asher Morgan all night."

Her eyebrows arch. "And he is?"

"A friend of mine." I'm digging myself a giant, coffin-sized hole.

Thankfully, the lunch bell rings. She writes *Asher Morgan* down at the top of the notebook and then tucks it in her pocket. Then she hands me her card. "We'll be in touch."

I take the card, stuff it into my back pocket, and leave the office, not looking back.

Chapter 7

Everyone in the school is calling Laden's disappearance the Angel of Death Killing. The rumor spread about the detective interrogating me. It's like I've relapsed back to three years ago, right after my dad vanished. The halls are fluttering with whispers of "Freak," Psychopath," and "Murderer." But I walk with my head held high. A little gossip and dirty looks is nothing compared to being plagued by death every day.

Raven still hasn't shown up at school and she hasn't called or replied to any of my texts, so I go to the cafeteria solo, crossing my fingers I'll make it out alive. I'm waiting in line, when Mackenzie Baker comes brushing by, knocks her shoulder into mine, and nearly breaks a high heel trying to recover her balance. *Ropes bind her wrist and mouth. Darkness devours her. Come out, come out, wherever you are.* It's a game and Mackenzie loses, lost in a sea of blood. I've seen her death before and it never gets easier.

"You better watch it," she says with edginess in her tone.

I stare at her expressionlessly and don't utter a word. She flips her hair and quickly returns to the conversation with her cluster of friends as they head for the tables.

"So was I right?" The soft touch of Cameron's voice sends a rush of adrenaline through my body.

I step back and elongate the distance between us. "Were you right about what?"

"About your poem," he says with a charming smile.

"You think I'm in pain?" I move forward with the movement of the line.

"I think your heart carries a lot of pain." He steps forward. "But that you hide it, just like you hide a lot of things."

He's striking a nerve. "Isn't everyone hiding something?" I ask.

"Now those are the words of a true writer." He reaches behind me, missing my arm by an inch, and grabs a tray. "But the question is, what are you hiding, Ember?"

There's accusation in his tone—he's heard the rumors. "Bodies in the basement of my house and a burner full of ashes," I say darkly.

He's unfazed. "Weird, because that's the same thing I have in my basement."

I collect a tray. "I'd be happy that we share something in common, but we both know that neither of our houses have basements."

"Yep, but they have attics," he says and it no longer sounds like he's joking. "And attics are excellent places to hide bodies too."

I pick up an apple and slide my tray down, unsure what to say.

He laughs. "Relax, I'm just kidding."

I offer him a small smile, and then pull a face at the food the lunch lady slops on my tray. *Raven, where are you? I need my McDonald's.*

"I think they forgot to kill it first." Cameron pulls a revolted face. "It looks like it's still moving."

"What? Don't they have mystery surprise Monday in New York?" I loosen up a little, grab a bottle of water, and pick up my tray. My eyes browse the room lined with tables separated by cliques and social status. There's a lot of chattering and wandering eyes at the accused killer standing in the center of the room. Who am I even looking for? I spot Asher in the far corner table sitting with the self-proclaimed artists of the school.

Asher's eyes find mine and light up. But then he notices Cameron standing next to me and he glares. Cameron returns the glare with equal animosity.

"I thought you said you didn't know him?" I ask Cameron with cynicism.

He blinks the glare away and smiles politely. "I don't know him. Now, if you'll excuse me, I've got places to be." He struts off to Mackenzie's corner table and immediately starts flirting with her.

"Hot and cold much," I mumble.

Asher waves me over. I hesitate, not at him, but at the rest of the people at the table who are just as afraid of me as Mackenzie is. But then Asher smiles and my doubting thoughts surrender.

I take a seat at the table and everyone gives me subtle nods, except for Farrah Taverson, who is the only girl at the table. And who dated Laden Miller up until a few weeks ago. She scowls at me, gathers her medieval era dress, and leaves the table.

"You looked like you needed help," Asher whispers in my ear.

I stir the slosh on my tray. "I don't usually eat in the cafeteria, especially without Raven."

"She's still not here?" he asks and I shake my head, frowning. He takes a bite of his sandwich. "Do you know that guy you were standing by?" He licks a dab of mayo from his lip. I imagine licking it off him, along with many other things.

"Ember." His voice is low. "Are you okay?" His gaze travels to my forehead. "Did you go to the hospital after the accident?"

"Yeah," I lie. "And I'm fine. No broken bones. No concussion. I'm like a walking miracle."

"What about your car?" he asks with concern.

My mood sinks lower. "That's definitely a goner."

"And how about... how are you doing with what everyone else is saying?"

I shrug. "It's not the first time they've wanted to burn me at the stake."

He takes another bite of his sandwich and changes the subject. "So you never answered my question."

I dare a bite of my own food and it tastes as bad as it looks. "About what?" I casually put a napkin to my mouth and gag out the slosh into it.

"About the guy you were with just now?"

"That's Cameron." I ball the napkin up and set in on the corner of my tray. "He's the other new guy here and coincidently, he's also from New York."

"That's weird." His jaw tightens and he throws the rest of his sandwich into his bag. "Would you do me a favor?" He stands up and collects his garbage. "Would you show me around a little bit?"

"Sure. But I'm surprised no one else has, especially Mackenzie," I say. "She seems to have made it her abiding duty to show Cameron more than he probably needs to see."

He laughs and we head across the cafeteria toward the trash cans. "I don't think I'm really Mackenzie's type."

I eye his Goth/emo style. He's not her type, but he's still beautiful, especially his eyes. "She may not admit you're her type, but trust me, deep down I'm sure she thinks about you."

He throws his garbage into the trash, but holds onto a mini bag of Doritos. "And what about you? What's your type?"

I dump my tray into the garbage and bite at my lip. "I don't have a type."

We walk for the exit door, side-by-side, and at that moment, everyone in the cafeteria doesn't exist. We are the only two people in this world where, for a split second, death doesn't prevail. Again, I crave to touch him, feel every inch of him, and understand what he's thinking.

He hands me the bag of chips, but I shake my head. "No, thanks. I'm okay."

"You didn't eat anything. Well, you did, but you spit it out," he says. My mouth waters as I eye the bag of chips and he laughs. "Just take them."

So I do and eat them as we roam up and down the halls. I explain where everything is—who everyone is. The two basic factors that everyone in high school needs to know to survive. After I've given him the grand tour, we stop in the fairly empty quad centered in the school. A large circle of pillars form the walls and there are benches in the middle.

"I used your name this morning," I say quietly. "When a cop brought me in for questioning." He appears mystified so I add, "Questioning for Laden's disappearance."

"I knew what you were talking about," he says, leaning against a pillar. "I was just wondering why you said it so guilty. I know you were with me."

"For part of the time," I clarify. "You dropped me off around three and she wanted to know where I was between the hours of two and four."

He gets this funny look on his face, like he might laugh. "So where were you for the extra hour? Or should I say we."

"You don't have to cover for me," I tell him. "Your name just slipped out because it seemed a lot better than telling her I was up in my room with a friend that was trashed out of her mind. And I've been through this before and excuses like that don't fly."

"When your dad disappeared?"

"How do you know about that?"

115

His face is guarded. "People like to talk a lot around here, I've noticed."

I shy away. "I'm sorry. I'll go find the detective and tell her the truth." I turn for the office, but he blocks my path.

"Last night was one of the best nights of my life," he starts. "I have never made out so long before. And the lake was beautiful, crystal clear with a bright moon setting. And Ember… she is the most amazing kisser."

"Yeah, I think you took it one step too far on the last sentence." I stifle a smile. "You might want to leave that part out."

He challenges me with a cock of his eyebrow. "Or find out for myself."

"You seriously don't have to cover for me." My phone rings inside my bag, but I ignore it. "I can figure out something else."

"It's fine," he insists. "I know you didn't do it."

There are no words to express my gratitude. "Thanks. I owe you big time."

He fiddles with his eyebrow ring, looping the tip of his pinkie through it then pulling it out. He stuffs his hands into his pockets and suddenly he looks nervous. "Okay, so I have to ask you something. And feel free to be completely honest with me."

"Okay…" I wait for the moment where he tells me he was kidding and he really thinks I'm a killer.

"Hypothetically, if I were to ask you on a date, what would you say?" he asks.

My heart erupts in my chest. "Well, if we were only speaking hypothetically, I'd say yes."

The corners of his mouth quirk. "And if I wasn't speaking hypothetically."

"Then I'd say I'd have to think about it." I've been spending way too much time watching Raven seduce guys.

He bites his bottom lip and reaches for my messenger bag. Before I can react, he extracts my cell phone. He punches a few buttons and hands me the phone. We stare at each other and I picture my lips pressed to his, tasting him thoroughly. He leans in like he might kiss me, then the bell rings and students pour into the quad.

He winks and backs away. "Think about it and let me know when the hypothetical can become a reality," he says before vanishing into the crowd.

It's probably the closest I've ever come to a perfect moment. And I'm actually happy. My happiness elates when I flick the screen on. He's added his phone number to my contacts.

When I look up, the quad is profoundly occupied with people standing along the wall, sitting on the benches, talking, laughing, yelling. With my shoulders slouched, I take a deep breath before carefully making my way toward the hall.

Someone slams into me from behind. *I want to die. Piercing. Heartache. An eternity of self-loathing finally reaching its end.*

I dodge to the side, but the crowd thickens. I'm bumped and prodded from all directions. My bag slips from my shoulder and falls to the floor. I scramble to pick it up. *Death. Everywhere.*

A thick-necked guy gives me a hard shove. "Watch it, killer."

I elbow the nearest person, trying to make room. *Bound, gagged, I see where you're hiding, blonde hair, blue eyes. I'm not going to hurt you.* I gasp.

Mackenzie's eyes bulge with terror. "What's the matter with you? Are you having, like, an episode or something?"

I snatch my bag, weave through the nearest gap, and burst out of the front door. The sunlight sparkles on my skin and I breathe in the fresh air. The bell rings and I cut across the grass and round the corner.

Raven is leaning against the side entrance. A guy with greasy hair and sideburns leans over her with his hands braced on the wall. Her eyes are locked on the guy like she is a love-struck puppy. He glances in my direction and I catch sight of the *X* on his eye—the sleazebag from the other night.

"What are you doing?" I hurry toward her.

Raven's eyes are red and swollen and her mascara is smudged. "I'm not doing anything. Now go away."

"You're not okay." I reach a hand for her. "What did he do to you?"

"She's fine," the sleazebag snarls and slaps my hand away. "Now get the hell out of here."

"Don't touch me, asshole," I warn, breathing through the stench of his death.

Raven wipes her tears away with the collar of her pink shirt. "Ember, just go inside. Please."

My muscles stiffen under the guy's powerful glare. "I will, but you're coming with me."

"You need to butt out of business that doesn't concern you." The guy prowls forward and shoves me backward.

"She's my friend," I say firmly, regaining my balance. "So therefore it is my business."

He glares at me with hatred. "Well, if you want, I could make it directly concern you." He lunges at me, grabs my arms, and thrusts me back against the brick wall.

His vile death chokes me. *He stands in the middle of a field. It's dark. A gunshot fires and he collapses to the ground.*

I blink, stunned. It's not the same death omen as the other night.

He smiles and a chill pricks at my skin. "What's wrong *Ember*? Are you scared?" He drops his voice as he leans in, his stale breath hot against my face. "Tell me, how was your drive home last night?"

"You tell me." I kick him in the shin, dodge to the side of him, and reach for Raven. "Come on, let's get out of here."

Raven shakes her head and skitters away from me. "I can't, Em. I have to stay here."

Rage flickers across his face. He hurdles for me and grips my wrists so tight my skin breaks. I groan as the venom of a thousand deaths paralyzes me: *self-inflicting, painful, too early, broken heart, old age, help me, help me, help me.* There are so many that I can't sort through all of them. It's crushing the oxygen from my lungs and strangles my heart. It's unbearable and ironic; what if death omens are the cause of my infinite death?

"Let her go," a deep, demanding voice chips the blackness and pain.

Sleazebag abandons my arms and I crumple to the ground. I clutch the grass, gasping for air. *Deep breaths. Deep breaths. Deep breaths.*

A hand appears in my vision, but I shake my head. "Let me help you up."

"Go away." I choke. "*Please.* I swear I'm fine."

"Ember, take my hand," Asher says and the resonance of his voice settles me down.

I slip my hand into his and contentment glides through my body, squelching the pain.

He helps me to my feet, his grey eyes searching me as he brushes grass out of my hair, off my shoulder, and the feel of his hands is invigorating. "Are you okay?"

Intoxication hums through my head. "I'm fine…"

He traces his fingers down my cheekbone, my neck, my throat, heating my skin in an unfamiliar way. "Ember…" He groans and lust fills his eyes.

I repress a moan. "I think I… I think I…"

"A little help here," Raven's sobs crash us back to reality.

"I think you'll be okay." His eyes focus on the doors of the school as he blinks the glazed look in his eyes away. "But I think you need to take your friend home."

Raven's curled up against the door, bawling her eyes out. "Em, help me. Please. I don't know what's going on."

I squat down in front of her. "Come on, let's get you home." When I get her to her feet, focusing past the pollution of her death, I notice both Asher and the sleazebag are gone. "Where'd that guy go? Rav, did you see where he went?"

"Take me home!" she screams psychotically, with her hands clenched. "Now!"

Sighing, I lead her toward the parking lot, picking up my bag along the way. Holding my breath, I exhale through her death omen: *blood under her head, pain in her body, rain falling from the sky.* I lower Raven into the passenger seat of her car and buckle the seatbelt for her, then climb into the driver's seat.

"Do you have your keys on you?" I adjust the seat back.

Tears rain from her eyes as she rummages the keys out of her shirt pocket. "I'm so sorry. I don't know why I yelled at you."

I press my lips together, fighting back the urge to yell at her, and turn the engine on. "Sorry for what?"

"For bailing on you so I could meet up with Garrick." She covers her face with her hands and cries.

"You bailed out on me this morning to be with that guy that has the X on his eye?" I'm stunned. "But he's a total creep."

"I like him," she says, blinking her tears back, looking possessed. "He's nice, has good teeth, and is courteous."

"No he's not." As I back the car out of the parking spot, I notice Asher's GTO peeling out of the parking lot. "Okay… where is he going?"

"Ember!" Raven shouts with terror in her eyes. "Please take me home!"

"Okay. Okay." What is going on with her?

I drive toward our neighborhood, letting her cry for a few minutes. Then I turn down the volume of the radio. "Okay, you have to tell me what the hell happened to you that night Laden vanished," I demand in a soft but determined tone. "And why you were just with a guy that probably slipped you a roofie."

"He didn't do that," she protests with a quick shake of her head. "It was another guy with the same kind of *X* in his eye."

"I know you're lying," I accuse. "Your eye just twitched."

She dabs her eyes with her fingers. "I'm crying. Of course my eye twitched."

"I don't believe you," I say. "You're lying and you've been lying to me since the other night. And you're not acting like yourself... You're not taking drugs again, are you?"

"Of course not." She rolls her eyes.

As we drive over the bridge, her eyes dart to the median. There's a faint scent of death in the air and on the lamppost is a blue flyer with Laden's face on it. His car is no longer in the street, but the large red X on the asphalt is still visible.

"Such a shame." Laughter hints her voice. Her eyes, smeared with mascara, widen as she gawks at the spot Laden vanished. "He was a really good kisser." She leans forward and relaxes her head on the dashboard. She shuts her eyes, sweeps her hair to the side, and fans her sweaty face. "It's so hot... Isn't it so hot?"

I notice the scratch on her shoulder blade looks a little infected. "What happened to your shoulder?"

She shelters the spot with her hand. "Things got a little rough between Laden and I, if you know what I mean."

I press my lips together. "How rough?"

Her head whips up and her eyes scorch fire. "What are you getting at exactly? That I might have had something to do with his death?"

"There's no proof he's dead yet." I veer down the road that leads to our houses. "And I didn't say anything about you being involved. It just looks infected."

"Yeah, whatever. If anyone should be accused of his murder it's you. Especially with the whole I-saw-him-standing-outside-my-house thing. You better watch what you say, *Ember*, or people are going to think you're as crazy as your dad. Oh wait, they already do."

At that moment, I hate her. She is not my best friend and I don't care if I ever see her again. I want to rip her hair out and hurt her.

"You need to tell me what happened. With the details," I demand as I turn into the driveway of her house. I force the shifter into park and place a hand on her arm. "It's like you're possessed by the devil or something."

She glances at my hand on her arm and then her eyes drain of emotion. "I have no idea what you're talking about." She jerks her arm away and jumps out of the car.

I remove the keys from the ignition and jump out after her. "Raven, we're not done with this conversation yet. I'm worried about you. You're acting like you've lost your mind."

"You would be the expert on that, Death Girl." She whisks around the front of the car and shoves her hand at me. "My keys, please." I slam the keys into her palm.

"Thanks, Emmy. And I mean for everything. But honestly, I really need a break from you. You're too much baggage. " She sashays into her house and slams the door, leaving me in the driveway, stirring in my own anger.

I storm for my house, but a flash of black in the trees sends me to an earthshattering halt. Laden's body hangs from the tree in my front yard, a rope around his neck, and blood dripping from his lips. His pale skin is blue and his eyes stare lifelessly at me.

Death. Silence.

Trying not to panic, I fumble my phone out of my bag and nearly drop it. I start to dial the police, but when I look back at the tree the phone falls from my hands. The body is gone, but his blood still stains the grass.

Chapter 8

I swivel in the computer chair with my fingers to my temples. I'm tucked in the corner desk just outside the living room. The words on the computer screen are blurry from the hours of searching on the internet. Ghost possession. Demon possession. Cult rituals. Nothing explains what's going on with Raven. Or what's going on with me.

So I shift the focus to Garrick. A death omen has never been that powerful before. It felt like a thousand deaths, each one a thorn on a dying rose, individualized but connected to the same vine of life. I start to type something on the keyboard when Ian's head appears over my shoulder and he reads the screen.

"Wow, should I be worried?" he asks, reading my search history on the sidebar.

"We're studying mythology and human nature in English class," I lie easily.

"Well, if you need any help, let me know," he says. "I had to study mythology for this oil-based painting class I took. The teacher was seriously into that crap."

"Yep, I sure will." I wait for him to leave and then type "X tattoo" into the search. Nothing pops out, so I delete "tattoo" and put "symbol." I scroll through the options and click on a link about execution.

I read through the article: "An *X* symbol has many representations, one being the elimination of a life." I slump back in the chair and cross my arms. "Well, look at that. It does have to do with death."

Still, why does Garrick have an *X* on his eye? Could Garrick be... could Garrick be causing the disappearances? But why does he have so many death omens?

I stretch my fingers and type: Death Omens. I highlight the search button with the cursor, and hesitate before clicking it. I skim through the search results, until I come across a sketch of an angel with her head tucked down, tears seeping from her eyes, and black smudges on her cheeks. Her dark wings elongate the page and a lifeless rose crumbles from her hand. A skeletal pattern tattoos her arms and legs and a circle rounds the stone floor beneath her bare feet.

"It's just like in Asher's painting of Angel," I mutter. Grim Angel is the title of the sketch. "It's like a mix between the Grim Reaper and an Angel."

I do a search on Grim Angel. "Grim Angels are a unique breed immune to most of the Angel of Deaths' and the Grim Reapers' gifts. Grim Angels are believed to be insane due to the curse of their hybrid breeding of an Angel of Death and a Grim Reaper, which plagues them with a constant burden of death. They may suffer from blackouts and lose track of their mind, if not properly taken care of." I read the note aloud again. "Blackouts and a general burden of constant death." I shiver and peek over my shoulder, just to make sure I'm not sprouting wings. But the inner voice deep inside me disagrees.

After reading a few more websites, and finding nothing else, I give up for the night. "What are these things, like some kind of hush-hush mythical species no one is supposed to talk about or something?"

I shove the chair back, shut off the computer, and flop down on the couch next to Ian. "Is mom home yet?"

He surfs through the channels with the remote. "Nah, she called and said she's going to be late."

"Did you check on her prescription to see if it was still full?"

"Yeah… and it's still full. She hasn't taken them for at least a week."

"We should talk to her about it," I say. "She came home last night totally wasted. And ranting about dad being a killer."

Ian turns down the volume of the TV and sets the remote down. "Where was I?"

I point over my shoulder at the staircase. "Upstairs in the attic with your '*muse.*'"

He squirms uneasily. "Did you get her upstairs okay?"

I grab a handful of skittles from the candy bowl on the coffee table and pop them into my mouth. "Yeah, I made do."

He slips off his beanie to ruffle his hair. "Was she nice to you?"

I seal my lips together and force the tears to back down. "She was fine, I guess."

"I can tell when you're lying." Ian pushes the sleeves of his shirt up and kicks his feet up on the table. "What did she say to you?"

Ian knows about my rough relationship with our mother to an extent, but there are pieces I omit from him, like her accusations that I killed Grandma Nelly.

"She was as nice as she always is." I scoop up another handful of skittles and get up from the couch. "I'm going to bed. I'll see you in the morning."

"Ember…" He struggles for words. "You know you can talk to me about stuff. My meds are helping a lot and I think I can handle things now."

"I know," I say, but he can't. It's in his eyes—the fear I might open up and he'll have to deal with it. So I bottle it up—the accident, Raven, death, that I saw Laden's body hanging from our tree. "And if I do ever feel like talking, you'll be the first one I come to."

He lets out a breath of relief and turns back to the TV. I trudge up to my room, wondering when I'll crack.

Chapter 9

Asher's not at school the next day. Or the next. It bothers me for some reason. I barely know him, yet knots wind in my stomach every time I think about him. It's like I've become obsessed and I don't like it.

I'm in the library, tucked in the table in the farthest corner, writing poetry about my frustration.

In the midst of a foggy field, the answers are hidden

But the impossible journey deems them forbidden

"Have I told you how much I'm sorry," Raven says, sliding a candy bar across the table.

I glance up from my journal. "How many times are you going to apologize?" I pick up the candy bar. "My teeth are going to rot out if you keep it up."

"As long as it takes for you to accept it." She takes a magazine out of her bag. "So what does Mr. Reynolds want us to do in here?"

"He said something about doing research on our science project." I point the pen at the computers. "But the computers are full, so I thought I'd hang out and do some writing instead."

"What are you writing about?" She moves the strap of her tank top over a little and peels a layer of skin off her shoulder blade.

I scratch the title *The Unknown* on the top of the page. "Stuff. Life… You know you should really get that looked at. I really do think it's infected."

She flicks the skin onto the floor. "I did and the doctor said it's fine." Her eye twitches and she pretends to pluck some mascara from her eyelashes.

Swirling the pen on the top of the paper, I sketch a poorly drawn angel. "You can die from infections. Do you know that?"

She peels another layer of skin off, and it's like she's molting. "But you know when I'm really going to die and if it was from the infection, you'd make me go to the hospital."

She has me there. Under the title of my poem, I write:

The Reaper of Death, the Angel of Life.

They walk together in day and night.

"Raven, have you ever heard of a Grim Angel?" I ask.

She drums her manicured nails on the table as she considers this. "Maybe… in one of the books I looked through when I was doing my angel painting project. But I can't remember exactly what it is. Why? What's up?"

"I was just looking through some stuff on the internet the other night and I came across a drawing of one. I've never heard of them before, though."

"Why were you looking up angel stuff on the internet?"

"For a poem I'm working on," I lie breezily. "Do you still have those books?"

She shakes her head as she twists her pink hair up. "I returned them to the town library and they had to special order them, so I don't even know if they're still there."

I drop my voice as the librarian walks by. "Do you remember anything about them at all?"

She turns a page of her magazine. "Only that they are a mix between a Grim Reaper and an Angel of Death. And that they're super crazy most of the time."

"How exactly are they supposed to be crazy?" I ask. "I mean, what defines them as being insane? Do they do weird things or rant incoherent thoughts?"

"The books said that they used to sneak around killing innocent people and stealing their souls," she explains. "Like it was a game or something. And they suffered from hallucinations."

I need to get my hands on those books. I make a note on the paper to go to the library and underline it.

"So what's up with you and Asher?" She abruptly changes the topic.

I stop drawing and glance up. "What do you mean?"

She presses me with a look from over the magazine. "Don't play dumb with me, *Ember Rose Edwards*. You know what I'm talking about—our knight in shining armor and the reason why you've been bummed out all week."

"I'm not playing dumb, *Raven Lilly Monroe*," I retort. "I have no clue what you're talking about."

She taps her lips with a wicked glint in her sapphire eyes. "So you don't have a thing for a dark-haired stranger who rescued you from your death omen spasm and who showed you his painting of an angel... Although, by how stuck you are on him, I'd guess he showed you other stuff of his, too."

I roll my eyes and focus on my poem. "I thought you had a thing for him. Wasn't he the reason for your melt-down in my closet... And wait, how do you even know about the painting?"

She giggles. "Oh Em, you are such a riot. You can't almost make out with someone in the art room and expect no one to know about it." She dabs the tears from the corner of her eyes. "And I'm totally over the Asher thing. Guys are like shoes to me, you know that. I wear them once and then get bored."

I press down so hard on the paper the pencil breaks. "Did you actually wear Asher?"

She points an accusing finger at me. "The very fact that you ask that means you like him. So I think it's time you found out where he is. And if he likes you."

"Raven, this isn't second grade." I tip back in the chair and throw the pencil in the trash bin.

She discounts me. "Call him. Didn't you say he gave you his phone number?"

"I already tried and he didn't answer," I lie to get her to drop it. The bell rings and I slam my journal shut. "Look, I think I need to just get over him. I have too much stuff going on in my life." I swing my bag over my shoulder, but she steals it away from me.

"Like what?" She backs away, jiggling the bag out in front of her. "Your life's pretty easy, Em."

"Raven," I warn as she backs down the nearest aisle between the bookshelves. "Don't even think about it. I swear to God, I'll never forgive you if you call him."

"Don't kid yourself, Em. You'll always forgive me, no matter what I do." She spins in her high-heeled boots and dashes off.

I chase after her, fuming as she pulls out my cell phone and drops my bag on the floor. I hop over my bag and reach for the back of her shirt as she punches the buttons. A girl at the end of the aisle backs away, eyes wide, legs trembling, probably thinking I'm trying to kill Raven. Raven laughs as she wiggles out of my fingers. She darts around the corner of the bookshelf, intentionally knocking some books off the shelf.

"Raven, please don't call him." I trip over the books and round the corner. She has the phone to her ear and dodges my advance. But her ankle rolls and she falls on her butt.

I jump on her, accidently bumping my knee into hers, and kicking a row of books to the floor with my boot. Her death pours through me, but I breathe through it. "Give me my phone back."

She giggles as I try to pry the phone from her fingers. On her back, she pushes herself across the floor with her feet and I crawl after her.

"Hi, Asher, this is Raven," she says into the phone and I narrow my eyes. "Call Ember when you get the chance. She needs to know if you're okay and if you like her, because it's driving her crazy. Literally."

I pinch her arm. "You are the worst friend ever."

"Ow…" She laughs, throwing her head back. Tears of laughter flood her eyes as she keeps talking in the phone.

"In fact, it's a matter of life or death—she has to know ASAP." She hangs up the phone.

I glare at her and rip the phone from her hand. "Thanks a lot. Now he's going to think I'm insane."

"Aren't you?" She flutters her eyelashes innocently. "Besides, I was just trying to help. And it shouldn't bother you what other people think. You've been through a lot worse than some guy thinking you're a stalker."

I roll to my back, putting distance from her and her death. "I don't know why I care, but I do."

"I wouldn't get your hopes up," she says in a heavy-weighted tone. "Guys like Asher don't really look at girls like you. They're more my type."

I wonder if this whole scene was to make Asher think I am insane, so she could have him. "Raven, are you sure—"

"Raven. Ember. Can you explain what on earth happened?"

We blink up at our science teacher, Mr. Reynolds. He's the kind of guy who always looks like he has a chip on his shoulder, like his face is permanently frozen in a scowl. He wears a lot of tweed suits with elbow patches.

He stares at us lying on the floor and then at the books strewn around us. "So which one of you wants to explain what happened?"

"Um… Would you believe me if I said the books pushed us over?" Raven suppresses a laugh.

He blinks through his thick-rimmed glasses. "This is going to cost you both after-school detention."

"Why?" Raven complains. "We were just messing around, Mr. R. And we didn't mean to knock over the books."

"And I'm going to add two more days for complaining." He extracts detention slips from his pocket, hands them to us, and walks to the checkout counter.

"You should have just let me call him." Raven pinches me on the arm.

I slap her hand and wince from the foul flicker of her death. "Why? I knew you'd make it as embarrassing as you did. You always do."

Just then, Cameron strolls by. His eyebrows dip together as he spots Raven and I tangled up in a pile of books.

He stops in front of us and his lips curl into impish grin. "I'm kind of curious what led up to this."

"We fell," I say, before Raven can feed him some dirty story. I grab the shelf and pull myself to my feet.

Raven sticks out her hand to Cameron and pouts her bottom lip. "A little help, please."

Cameron takes her hand and tugs her up. She intentionally trips and braces herself with his shoulders. "Oh my goodness." She squeezes his shoulder. "You must work out."

He removes her hand from his arm. "Not really."

"We should get to class," I tell Raven before she can further embarrass herself.

She seductively smiles at Cameron and flips her hair before walking past him. "See you after school, Em." She waggles her finger at me and turns the corner.

"Sorry about that," I say to Cameron. I round the bookshelf and collect my bag from the floor where Raven dropped it. When I turn back around, I almost run into him.

He watches me with his haunting eyes, like he could eat me up. "You dropped this." He hands me my phone.

I drop the phone in my bag and back up. "I'm real sorry about Raven. She can kind of be a little… overly friendly sometimes."

"I think she might have some issues," he informs me with a lazy grin.

"Doesn't everyone?" I pick up a book to divert my attention away from the heat in his eyes.

He takes the book from my hands and discards it onto the shelf. "Okay, I'm going to get straight to the point. I think we should go out on a date."

"Go out on a date?" I elevate my eyebrows. "Really? You and me?"

"Why do you sound so surprised?" he asks, amused.

I glance at my black jeans, my fingerless arm warmers, and my black and red striped tank top, then at his black button-down shirt and his name brand jeans. "I think it's kind of obvious."

"We're not as different as you think," he assures me confidently. "You like poetry, right? So I was thinking that you and I could go to a poetry slam."

I sputter a laugh. "Sorry to burst your bubble, but there aren't poetry slams around here. In fact, the closest thing you'll probably find is banjo night down at Mamma's House of Cheese Fries."

He laughs and it erases the misery in his eyes. "You don't think I know that." He inches forward and the tips of his shoes clip the tips of mine. "There is, however, a Saturday night poetry slam in Jackson."

I casually step back, seeking room before an accidental touch happens. "What about Mackenzie?"

He matches my step, closing in on me, the heat of his body radiating all over me. "What about her?"

"Are you two like, dating or something?" My elbow bumps the shelf and books topple over.

"We're just friends." He crosses his arms and leans against the bookshelf.

"Yeah, but you guys won't be, if you go out with me," I say and he fakes a befuddled look. "Oh, don't pretend like you haven't heard what people say about me: cult member, Satan worshiper, *murderer*."

"And haven't you heard that I like to spend time in the cemetery digging up graves." He dips his head in and his warm breath embraces my cheeks. "Say yes, Ember. *Please*."

The back of my mind screams that this is wrong, that something is off about the whole situation. But there's a pull toward him, like a magnet to metal.

"Okay," I say, startled by my answer. "It's a date, then."

The bell screeches and he backs toward the door. "I'll pick you up tomorrow at eight." He winks at me and pushes out the door.

***

"I hate this," Raven complains as we take a seat at a table.

School is over, but Raven and I have detention with Mr. Reynolds, which is held in the library. I haven't told her yet about my date with Cameron, because I know she'll freak out and make a scene.

"It's only for an hour," I say. "You'll survive."

Her face scrunches at the science book in front of me. "I have much better things I could be doing than homework."

I take out the assignment. "You'll survive."

Mr. Reynolds comes up to our table with his arms crossed. "You two are not allowed to sit near each other." He points a finger at a table across the room. "Raven, get your stuff and move over there."

"We promise we won't talk." She smiles innocently.

Mr. Reynolds narrows his eyes. "Get your stuff and move over there. Now."

Raven huffs, grabs her purse and a magazine, and stomps over to the table across the room. Mr. Reynolds heads back behind the counter to chat with the librarian. I start working on my homework, but anxious energy thrums through me.

When Mr. Reynolds steps out for a moment, I walk up to the counter. Ms. Kinsley, the middle-aged librarian with auburn hair and green eyes, looks up from her computer.

"Can I help you?" Her standoffish tone probably means she knows who I am.

"Do you have any books," I say, "that perhaps focus on the more uncommon creatures of mythology?"

She types something on the keyboard. "There might be some in the back, in the mythology section, but I don't know what they focus on."

"Thanks," I say and walk for the bookshelves. At the back, I find the mythology section. I pull out the heaviest book, and camp down on the floor with it. The index has nothing titled Grim Angels, however there is a section on "The Curse of the Angels."

The curse of the Angels is a result of a battle that took place a long time ago. Most refer to it as the battle between good and evil, but during the era, people believed the only theme to be evil.

The battle allegedly started from a dispute over souls. Angels of Death were the carriers of the innocent souls, and Grim Reapers the carriers of the evil souls. However, when the Reapers became greedy and began stealing the souls of the innocent, a battle broke out between the two. As a form of punishment, Michael, the ruler of the Angels of Death, and Abaddon, the ruler of the Grim Reapers, cursed the warriors to Earth and bound them there with a breed that carried both groups blood.

Grim Angels—half Grim Reaper, half Angel of Death—have walked the earth for centuries undetected by humans. Only would they be free when the last Grim Angel made the choice between good and evil.

The next section switches to Legend of Faeries. I thrum my finger on top of the book, having no idea what to do with what I read. I start to put the book back on the shelf when wet droplets trickle down the back of my neck.

I wipe them away, looking behind me, and then at my hand. "Blood?"

I glance up at the ceiling and blood splatters against my forehead. I quickly smear it away and jump to my feet. Hanging by a rope from the ceiling is the body of Farrah Taverson. Her medieval dress is soaked with blood and her eyes are bleeding.

"Oh my God." I breathe, backing away. *What do I do? What do I do?* I rub my eyes, but she stays there, her feet swaying from the breeze of the vent next to her head.

I back away toward the edge of the shelf, when I crash into someone. I whirl around with ragged breaths.

"Ember, are you okay?" Cameron asks. He has a book in his hand and a backpack on his shoulder. He reaches for my head and wipes his fingers across my skin. When he pulls back there's blood on them. "Did you hurt yourself?"

I wipe my forehead with my sleeve, and glance behind me at the ceiling. Her body is gone, but the blood is real. What does that mean?

"I must have scratched myself on the edge of the shelf when I was pulling the book out," I tell Cameron.

He looks at me warily. "Are you sure you're okay? You look like you're going to be sick or something."

Suddenly the intercom screeches on. "Any faculty left in the building need to report to the main office immediately." It statics off.

"I wonder what that was about," Cameron says as we walk out of the shelves.

"I'm not sure," I say, heading back to the table with a permanent chill in my body.

"Are you planning on going to the cemetery tonight?"

"I don't think so… I really think I might need to get some rest."

"Alright, everyone," Ms. Kinsley stands up from her chair and shuts her computer off. "Everyone needs to get there stuff and exit the library. I need to lock up so I can go the main office."

As I gather my books and bag from the table, Cameron wipes some remaining blood from my hair with the sleeve of his shirt. "Such a shame." He grins slyly. "I've been dying to get you alone again. But I guess I can wait until tomorrow."

"About that," I start to cancel, not wanting to add more to my cracking plate. "I think I—"

"I'll pick you up at eight," he cuts me off, sensing a rejection. Backing away, he runs his fingers through his hair and smiles. "I promise, I'll give you the time of your life." The way he says it sends a chill over my skin.

"Oh my God." Raven comes running up to me, her purse on her shoulder and the car keys in her hand. "Did you hear?"

I shake my head, my eyes locked on Cameron as he shoves through the exit doors.

"Farrah Taverson's body was found next to the lake." Raven says as we walk out the door of the library. The hallway is empty, and most of the lights have been shut off. "I guess she told a few friends she was going to go looking for Laden. Some boaters found her floating in the water, and she had stab wounds and there were feathers in the pockets of her dress. They think it's murder. And probably the same one who killed Laden and your—"

"Neither of their bodies have been found." My heart crushes into tiny bits and pieces that stab into my stomach. "So they might not be dead."

She gives me a look of pity. "Yeah, maybe."

I swallow hard. "How do you know this?"

She leans in and whispers, "I overheard Mr. Reynolds talking to the cops about it when I snuck out to go to the bathroom."

We push through the side doors. Parked in the fire zone in front of the school are two police cars. But if what Raven says is true, then how did I see her body? Could my death omen abilities have cranked up and now I can see death without touching someone? I'm not sure—I'm not sure about anything anymore.

"What's wrong, Em?" Raven asks, unlocking her car. "You look like you saw a ghost or something."

Or something. "I'm fine."

She frowns at me with doubt from over the top of the car. "Are you sure?"

I nod, ducking into the car. "Yeah, absolutely one hundred percent fine."

"Want to know something really creepy," Raven says, swinging the keychain around her finger. "I got this really strange text from Farrah and now I'm wondering if it had something to do with this. Like maybe she was being stalked by the murderer and was starting to get scared."

"Why would she send you a text?" I take out my cell phone and check my messages. "I didn't know you guys were friends."

"We talk a lot in art class." She cranes her head and backs out of the parking spot.

I toss my cell phone into my bag. "What did the message say?"

She shoots me a haunting look. "*Fear the Reaper.*"

***

"Oh my God! Oh my God!" Raven bounces up and down in the middle of my bedroom, holding my unenthusiastic hands. Her bangle bracelets jingle and her eyes are as sparkly as her glitter eyeliner. "This is *so* amazing. Why didn't you tell me in the car?"

"Because I knew you'd want to bounce up and down, which is a total road hazard." I wiggle my hands free. She's been really bad lately about touching me. "But don't you think it's a little weird that he asked me out? I mean, I really don't seem like his type."

She flops down on my bed and dramatically drapes her arm over her head. "Oh Em, you are so naïve sometimes." She peeks out from underneath her arm. "Did you ever read that romance book I gave you? It has a lot of good tips in it."

"I'm sure it does." I try not to roll my eyes. I feel like shit, but try to play it off, convincing myself that what happened with Farrah was just my death omen evolving. "But I still don't know if I should go…"

"Are you having second thoughts because of Asher?" She frowns. "Because I don't think you should date him."

I check my messages and then toss the phone on the dresser. "At the library you said the opposite."

"No, I said you should call him and find out if he likes you. And obviously he doesn't, since he hasn't called back." Her lips curl to a smile. "And now you have tall, blonde, and sexy wanting you."

"It's just a date." I write the word *solitude* on my wall and then below it: *Do you know me at all? Are my words just air? Is my heart easy to spare?* "I don't *have* him."

She slants up on her elbows and scowls at my words. "Why did you just write that?"

I shrug and circle the words: *you, are, my,* and *heart.* "Why do I write anything?"

She leaps off the bed, steals the marker from my hands, and traces over the letters until the words transform into a small sketch of an intricate angel. She clicks the cap on and hands the marker to me. "There. That's much better."

We grow silent and she gathers her purse from the bed. "I'm going to take off. Call me tomorrow before you go on your big date. And wear something sexy." She eyes my clothes and slips out into the hallway.

I drop down on the bed and pick up the romance novel from my nightstand. Each and every page has me pulling faces. It's a relief when my phone rings. I chuck the book aside and grab my phone off the dresser.

I yawn and stretch out my arms. "Hello."

"Hey, it's me," Asher says.

A pause.

"You haven't been at school," I finally say. "Were you sick or something? You ran off so quickly after Garrick, umm... tried to hurt Raven and I."

"I was... Look, Ember, can we talk about this in person?"

"Umm... is this about the message Raven left you?"

"Kind of." He speaks cautiously. "But there's also something I want to show you."

"Sure," I tell him. "What time are you going to be here?"

His somber tone doesn't alleviate the tension. "Can I pick you up in like fifteen minutes?"

I tell him yes and we say goodbye. I pull my black vest over my red and black striped top and lose the arm warmers. Then I wait for Asher on the living room couch, trying not to get too pumped up about seeing him. Ian's not at home and I haven't seen my mom since she told me I'd turn into a killer like my dad. But that happens when she drinks a lot. My dad wasn't a killer. He liked his bar fights, and did some questionable things, but he never sent anyone to their grave.

I turn on the TV, but the satellite's been disconnected. "Did she forget to pay the bill again?" I dial my mom's cell, but it sends me straight to voicemail. I hang up and search the cabinet drawers for the bill. There are stacks and stacks of papers, batteries, tacks, pens, but no bills.

Suddenly the lights flip off and the house suffocates in darkness, except for the faint cast of the outside light filtering through the curtains.

"Okay… did she forget to pay the power bill too?" I fumble through the drawer and pull out a flashlight. I shine the light around the room as I walk toward the front door. The floorboards creak under my feet and I can hear heavy breathing.

I'm not alone.

My boot catches on something solid and I fall flat on my face. The flashlight flies out of my hand and rolls across the floor. My legs tangle with something and the silence of their body is more frightening than if I felt their death.

"Asher?" I squint through the dark down at my legs.

A dark figure slowly rises from the floor. The head is enormous, its arms long, and its body stretches to the ceiling. A cape flows to the ground and armors its face. Nope, not Asher.

"Ember," it breathes, reaching for me. "Don't be afraid. You know I'd never hurt you."

"You stay the hell away from me." I flip over onto my stomach, taking out the table. I scramble to my feet and sprint across the room for the flashlight. I scoop it up and spin around, sweeping the light across the room.

But he's gone.

I back for the door, sliding my phone out of my pocket. I dial Ian's number. "Come on, come on, come—"

The doorbell rings. Startled, I drop my phone on the floor and the back pops off. I snatch up the pieces and quickly throw open the door.

Asher looks sexy as hell. His inky black hair dangles in his gorgeous slate eyes and the sleeves of his plaid shirt are pushed up, showing off his lean arms. My eyes stray down lower, to where his jeans ride low on his hips, and I picture myself trailing kisses down his abs.

Damn Raven and her dirty books. They're messing with my head.

He shields his eyes with his hands. "Do you blind every guy that shows up on your porch?" he jokes.

I click off the flashlight and toss it on the end table. "Sorry, the power went out."

I shut the door behind me as I step outside. We walk silently to his car and get in. Through my living room window, the caped visitor watches me and I can't seem to take my eyes off him.

Asher turns the stereo down and rotates in his seat to face me. "Is something wrong?" He tracks the course of my gaze. "What are you looking at? Did you forget to turn something off?"

I tear my attention away from the house. Away from *him.* "No, everything's good. So what did you want to show me?"

He grins as he backs down the driveway. "It's a surprise."

I try to be happy, but I'm severely distracted by the return of an old friend, the Grim Reaper. The last time he showed up, he ruined my life.

Chapter 10

I first met the mysterious cloaked creature when I went to live with my dad. I named him the Grim Reaper, but only because he looked like Death. When I was little, I thought he was my imaginary friend because no one could see him but me. After he vanished from my life, he reappeared once, right before my dad vanished. He told me my dad was going to die within minutes. I panicked and called the cops, telling them Patrick Edwards was about to die. It was one of the biggest mistakes of my life and put me under high suspicion.

I watch the trees blur by, trying to convince myself that I didn't see the Grim Reaper, that he was just a figment of my imagination. The sky is masked with darkness and the fields and yards are shadows.

"Are you sure you're okay?" Asher drives down the main road toward the outskirts of town. "You seem a little distracted tonight."

"What?" I turn away from the window.

Asher sighs. Keeping one hand on the steering wheel, he reaches over and takes my hand. "You're probably wondering where I've been for the last few days and why I ran off after that thing with that man who had the *X* on his eye."

"You mean Garrick," I clarify.

He entwines our fingers and tranquility envelops my over-thinking brain. Suddenly, my Grim Reaper and my Death problem are insignificant.

Asher asks, "Do you know Garrick?"

"Yeah, I met him at the party," I explain. "The one that I met you at."

He sketches along the folds of my fingers, sending tingles all over my skin. "Did you meet him before or after I talked to you that night?"

"After," I reply. "It was right before I left to chase down Raven… He told me someone was messing around with my car."

"And then your car's brakes went out." He cracks his knuckles on the steering wheel as he cogitates. "I wonder if…"

"If what?" I press. "Asher, do you know this guy? And did he mess with my brakes that night? Because he told me someone else was messing with my car, and I'm starting to wonder if it was him and maybe he was also the tailgater."

He slips his hand from mine and places it on the shifter; it feels like a glove slipped off my fingers and my hand feels bare. "Ember, have you ever heard of the Anamotti?" he asks and I shake my head. "Well, it's this term that got thrown around a lot in the neighborhood I lived in New York… It's kind of like this hush-hush secret society thing."

"What kind of a neighborhood did you live in?" I wonder.

He hesitates. "The Upper East Side."

"So it's a secret society for rich people."

"Kind of."

"I'm confused," I confess. "What does this have to do with Garrick? Is he part of it?"

He fiddles anxiously with the air freshener on the rearview mirror. "Yeah, he was… He is part of it."

"So Garrick's from New York too?" I question. "I don't mean to sound rude, but I'm not sure I believe that you, Cameron, and Garrick, all moved here at the same time and from New York."

"Garrick didn't move here from New York," Asher discloses in a subdued voice. "I said the term got thrown around a lot in my neighborhood, but it doesn't mean every member from the Anamotti lives there."

I ask, "But then how do you know Garrick is part of the Anamotti?"

"That X tattoo he has," Asher makes an X motion over his eye with his finger, "is the symbol of the Anamotti."

"So what are they?" I inquire, thinking about what I read on the internet about X symbols. "What is their secret society all about? And why do they have X's?"

He restlessly drums his fingers on the shifter, lets out a shaky breath, and laces his fingers with mine again. "I'm afraid it might scare you, especially because Garrick is interested in you."

"No, he seems interested in Raven." Unable to help myself, I caress his palm with my thumb. "I think he was with her that night when Laden disappeared."

"Maybe," he says sadly. "But I think he's using Raven to get to you."

"For what?" I begin to pull my hand away. "And how do you know all this… Are you part of this Anamotti?"

"I can't tell you that right now." His hand tightens on mine. "Trust me, I want to. Desperately. But not yet, okay? I need to… we need to spend some time together first. " Honesty blazes in his eyes like smoke over a fire. "Please just trust me, Ember."

It's a strange answer, but not accepting it would be like the pot calling the kettle black. "Okay, I can wait, I guess."

He runs his fingers through my hair, gently tugging at the roots and sending a shock of pleasure through my body. *Wow. Dear God Almighty.*

"Thank you for trusting me," his voice perpetuates my body with heat.

We leave the sunnier part of town behind and enter the rougher side. The old-fashioned shops and restaurants become old and dilapidated houses. Rusted cars clutter the yards and bars and smoke shops fill up the business areas. It's frightening how much this side of town feels like home.

My concentration centers on Asher. "So where's this mysterious place you're taking me?"

Still holding my hand, he downshifts. "That's kind of a surprise, but I thought we could get something to eat first. I mean, if that's okay with you."

I crack the window and let in a cool breeze. "Yeah, that's fine with me."

"Are you sure there's nothing bothering you?" he asks. "You seem a little… sad. Or sadder than usual."

The wind gusts through my hair and I shut my eyes, breathing in deeply. "I'm fine. I promise." I erase my sadness as much as possible, and open my eyes, summoning up a small smile. "I'm actually just really hungry."

"Good." He grins and turns the car into the crowded parking lot of Phil's Shenanigans and Fun. "Hmm…" Asher observes the sign. "I wonder what kind of fun it's referring to."

"No, you don't," I say unintentionally. It's the bar where my dad hung out.

"You've been here?" Asher shuts off the engine.

"Once or twice." I omit some of the truth. "And I think they card here."

"I heard they don't." He points a finger at the front door where a young couple is walking inside. "And I think we go to school with them."

"Yeah, you're probably right." I sigh heavily. "I think they do let in minors."

My dad came here a lot and brought me with him. I'd sit in the corner booth, coloring, while he drank himself into a stupor, ranting about his philosophical ideas on life and death until he'd piss off someone enough that they'd take a swing at him. Then Phil, the owner—who was like a second father to me—would load us up in his Chevy and drive us home.

"Do you know if the food's good here?" Asher opens the car door.

"Yeah, the food, the service—it's all great." *Except for the memories.*

Before I can climb out of the car, Asher hurries around, opens the door, and helps me out. The boy blows my mind with his gentleman skills. He holds my hand as we walk across the parking lot. There is a row of motorcycles in front and a bench where people are smoking. The windows of the bar are shielded with flashing neon signs and flyers. At the entrance Asher releases my hand, but only to open the door.

I fan the smoke from my face as the door swings closed. Asher returns his hand to mine. The bar is packed, the music's loud, and there are no barstools available. Paper-mache spiders and witches hang from the ceiling and each table has a miniature pumpkin.

"Hi y'all. My name is Amy and I'll be your waitress today." A perky girl in her early twenties appears in front of us. Her black skirt barely covers her legs and her white shirt is tight enough that the poor girl probably can't breathe. "We only got booths tonight. Is that okay?"

"What do you think?" Asher asks me. "Is a booth good?"

"A booth's better," I answer.

"Okay." The waitress leads us through the smoke and people with a cheery skip in her walk. We settle in the corner booth, sitting across from each other, and she hands us our menus and sashays toward the bar. Phil's the bartender tonight. He's a large man with tattoos casing his arms and neck. His shaved head reflects in the low light and his goatee touches the bottom of his neck. He has a T-shirt on with the sleeves torn off, jeans, and biker boots. He's pouring a shot when the waitress says something to him. His eyes lift to me and I slump down in the booth, holding the menu in front of my face, ducking for cover.

"Please don't come over here. Please don't come over here," I chant under my breath.

Asher guides the menu away from my face. "Okay, what's up?"

I pretend to be very interested in the list of appetizers. "Nothing. I'm just reading the menu."

He eyes me suspiciously and aims his attention to a person standing next to our table.

"Holy biscuits and gravy, it is you."

I know that voice. "Hey, Phil." I plaster a fake smile on my face and look up at him.

He grins and opens his arms, waiting for a hug. Internally cringing, I get to my feet and wrap my arms around him. He smells like cigars and booze. Both will be the cause of his death, something I've known for years.

I pull away and drop back down in the booth. "I thought you were going to quit smoking."

He rubs his neck tensely. "I did for a while, but old habits die hard. But look at you. All grown up. I haven't seen you since the night your…" he trails off. "Well, anyway. How are you doing? And how's your mama doing?"

"She's doing good." I pick at the peanut shells wedged in the cracks of the tabletop.

"Is she still working down at the diner?" he asks. "Or did she finally get away from that shithole."

"No, she's still doing the waitress thing," I say and his eyes wander to Asher. "Oh, this is Asher. Asher, this is Phil."

They nod and say their "how do you do's."

I grow fidgety and fiddle with the pumpkin, spinning it on the table. Being around Phil brings back the memories of the nights at the bar with my dad. When Phil would drive me and my dad home, he'd tell me things would get better—that eventually my dad would get his life together. It's not Phil's fault it never happened, but it reminds me of a time when I was naïve enough to believe it would.

He can tell I'm uncomfortable. "Alright, well if you need anything, let me know." I nod and he returns to his position behind the counter.

Asher turns the page of the menu. "I thought you said you'd been here once or twice."

I shrug, not ready to veer down that path. Awkward silence builds and we flip through the menus. By the time the waitress shows up to take our order, I wonder if Asher's going to tell her we're leaving.

She poises her pen above the order book. "What can I get y'all?"

Asher taps his fingers on his lips and I catch Amy licking her own as she eyes his. "What exactly are Rocky Mountain oysters?" he asks.

I restrain a laugh as Amy's face twists in confusion.

"Well… I think they're a kind of meat. I'm not sure what kind, but I like them." She presses the end of the pen against her chin.

I shake my head at Asher. "You don't want those. Trust me."

Amy shoots me an aggravated look. "They're not bad. I mean, the meat's a little tough, but they taste good." I feel bad for her. Kind of. She leans over the table and her boobs practically pop out of her top. "Look sweetie, get whatever you want, okay?" she says to Asher.

Asher's gaze connects with mine. "I kind of like to know what I'm eating."

I lean over the table, cup my hand around Asher's ear, and whisper what Rocky Mountain oysters are.

His eyes bulge. "Yeah, I'll have water, cheese fries, and a hamburger with extra mayo."

"I'll have the chicken sandwich and a coke." I shut my menu and Amy snatches it out of my hand. She takes Asher's menu more delicately and saunters off to the order window.

"Thank you," he says with a smile.

I rest my elbows on the table. "For what?"

"For not letting me eat that crap."

We laugh quietly and then silence builds again. A woman in a bright red dress and cowgirl boots is belting out the lyrics to Faith Hill's "This Kiss" from the stage. The whole scene is super cheesy, but I start to relax, like I'm finally home after being gone for three years.

"My dad and I used to come here," I finally say over the music.

He gives me his undivided attention. "Really." He glances at the rough people, the smoky atmosphere, and the bar lined with bikers. "How old were you?"

"I was four the first time he brought me down here, and it kept up until I was thirteen—until he died, basically," I say. "My dad really liked his Jack Daniels."

"So did my dad... Well, actually it was Jim Bean." He pauses and his smile brings soft invisible kisses to my skin. "See, that wasn't so hard. And we learned we have something in common."

"I'm not socially impaired," I retort, dusting some salt off the table. "I just like my space... for personal reasons."

He crosses his arms on the table. "I know you do and I actually kind of like that about you. You're not always giggling and trying to run your fingers through my hair."

I wonder if he's talking about Raven. "Some guys like that."

"No they don't." He flicks his tongue ring against his teeth. "I want you to give me a shot—I want you to let me in and let me get to know you."

My chest squeezes with elation, but thankfully my voice holds rhythm. "What do you want to know about me?"

He rolls the pepper shaker between his hands. "How long have you known Raven?"

I shrug. "Since we were born."

"Does she always act so…" he bites back.

"Slutty?" I finish for him.

He laughs and it's the most beautiful sound that's ever touched my ears. "I was going to say guy crazy, but I thought that'd make me sound like a jerk. She's a little intense, and that whole thing with Garrick. How did she even meet him?"

"At the same party I met him," I explain. "But I have no idea why she was with him that day at school."

He zips his lips together and studies the cracks in the table. "When Garrick had a hold of you at school… you looked like you were going to pass out."

"I just don't like being close to people like that." I tousle my hair with my fingers and stare at the karaoke stage area in the corner.

He slides his hand across the table and interlaces our fingers. "But you don't seem to mind when I touch you. In fact, I have this idea in my head—and please let me know if I'm overshooting it here—that you like me a little."

I shrug. "I guess you could say that… You make me feel calm."

"Calm, huh?" he muses. "And that's a good thing?"

"Yeah, that's a good thing." I smile and his eyes zone in on my lips.

"You have a beautiful smile," he says sensually. "And beautiful lips. I wonder what they—"

The waitress interrupts us with our food. "Here ya go, honey." She slides Asher's food in front of him. Then she drops my plate in front of me and it clanks loudly against the table. "If you need anything, let me know."

"I think she might have a thing for you," I say, dipping a fry into the ranch.

Asher looks like he's about to laugh. "You think?"

"I do." I pick the onions off my chicken sandwich. "Why's that so funny?"

He pours ketchup on his burger. "Because you're probably right, but she doesn't stand a chance. She's not really my type." He glances at the disposed onions on my plate. "You don't like *onions*?"

"You said that like I just admitted I hate chocolate. And onions and chocolate are on two very different levels."

"Yeah, onions are much better."

"You can eat them if you want." I motion at my plate. "What's mine is yours."

He picks up the onion, tips his head back, and spirals it into his mouth. "I might hold you to that a little bit later." His eyes darken with hunger.

A tingling sensation coils inside my stomach. I clear my throat and take a bite of my chicken sandwich. "So, you like the band From Autumn to Ashes?"

He glances down at his shirt. "Yeah, I got this shirt at one of their concerts. They're pretty good. Have you heard them play?"

"Not in person." I pop a fry into my mouth. "But I have a lot of their songs downloaded."

He bites into his hamburger and a droplet of ketchup stays on his lip. The urge to lean over and suck it off his lip surfaces again. He licks it off, leisurely, watching me like he knows exactly what I'm thinking.

We stare at each other with heat in our eyes and desire throbbing in our bodies. It's something I don't quite understand, because I barely know him. But I don't want the feeling to ever leave.

"So what is there to do around here?" Asher's voice sounds high and he clears his throat. "Besides hanging out at bars."

"You're asking the wrong person," I tell him. "Honestly, the only thing I do is follow Raven to her parties."

"Yeah, what's up with that?" He picks a flake of lettuce off his hamburger. "It doesn't seem like you're really the partying type. Or the following type?"

"I'm not, but…"

"But Raven is, and she's the boss," he finishes for me.

"She's not the boss… Okay, well maybe she is, but it's just her personality."

He chews slowly. "I had this friend back in New York who was a little bit bossy, so finally one day I told him to shove it. You know what, we still stayed friends."

"I'm sure you didn't tell him to shove it," I remark. "You seem way too nice for that."

A smile plays at his lips as he reaches over and steals another onion off my plate. "Do I?"

I take a sip of my coke. "Are you trying to tell me that you're secretly mean?"

"I have a mean… side." He wavers. "I guess. But it doesn't come out a lot."

"I think everyone has sides of them that rarely come out." I stir the straw in my drink.

He nods. "So what's yours?"

Crazy. "I don't know…"

"You don't have to share it with me if you don't want to." He takes a sip of his water. "I won't make you do anything you don't want to."

It feels like there's a hidden meaning in his words. "So what made you want to be an artist?"

His jaw clamps tight. "My father was an artist and he passed along his gift to me."

"You sound upset about that. Did you fight a lot with your dad or something?"

"My dad wasn't around a lot, but I love painting—it helps me get out what I'm feeling."

"I know what you mean." I think of his angel drawing and wonder what he was feeling when he painted it—I wonder if he knows stuff about angels. "It's why I write poetry."

"I'd love to read some of your poetry," he says.

I stare down at my chicken sandwich and my hair falls around my face. "I usually don't let people read it. Well, except for Raven, but she's only read what I've written on my walls." And Cameron, but that was by accident.

"You write on your walls?" He sprinkles some salt on his fries. "Now that is something you'll have to let me see."

"Sure." I tuck my hair back. "There's artwork on the walls, too—Raven's and my brother's."

He wipes his hand on a napkin. "Maybe you'll be nice enough to let me put something up on it."

"Like a painting of your sad angel."

"Would you want that? A drawing of an angel that would always be on your wall?"

"There's already one on there. Raven put it up when we were like, eight." I take another bite of my chicken sandwich. "And my brother put the Grim Reaper on it for who knows what reasons, so I have the good version of death and the evil one." As I say it aloud, I think of the book I read. A battle between good and evil. Between Angels of Death and Grim Reapers. I have the battle on my walls.

Asher's expression falls. "But which one's evil and which one's good?"

It's an obvious answer, but my lips decline to utter the words, and an image of my imaginary childhood friend pops into my head.

The waitress arrives with the bill. I try to pay for my half, but Asher won't allow it. While we're waiting for the waitress to bring the change, two men walk inside the bar that catch my attention. They stand out in their business attire and fancy haircuts. The taller of the two has blonde hair and dark eyes that look really familiar. Then it clicks. Cameron's dad. I don't recognize the man who's with him, but I notice him glance our way.

Asher's eyes find them and his eyes darken. Cameron's dad returns the look with equivalent revulsion.

"Do you know them?" I nod my head toward the two men.

Asher's eyes stay on them as he shakes his head. "No, I don't," he says through gritted teeth. He rips his gaze away and his expression is feral.

"Asher, what's wrong." I start to turn my head back to the men, but a man with long brown hair and a stocky body stumbles from a barstool, waving his finger at me.

"Ain't you that girl who killed her father?" he slurs.

"I didn't kill him." I cringe uncomfortably. "The cops just thought I did for a while."

His thigh bumps the table and knocks my coke over, spilling ice all over the table. "But didn't you run away after you called the cops and reported his murder? Yeah, yeah, and they took you to jail."

"That's not how it happened," I lie, scooping up the ice and dropping it in the cup.

The waitress returns with the change. "Gary, you aren't causing trouble, are you?"

He bobs his drunken head. "Nah, just chattin' with my good friends. This is that girl who killed her father."

"I didn't kill him!" I raise my voice louder than I meant to.

Now more people than Gary are staring at me. The waitress gives Asher a concerned pat on the shoulder, like she thinks I'm going to kill him.

"If you need anything else at all, just let me know." She tugs on Gary's arm. "Come on, Gary. Let's get you home."

But he won't budge. "You know I used to work at the same shop as your dad." He wipes the sweat from his forehead. "We were pretty good buddies."

"That's great." I put some money down for a tip.

Asher slides the money back. "No way."

I push it back in the center of the table. "You paid for dinner and the least I can do is pay for the tip."

He struggles and then gives in. "Fine, but next time you're letting me pay for the whole thing."

"Is there going to be a next time?" I doubt.

"Absolutely." He smiles.

I begin to stand up, but Gary blocks the end of my booth and Amy hurries back to the counter to get some assistance. "Can you please move so I can get up?" I ask as politely as I can.

His feet stay planted. "You know he used to talk about you when we'd go out drinking after work." He leans down in my face, his breath reeking of booze as he whispers in my ear. "He told me your little secret—how you could cause death."

"I don't know what you're talking about." I start to stand again, but he shoves me down and my elbow cracks against the table and the faint scent of his death pollutes my lungs: *electricity, chair, people watch, grateful he's dying.* It's vile and knocks the breath out of me.

The next thing I know Gary is on the floor clutching his jaw and Asher is standing over him.

"If you ever touch her again, you won't be walking out of here alive." He extends his hand to me and I happily take it. Calmness rushes through me as we swiftly weave through the tables. A group of men push up from the barstools and follow us. Trouble lingers in the air, like a warning before a storm. Some of the men are as weak look-ing as Gary, but some are large, beefy, and have scars all over their arms and faces, probably old wounds from bar fights.

People eating dinner at the tables watch us nervously—they smell what's coming. And so do I. Asher and I speed up as we near the door.

"Where do you think you're going?" one of the larger men calls out.

Asher pauses at the door, deliberating something intensely. Then he slowly turns around. "We are leaving. Do you have a problem with that?"

A bulky man, sporting leather pants and a vest crosses his arms. "Yeah. You can't just knock out one of my friends and then walk away without paying the consequences." He waves his finger at me. "And that one… well, she's just a downright filthy murderer who gets to walk off easy."

"You didn't even know my dad," I state. "So shut the hell up."

"I'm not talking about your dad," he growls. "I'm talking about my nephew, Laden Miller."

"I had nothing to do with that." My legs tremble but I refuse to cower back. "I barely knew him."

"So you say." His eyes burn with a loathing so powerful, I want to run. "But you did know your daddy and you probably killed him just like you killed my nephew. I bet you even had somethin' to do with that girl he was always hangin' out with. That Farrah girl. Yeah, I bet you killed her too."

Asher drops my hand. His muscles are tense as if he's trying to channel all his anger to stay in his body. He steps toward the man and spreads his arms open. "The next word that comes out of your mouth better be an apology."

The man cracks his knuckles and neck. "Or what?"

I eye the men, who are twice Asher's size, and then tug on Asher's sleeve, trying to lure him back. "Asher, I think we should go."

Laden's uncle laughs and the rest of the men join in. "Ooo, little murder girl said it's time to go. You better listen." Suddenly, he clocks Asher in the face.

Asher crumples to the ground, holding his cheek. "Well, that was a cheap shot."

"Oh my God." I hover over Asher. "Are you okay?"

His grey eyes darken as he starts to stand up. "Stand back," he warns.

"Are you being serious?" I ask. "They'll kill you."

"Ember, please stand back," he says, not looking *at* me, but at Laden's uncle with a ravage glint in his eyes. "I don't want you to get hurt."

I don't move. From the corner of the bar, Cameron's dad is watching Asher with fascination as he sips out of a martini glass. Asher stands up and pops his knuckles. With one swing, he knocks Laden's uncle out.

"Holy shit," I breathe, staring down at the unconscious man, his legs and arms sprawled across the floor, and there is a little bit of drool pooling at his lips.

Then all hell breaks loose.

The rest of the men charge at full speed. Asher dodges to the side and nudges me out of the way with his elbow. A few men bump into tables, sending people springing from their chairs and plates flying through the air. The whole bar scatters for safety, screaming, and dashing for the front door. The music switches to a heavy metal song and abruptly, the small fight becomes a full-on brawl. I'm not surprised. I've seen it happen many times. Men take swings at each other and even a few buffer females get in on the action. Bottles are being smashed over heads and chairs are getting clobbered.

A tall, lanky man comes strutting up to me with a smirk on his face. "What's the matter, sweetheart? You scared?" He steps closer and exhales beer breath in my face. His hands touch my waist and I knee him between the legs. Death flashes through me, but it was worth it.

He collapses to the floor, groaning and clutching his manly parts.

"Do I look like someone who'd be frightened by a little bar fight?" Shaking my head, I step over him. Phil hurries out of the back room with a baseball bat and his cell phone. "Shit." I duck through the flying glass and fists. "Asher!" I trip over an unconscious man and glass slices my palms. Keeping my head low, I dash across the room, leaping over chairs and weaving around broken tables.

Asher is near the back door, exchanging punches with a guy with a bald head and a snake tattoo coiling his upper arm. Asher's lip is split open and his cheekbone is swollen. He throws jab after jab and his movements are almost inhuman, swifter and stronger.

I'm impressed and terrified.

A tall guy with a thick neck sneaks up behind Asher, holding a beer bottle in his hand. I pick a glass cup off the floor and throw it at the guy's head. It slams him in the forehead, he drops the beer bottle, and falls to the floor like a bag of bricks.

Asher slams his opponent in the face and blood spurts from his mouth. He repeats the movement over and over again, until the guy passes out.

Asher breathes violently as he clutches his hands. "I'm sorry, Ember… I just."

I grab his hand and lead him toward the backdoor. "Phil's about to call the cops… I can't get caught in this mess. I'm already on probation."

I shove open the door and we breathe in fresh air. The door slams shut and the noise from the bar fight is suffocated. The back parking lot is secluded from the highway and the sky is black. The lights from the neon signs flash across our faces, making us look ghostly.

Asher faces me, breathing heavily, his eyes untamed. "I'm sorry, Ember. I didn't mean for things to get so out of hand."

My heart knocks energetically in my chest. I feel alive, high on adrenaline, like I could conquer the world. "It's okay. Trust me when I say I'm used to bar fights." I touch the tip of my finger to his bottom lip. "You cut your lip open." I wipe the blood away and I start to pull my hand back. But he covers it with his and presses it against his lips. He kisses my palm and his eyes penetrate me, making me feel exposed. Our breaths quicken, in sync and matching each other's desire.

"Can I kiss you?" he whispers with begging eyes.

I nod my head once and his lips crash into mine.

My first kiss. And it's as beautiful and exciting as everyone makes it out to be.

Maybe even better.

He covers my lips with his, quickly, like how he moved during the fight. But his touch is gentle. My skin ignites with heat and I wrap my hands around his waist. My lips part and his tongue slides in. He caresses the roof of my mouth with his tongue ring and I let out a moan.

He withdraws slightly, and I worry he's repulsed by my enjoyment. But then he growls, wraps his fingers around my thighs, and picks me up. I enclose my legs around his waist as he continues to taste every inch of my mouth and backs us against the wall, beneath the shadows and florescent lights. There's no space remaining between our bodies and I can feel every inch of him. His kisses bring me a feeling of ecstasy for the first time in my life.

His hands are tangled in my hair. They trail down my neck, finally settling on my hips. He slips a hand up the back of my shirt and the contact sends a jolt of electricity down my spine. He holds onto me like I'm his lifeline, as if letting me go will kill him.

"I've wanted to kiss you forever." He groans against my lips and steals my breath away. It's like we've unleashed a hungry animal in each of us. But the sound of the sirens makes him pull back, although it looks like he doesn't want to. His eyes are as black as coals and his lips are swollen.

"We should get out of here," he whispers, looking like he might kiss me again.

I nod and untangle my legs from his waist. Holding hands, we sneak around the side of the building and quickly hop into the car. Red and blue lights flash through the dark parking lot and cops hop out of squad cars. A swarm of people are barreling out the front door, distracting the cops enough for us to drive off into the night unnoticed.

From the corner of my eye, I watch Asher. He meets my eyes and gives me this look that makes me wonder what he could possibly want to show me.

"Now where are we going?" I ask, buckling my seat belt.

He smiles and winks at me. "You'll just have to wait and see."

I lean back in the seat and watch the trees blur by, feeling alive and carefree for the first time in my life. I wish I had a pen so I could write about this moment and preserve it forever. Then I could remember what it felt like when it vanishes.

Chapter 11

We drive along the highway, making small chitchat about the fight. Asher doesn't ask questions about what was said. When he looks at me, it feels like he's really looking at me, instead of at the girl who was brought in to the police station for the suspicion of her dad's disappearance.

Asher finally turns off the main road and parks his car in a gravel turnout overlooking the lake. He turns the car off and dabs the cut on his lip with the collar of his shirt.

"You know, this whole night really didn't turn out how I was planning it," he says.

The lake shimmers and the moon reflects against the surface, the water rippling a dance against the breeze. The mountains are black and the trees dark silhouettes.

"How were you planning it to go?" I ask.

He puts the parking brake on. "A little less bar fighting and a lot more making out in the back of the bar."

Ember

I look at him to see if he's being serious. He stares at me with hunger in his eyes. I touch my lips. "How did you learn to fight like that?"

His jaw tenses. "My dad taught me."

"Yeah, mine too," I mumble, lowering my hand from my lips.

He relaxes a little. "Yeah, I saw you knee that guy… You didn't so much as hesitate."

"Hesitation shows weakness." I sigh. "At least that's what my dad used to say. He was a do-or-die kind of guy." I pause. "I didn't kill him."

"I know." His voice and gaze is rock steady.

"So you don't believe the rumors at school?"

He shakes his head and a wisp of his inky black hair falls into his eyes. He leans over and tucks a strand of my hair behind my ear. "Come on, there's something I want to show you." He grabs a flashlight out of the glove box and hops out of the car.

I climb out and meet him at the front of the car. We walk down a dirt path, holding hands. It's pitch dark and he lights the way with the beam of the flashlight. An owl hoots from in a tree and the crickets' melody haunts the night. It's strange but peaceful knowing we're the only two out here and that we are sharing a private moment no one else can ever touch.

Asher unexpectedly makes a sharp veer off the path into the trees. The leaves and twigs crunch under our shoes as we hike deeper into the woods.

"Where are we going?" I whisper, forcing my eyes to adjust to the night. The branches form eerie shadows above our heads and the soft swish of the lake's waves whisper in my ears.

He shoves a branch aside and lets me walk through first. "There's something out here I want to show you."

"What? A roll of tape and a shovel," I say sarcastically.

He spots the flashlight on my face. "Am I scaring you?"

I shake my head. "I think it would take a hell of a lot more than a creepy walk in the forest with a really hot guy to scare me."

"You think I'm hot, huh?" It's nearly pitch black, but I hear the smile in his voice.

I roll my eyes, playing off my slipup. "So what's really—"

He silences me with his lips crushing into mine. We melt together, steaming up the woods as he presses his body against mine. His fingers find my waist and I wonder if it's possible to stay like this forever, in the darkness of the woods, away from the world and death.

He pulls back, breathing ravenously. "You're beautiful, you know that? Especially when you're embarrassed."

"I don't get embarrassed," I assure him. "Only uncomfortable."

We finish the rest of the walk holding hands and taking in the serenity of each other's company. We finally emerge out of the trees and onto a flat spot of land. Asher sweeps the light across the area, highlighting a stone statue of an angel with wings pointing at the sky and its head and back is curled toward the earth. Surrounding it are small wooden crosses staked in the ground, covered with vines of rose bushes.

"How did you know this was here?" I roam through the tiny cemetery, feeling as though I'm stepping on forbidden territory. "And does anyone else know it's back here?"

"My father took me here when I was younger." He watches me with the flashlight in his hand. "And I don't think anyone else knows it exists."

"How'd your father know about it?" I stare up at the angel statue.

"His father showed it to him." He spotlights an engraving on the foot of the statue.

I read it aloud, "To guard the Earth from the wrath of death, we must use vigilance. For those we seek to guard could destroy us and themselves."

"Do you know what it means?" I run my fingers along the elaborate lettering. "It feels like I've heard it before."

His mouth moves next my ear. "Some people believe that angels are the guardians of humans' deaths. However, most humans have a general fear of anything involving death. They have the potential to destroy themselves and their protectors. A long time ago people used to slay anyone they suspected were Angels of Death."

"Did they have black-winged feathers," I half joke, but am half serious, thinking of all the feathers I've come across during my life.

"Are you speaking of Laden's crime scene?" Asher asks gravely. "Or of something else?"

"You know about the feathers on Laden's crime scene?"

"Everyone knows about the crime scene."

I unintentionally bump a cross with my boot. "Do you know it was almost exactly like my dad's crime scene?"

He places a hand on my hip and gives it a gentle squeeze. "Yeah, I heard that."

Silence capes us as my memories drift back to the night my dad disappeared; the panic that led to my stupid decision to run away and who ran away with me.

"Do you know that some people believe that angels exist?" he asks. "And that they walk in disguise, looking for the Grim Angel who will save them?"

"That's not too hard to believe, I guess. I mean, there are a ton of strange things in this world." *Like me.* I lean back against his chest, breathing in his proximity. "But what's the wrath of death?"

His fingers coast up my forearm and my stomach quivers with desire. "The Grim Reaper," he whispers and I'm slapped back to reality.

I jolt away, stepping on a cross. I quickly pick it up and stab it back into the moist dirt.

"What's wrong?" Asher asks. "Did I say something that makes you uneasy? Because if I did, you can tell me."

It's like he knows. I gaze up at the statue and then at the crosses in the ground around it. "No… it's just getting late. I should probably get home."

He nods, not pushing me to tell him. "Yeah, we can go back."

As we backtrack through the trees, I think about the Grim Reaper. In my head, I picture walking inside my house and he's waiting for me on the couch with a cup of tea, like we're old friends. But I'm too old to be seeing imaginary people.

"Do you think that… do I come off as a little crazy?" I ask.

We edge along the turnout and he pulls me close so I can see the genuine expression on his face. "I think there are a lot of people that are considered insane, but they just see and go through more than the average person can understand." He kisses me on the forehead and I breathe in the warmth and silence of his lips.

We move away from each other and climb in the car. He starts up the engine and places the flashlight back in the glove box.

I watch him with a guarded expression. "Asher, why did you bring me here?"

He places an arm on the back of the head rest behind me. "Because I wanted to show you that people tend to fear the different, even when the different is good."

"Like Angels," I make sure.

He nods expectantly. "Like Angels, and like people who are out of the ordinary."

"But what does this have to do with Garrick and the Anamotti? Or can you not tell me that yet?"

"Do you want me to tell you now?" He waits patiently for my answer.

I hesitate briefly, nervous what the answer could be. "Umm... yeah?"

"The word 'Anamotti' means death. And they believe that angels exist," he says. "And they want to destroy them."

Angels? "Are you part of this group?" I tread with caution.

He shakes his head. "I'm not, but I know people who are."

I take in the dark alteration of the night. "What does that have to do with me?"

He tips my chin up and claims my gaze, looking past my eyes and into my soul. "I can tell you, but I want you to make sure you're ready for that answer, because it's… it might be hard for you to take in, especially when you've got so much stress in your life already. I want you to really make sure, whether you believe me or not, that you can handle whatever it is I tell you."

"How do you know about my *stress*?" I say, unable to look away from him.

"Because of the sadness you always carry." He brushes the tip of his fingers along the corner of my eye. "It's in here, all the time. So please, if you're not ready, it can wait."

It's frightening how much he *sees* me.

He gives me a moment to contemplate. My mind reflects back to Garrick and his multiple death omens. To Raven. And Ian. My alcoholic, manic-depressant mother. My dad's disappearance. *Angels and secret societies?* There is so much going on in my life and for once I have an escape— Asher. Tonight has been one of the best nights of my life and I want to hold onto the feeling of bliss for as long as I can. Whatever he's about to say will change it. Perhaps even destroy it—I can sense it through the tone in his voice, the way he moves, and the way his eyes watch me.

"Can you take me home?" I ask, fearing having to deal with what's before me, worrying that I'll crack and end up insane. "It's getting late."

He nods with understanding in his eyes and pulls his hand away from the head rest. "Whatever you want, Ember. And I mean that. Whatever you want, I'll give it to you."

I wonder if he really means it.

***

All the interior lights in my house are off. Either the power is still out, my mom and Ian are in bed, or no one's home.

"Is anyone here?" Asher stares at the house. "It doesn't look like anyone is."

"Well, it is," I glance at my watch and my eyes spring wide. "One in the morning. Jesus, how'd it get to be that late?"

"Time flies when you're having fun," he teases with a soft laugh.

The darker side of tonight has dissolved. The ride home was filled with light conversation about music, school, art, writing. And I refuse to think about Angels, the Grim Reaper, and the Anamotti.

"Tonight was fun though." I push the car door open. "And I needed some fun."

He captures the hem of my tank top and his knuckles brush the side of my stomach. He draws me back into the car. "Then why does it have to end?"

Is he asking what I think he is? My eyes travel to Raven's second-floor bedroom window. The light is on and I can almost hear her voice: *Do it, do it, do it!*

"You want to come in?" I involuntarily glance at his lustrous lips.

He nods slowly, his compelling gaze penetrating me. "At least until someone comes home—you shouldn't be here alone."

I look back at my house. "Let me just run in and check first. My brother might be here."

He smiles and releases me. I run inside and flick on the light. "Well, the power's back on." I check in the living room, half expecting to find the Grim Reaper waiting for me. But it's empty and the house is quiet. So is my mom's bedroom, Ian's room, his studio. I trot back downstairs and wave Asher inside.

He climbs out of the car and strolls up the sidewalk. He watches me with every step and I realize how happy I am he's staying. If he wasn't, I'd probably wake up in a few hours, dripping with the sweat of death. I'd grab my notebook and go to the cemetery, where I'd jot notes about loneliness and pain. Asher has the ability to distract me from death.

I shut the door behind him and he scales up my house. There are photos of me as a baby hanging on the foyer wall. Some I'm with Raven, some I'm with Ian. There are even a few I'm with my mom and dad, back when life was all rainbows and sunshine, or at least when I believed it was. But life was just waiting for me to pass it.

"You look like your dad." He squints at a photo of me as a two-year-old sitting on my dad's lap. My mom is leaning over his shoulder whispering something in his ear. Ian is in the back, swinging plastic nunchucks at an inflatable Santa Claus. There is a Christmas tree in the background, flashing with red twinkling lights. The picture's candid, and we look happy.

I want the moment back.

I head for the stairs and Asher follows. I'm aware of everything as we ascend the staircase; the movement of his body, the slightest elevation in temperature, the rhythm of his heart.

I open my bedroom door and he glances at the drawings on the wall, the poems, the pictures of the dead poets. He gives a lengthy gaze at the Reaper and then at the angel on the wall across from it, before he focuses on a picture of Edgar Allan Poe tacked to the closet doorframe.

"If I didn't know better, I'd think you have a crush on him," he says with a drop of amusement. "But then again, I really don't know you." He faces me with a smile tickling his lips. "So is this my competition?"

"I'm not in love with him," I reply, picking up the raven feather off my dresser. *Weird. I thought I put this away.* "I'm in love with his work."

"I remember from the party. You practically fell into my arms when I quoted the only line I know of his poetry." He teases me with a smug smile.

I narrow my eyes and try not to smile. "So you were playing me."

He shrugs, still grinning, and takes the feather from my hands. He spins it in-between his fingers and his eyebrows furrow as he stares at the feather. "Is this a raven's feather?"

"Yeah, why?"

He shakes his head and hands the feather back to me. "Where'd you get it?"

"From the ceme—the park." I set the feather on my dresser, wondering what an angel feather would look like. "They're a pretty common bird."

The seriousness in his face fades into mischievousness. "I was just wondering how hard you went looking for it— how deep your obsession is with Edgar Allan Poe."

"Ha, ha," I say sarcastically, giving him a playful shove. He traps my hand against his chest and the mood takes an impulsive shift. "Am I allowed to kiss you in here?"

"No one's home," I say. "You can do whatever you want."

"Can I?" He steers me to him. Our lips and bodies collide and liquefy with lust.

We fall onto my bed with our bodies entangled. My heart races with rapture and my skin flames with a burning need. He rolls us over, so he's on top of me, and his tongue ring inspects every single inch inside my mouth. My legs snake around his waist and he lets out a low growl as he sucks on my bottom lip. He traces kisses down my neck and my breath hitches. I slant my head back as his lips trail lower and lower. But my mind panics with self-doubting thoughts, not about Asher, but about myself, and I pull back.

He doesn't look mad or angry. In fact, he looks grateful. "Why don't we lie down?" He gently kisses my cheek and I shiver. "And I'll stay with you until you fall asleep."

"Let me go change into my pajamas first," I say, only to allow myself time to cool down.

He rolls off me and I climb off the bed, ignoring the thunder of my heart. I grab some pajamas out of the dresser and duck into the closet.

"You know that curtain is pretty thin," he says, humor hinting his tone. My iPod flips on and the sound of "Hands Down," by Dashboard Confessional drums through the room. I quickly slip on a tank top and a pair of plaid shorts. I unclasp my studded bracelets and drop them in the corner of the closet floor, right by the insane drawing of *X*'s. I barely remember drawing it, like how I barely remember being rescued from drowning. *Feathers all over his crime scene*. I shut my eyes and try to summon more details. Dark water. My necklace floating away. The black mass—the Grim Reaper.

I open my eyes. Am I losing my mind just like my dad? Or is everything real, just confusing?

I return to the room in a miserable mood. Asher is lying on my bed reading a book with his boots kicked off and his jacket thrown on the floor. My smile breaks through, until I see what he's reading.

"Wait a minute… is that…" I reach for the book, but he rolls to his side, laughing as he reads a line from Raven's romance novel. "'And then he takes his hand and slides it onto my—'"

I hop on him and steal the book away. "This is not mine. It's Raven's." I chuck the book across the room and it lands in the garbage.

He laughs and situates his hands on my hips as I straddle him. "So you don't want me to slide my hand on you—"

I conceal my hand over his mouth and shake my head. I wait until he stops laughing and then I remove it. He situates on the bed and then steers me down beside him. I rest my head on his chest.

"*So won't you kill me, so I die happy*," Asher sings quietly along with the song in an angelic voice. "You should get some sleep." He plays with my hair. "I'll leave when you do. That way no one will walk in us."

"You don't have to worry about that," I yawn. "No one ever checks in on me…" I lift my head up. "Won't your mom worry about where you are? It's late."

He shakes his head. "She's gone for the weekend, back to New York to close up one of her… accounts."

I press my cheek against his chest and his heart skips against it. "Asher, why did you take off the other day? After you got Garrick away from me?"

"That's another question you may really want to think about and make sure you want me to answer it."

I deliberate. "I want to know."

He lets out an uneven breath. "Because if I didn't leave I would have chased Garrick down and killed him."

Perhaps I should have got up and ran, but the silence of his body is my sanctuary. "Why would you have killed him?"

"For a few reasons," he whispers. "One of them being because he tried to hurt you." He pauses. "Does that scare you?"

"Do you think it scares me?"

"No."

"Then you're right."

Stillness takes over, along with the sound of the music. Moments later, I drift off to one of the most peaceful nights of my existence.

Chapter 12

I open my eyes to the warmth of Asher's arms wrapped around me. A rare smile graces my lips, and I'm glad he fell asleep and never left. The scent of freshly fallen rain and a bird's melody flows through my open bedroom window. I sit up and spot a raven suspended on a tree branch. Its black eyes watch me and I stick my arm out the window, trying to coax it closer.

"Hello, little minion of death," I whisper with my eyes narrowed. "Why won't you leave me alone? Are you trying to tell me something about my death? Because I'm sorry to break it to you, but I already died and now it looks like there is no death in my future."

That's when I notice Cameron's Jeep parked in front of my house.

I glance down at Asher sleeping in my bed and then back at the Jeep, remembering the date with him. Carefully,

I slip out from under his arm and sneak into the hall. I soundlessly close my door and walk to the top of the stairs.

Cameron and Ian are chatting in the foyer. Ian is telling him about this slammin' new art exhibit tonight in Jackson.

Cameron's ash black eyes instantly find me and a smile curves at his lips. "Good morning, princess."

Princess? I smooth my hair down and trot down the stairs. "What are you doing here?"

Cameron is dressed in black jeans, a grey Henley, and boots, with leather bands on his wrist. But with his blonde hair and tan skin, he looks more vintage than gothic. "I came to see you."

The beanie on Ian's head covers his eyebrows and his jeans are smudged with charcoal. He looks uncomfortable, standing next to Cameron, who's about six inches taller than him. "Well, I'll let you two chat or whatever." He raises his eyebrows at me and something in his eyes flash. He doesn't like Cameron. I find it odd because Ian usually is "all about the love."

"If you need anything, just holler." Ian heads upstairs and seconds later the door to his studio slams shut.

"I thought we weren't going out until later," I say quickly and run my fingers tensely through my hair. "And I was actually going to call you. Something came up and I don't think I'm going to be able to make it to the poetry slam tonight."

"Are you blowing me off?" His tone is clipped.

"No." I'm thrown off by his sullen attitude. "I just had something come up... My mom needs my help with something."

"That's funny, because your brother just told me your mom's out of town." He sounds irritated.

"Did he…" I search for another excuse.

"Does this have anything to do with the owner of the GTO in your driveway?" he asks bluntly.

"Um…" I don't know what to say.

Thankfully, the front door swings open and Raven pops her head in. Her pink hair is fluffed up in the front and pulled up into a ponytail. Neon pink eyeliner frames her eyes and she's wearing a black dress trimmed with pink leather.

"Hey, chica," she chirps. "Thanks for letting Asher and I meet at your house. It totally sucks that my brother doesn't approve of him." She gives me a secret wink, then grabs my hand and says to Cameron, "Can you hold on, hun? I gotta borrow her for just a second."

Cameron motions at the stairway and smiles. "By all means go ahead. I can wait."

"Thank you, sweetie." Raven drags me up the stairs and stops once we're in the hall out of Cameron's sight. She slaps my arm. "You slut. Please tell me he's still naked in your bed."

"What are you talking about?" I play dumb.

She rolls her eyes. "The hot sexy guy who had his car parked in your driveway all night."

"I didn't sleep with him." I lower my voice. "Well, not in the way you're thinking. We just fell asleep in my bed."

She eyes me like a cop trying to break down a criminal. "So nothing happened at all?"

"We kissed," I say. "And that's all."

She frowns, disappointed. "Okay, well here's what we're going to do. I'm going to get Asher to agree to come with me and then Cameron won't ever have to know about this."

"But I don't think I want to go out with Cameron," I protest. "I really like Asher."

"So," she says baffled. "It's not like you're dating. You've been out with him once."

"And he saved me from drowning in the lake." I let it slip out.

She slaps my arm again and I flinch from the spark of her death. "Why the hell didn't you tell me?"

I rub my arm and shrug. "You were talking about how much you wanted him and I don't know…"

"You just kept your mouth shut, like you always do." She takes me by the shoulders and looks me straight in the eyes, as if her next words are the most important thing I will ever hear. "Look, Em, I love you so much and that's why I'm going to do you this favor. You're going to go out on a date with Cameron." I open my mouth to argue but she shushes me. "You owe it to yourself not to get serious with anyone yet. Serious relationships mean things I don't think you're ready for."

The door of my bedroom opens up and Asher walks out, slipping on his jacket. He's got bed-head, but it's ridiculously sexy. "So that went a little differently than I planned. I don't even remember falling asleep." He shoves up the sleeves of his jacket, ignoring Raven. "So I want to take you somewhere today, if that's okay."

I open my mouth to say yes, but Raven interposes. "Em's already got plans."

I glare at her and she fires one right back at me.

Asher looks at Raven. "With you?"

She aims a conniving look at him. "No, with Cameron. You know, the other new kid."

Asher scowls at her. "I know who he is."

"Good, then I don't have to stand here and explain it to you." She links arms with him. "You can hang out with me today."

She leads him toward the stairs and I'm surprised by how little of a fight Asher puts up. When Asher and Cameron see each other, the air chills. We all stand awkwardly in the foyer.

"Well, you two have fun," Raven singsongs, tugging Asher toward the door.

Asher won't meet my eyes. "I'll see you later, Ember," he says, like we're acquaintances.

I open my mouth to tell him to stay, but my lips are incompetent. The pair leaves and Asher takes my calm and peace from death along with him. I'm dumbstruck. Thoughts of the two of them making out infest my brain.

"So I thought we could spend the day at the lake," Cameron's voice intervenes my thoughts. There's something about his demeanor that's off today; the sadness and pain he so often carries has evaporated into an intimidating level of cockiness.

"Yeah… I just need to change first." I withdraw toward the stairs, wishing I'd never agreed to the date in the first place. Cameron can't touch me without driving me insane, so what's the point of doe-eyed looks and flirty conversation? That's not what I want.

What I want is Asher.

I hurry up to my room and throw on a pair of black shorts, knee-high sneakers, and a maroon top tied together with a ribbon. I clip on my bracelets, grab my leather jacket and meet Cameron downstairs. He's looking at the same baby photo as Asher did last night.

"You look happy in this one," he observes.

"I was two," I say, flipping my hair out of the collar of my jacket. "A cardboard box could make me smile."

"Yeah, you're probably right." He turns away from the photo and opens the front door. "After you."

I walk outside and frown at the empty driveway. Raven's silver car is still parked in her driveway next door. I wonder if they really left together. This bothers me. A lot. Maybe more than anything in my life.

Chapter 13

The first half of the drive with Cameron is awkward, but mostly because Cameron's dad calls and chews him out over the phone. I don't know what for, but it's none of my business.

By the time he hangs up, we're at the mouth of the canyon that encircles the lake. The heat is on, but it's hot out and a layer of sweat coats my skin underneath my leather jacket.

"So your friend finally found someone interested in her, huh?" Cameron tosses his phone into the console.

I crack the window and suck in some fresh air. "Asher's not interested in her that way. They're just friends."

He turns down the heat. "Hmm… that's not what I saw. It looked to me like they were both happy to be leaving with each other."

"I don't agree with you," I say through gritted teeth. "And Asher's not really her type."

"It seems like everyone's her type if you ask me," he comments, downshifting. "Ember, is something wrong? You seem mad at me for some reason."

I encounter his gaze and the hurt in his eyes makes me feel bad. "Sorry, I just didn't sleep very well last night."

The pain in his eyes subsides. "Well, you could have always came down to the cemetery and kept me company."

"Why were you there?" I lighten up. "Were you looking for the family jewel again?"

"No, I gave up on that," he says. "I was actually there, hoping you'd show up again."

"Sure you were." My tone is cheerful, but I fidget unnervingly. Unlike Asher, Cameron is making me feel uneasy, in both good ways and bad. "And now you're going to tell me that you can't stop thinking about me."

His expression intensifies and his voice lowers to an intimate level. "Actually, I was going to tell you how much I like that shirt on you."

I glance down at the lace-up shirt Raven gave me that I've never worn until now. I don't even understand why I chose to wear it. Maybe subconsciously to live up to Cameron's flashy standards, and if it is, I'm disappointed in myself.

He reaches over and fiddles with the ribbon on the front. "You're so much different from the other girls I've dated." He curls the ribbon around his finger and pulls on it. "There's so much substance to you." He gives it another tug and it loosens the shirt slightly. "And innocence."

My black bra is starting to show through. I lean away and quickly tie the ribbon back up. "I'm not innocent."

He glances down at the ribbon and then inclines his eyebrows. *"Really."*

I hug the jacket to my chest. "Don't pretend like you know me."

He sighs and flips on the blinker. "Look, Ember, I'm sorry. I can be kind of cocky sometimes, but I promise I'll try to tone it down for today."

I sigh, slip off my jacket, and ball it on my lap. "No, I'm sorry. I'm acting rude again and I don't know why." *Because I want to be with Asher.*

"Because I make you nervous," he says simply and slows the car. He turns down a bumpy, dirt road that inclines to the shore of the lake. The steep, rocky hillside is covered with debris. My dad's Challenger. This is the exact spot where the accident happened.

"What's the matter?" Cameron silences the engine.

I rip my gaze from the lake. "Nothing. So what are we doing here?"

He points at a fire pit in the center of the shore. "Some people told me this was a good place to go."

"Yeah, to get wasted and have sex," I say, thinking of all the lake parties Raven has dragged me to.

He shoves open the car door. "You say that like it's a bad thing." He slams the door and walks toward the lake.

I think I might be in over my head. I slip on my jacket and hop out of the car. The silver pieces of the Challenger glimmer in the sunlight like nickels. The biggest one is about the size of a tire. I pluck a piece from the rocks and turn it in my hand.

"Looks like someone had a bad accident." He takes the piece of metal from my hand. "They must have been driving really fast to shatter the car so bad."

"Yeah, probably." I walk to the edge of the shore where the water meets the sand. Is the necklace still down there, trapped in the car?

Cameron comes up behind me and whispers in my ear, "Tell me what you're thinking." He uses the same purr as he did in the cemetery, the one that pulled me to him, that begged me to touch him.

I feel lightheaded. "I'm just sad…" I murmur.

"Tell me why," he purrs. "Maybe I can help."

It feels like I've drank a gallon of wine. "I was the one who wrecked… and my car, it's at the bottom of the lake."

"There was something important in it, wasn't there?"

I nod absentmindedly. "A necklace my grandmother gave me."

He moves to the side of me and tugs off his black Henley. He discards it on the ground and the sun glistens against his tan skin. He wades into the water until it is waist deep.

"Cameron, what are you doing?" I call out. "You can't—" He swan-dives in and vanishes under the water. I stand on the shore, searching for a glimpse of him resurfacing. Too much time ticks by for a normal person to breathe underwater. I pat my pockets for my phone. "Dammit. I left it at home."

I race for the Jeep to grab Cameron's phone he had tossed in the console to call Search and Rescue, but something darts behind the Jeep and I freeze. I glance back at the lake and then at the car. Dark boots stand behind the car.

I'm not alone.

"Shit." I dither and then sprint for the car. I scoop up a long, sharp stick as I cautiously open the passenger door. Without taking my eyes off the rear end of the Jeep, I feel around the inside of the cab until I snag Cameron's cell phone.

I flip the screen off lock and search for the dial pad. A tall figure steps out from the back of the Jeep. He's dressed in his usual back cloak that shields his eyes, but I know he's looking at me.

"I told you to go away last night." I back away from the Grim Reaper with the stick out in front of me. "And you have to leave because I told you to."

"You didn't mean it," he purrs softly, stepping toward me.

I throw the stick at him. "Yes I did. And I told you to go. I'm not a child and I can't see you anymore."

"You'll see me forever." He prowls toward me, step after step.

My feet are frozen in place, but not out of fear. In a weird, twisted way I've always wanted to find out what's beneath the hood. I reach my fingers toward him and he allows me to grab the brim. I begin to lift it back, but I hear water splashing and reel around. Cameron floats in the water, his lengthy arms guiding him to the shore. I glance back and the Grim Reaper is gone.

"I got it for you," Cameron calls out as he wades out of the lake. Beads of water trickle from his hair and down his well-defined abs and the sun lights up the sky behind him. It's straight out of cheesy movie scene, where everything is fake. *Fake.*

The nearer Cameron gets, the more my nervous energy charges. His soaked jeans ride low on his hips and the first word that comes to mind when I take him in is *perfection.* Then *fake, plastic, nonexistent.*

Dangling from his fingers is my grandma's necklace. "Did I mention that I'm an excellent swimmer?" He stops in front of me and hooks the necklace around my neck without touching me.

The maroon gem shimmers in the sunlight. I'm speechless, not because he brought me the necklace, but because he was able to retrieve it from the bottom of the lake.

He places his hands on my arms and I stiffen. "You don't have to say anything." His hands travel up my arms, over my shoulders, and down just below my neck, leaving a trail of water on my skin. My heart pounds in my chest. He's touching me and I can't feel the noise of death, just like with Asher. But it's a different kind of quiet than Asher. There's a hint of static and instead of calm, I feel out of control, like when my car went over the cliff.

"Your heart's racing," he whispers with an arrogant smirk. He dips his head down and sucks the water off the hollow of my neck. It feels wrong, yet right somehow. His lips inch closer and closer, and an involuntary moan escapes my lips. I feel hypnotized and start to surrender in his arms.

But he swiftly pulls away with his forehead furrowed. He peers over my shoulder and I turn around to see what he's looking at: Mackenzie's shiny Mercedes winding down the road.

"Did you invite her here?" I ask with a frown.

His eyes are locked on the car as he shakes his head. "Nope, I'm just as surprised as you."

The car slams to a stop beside the Jeep and kicks up a cloud of dust. The door opens and Mackenzie steps out. She adjusts her neon pink dress and struts forward, her high heels wobbling over the rocks. The passenger door flies open and her best friend Dana Millard swings her legs out. They both shoot me dirty looks.

"You have got to be kidding me," I mutter.

Cameron raises his eyebrows. "What? You don't like her?"

Mackenzie waves her hand. "Hey, I didn't know you were coming to this." She marches straight up to Cameron without so much as giving me an acknowledging glance. "I thought you said you were busy tonight."

A lifted truck rolls down the road, followed by a line of fancy SUVs, trucks, and cars. It's Saturday night and the whole teenage population is arriving.

Cameron glances at me. "I am busy."

She pouts her glossy bottom lip. "So you're not staying for the bonfire?"

"Maybe we could stay," he wavers, waiting for me to offer my okay.

"If you want to stay, that's fine with me," I say, my eyes skimming the forest as I try to determine how long it would take me to walk back to the house.

He smiles and pats my arm. "Sounds good." He backtracks toward the shore to pick up his shirt.

Mackenzie shadows him like a lovesick puppy, knocking her shoulder into mine as she passes by me; *bound and gagged, hands tied, are you ready to die, pretty girl?*

"Watch it, killer." Her eyes sparkle with a hatred she doesn't understand. I flip her the finger and she rolls her eyes, chasing after Cameron. "Why are you all wet?" She giggles and gives him a flirty pat on the chest.

I wipe the areas where Cameron touched me, erasing the water and the feel of his touch. Cameron's phone is lying on the ground and I pick it up. I dial Raven's number as more cars and trucks roll up. Mobs of people hop out of the cars; some I go to high school with and some are older.

"Hey Rav," I say when she answers. "I need you to pick me up."

"What?" She hollers in the phone. "Em, what are you saying? Aren't you having fun?"

Cameron seems to be. Over by the shore, he slips his shirt on, letting Mackenzie ogle him with a ravenous look in his eyes, like he might rip her dress off at any moment.

"Can you just come get me?" I beg. "Please."

"Yeah, sure, hun," she yells over the music in the background. "Where are you?"

The connection statics so I head toward the road, tucking in my shoulders as two guys pass by carrying a keg. "I'm at the lake," I say, but her voice cuts out. I head higher up the road. "Rav, can you hear me?" The signal dies. I trek up to the top of the road right at the border of the asphalt. There's still no signal, so I walk up the highway.

About a mile later, I still don't have a signal. It's midday, but the clouds are rumbling and the air is tinted with the smell of an impending rainstorm. But I keep walking with no desire to turn around, watching a raven soar menacingly above my head.

"Leave me alone, you stupid bird," I call out. "Go haunt someone else."

It keeps circling and cawing. Feathers fall from its wings and I catch one. I twirl it between my fingers, trying to remember if these were the same as the ones from my dad's crime scene. I saw a bag of them once, while I was being interrogated. But I think they were a little bit bigger.

I swing to the side as a black car with tinted windows rolls around a corner. The engine roars as it speeds up. Music bumps and vibrates the ground. The tires screech. Inching further to the side of the road, I tuck my jacket around me. I focus on seeing my death, but again there's only blackness.

The car suddenly swerves into the wrong lane, intentionally taking aim at me. There's little time to react. I scramble to the railing, but it slams into my legs and flips me onto the hood. I roll over the top and fly off the side of the road and over the edge of the cliff, bouncing off the rocks all the way to the bottom. Bones break and the rocks rip at my skin. When I finally stop, I'm lying next to the angel statue Asher took me to, surrounded by crosses and beautiful red roses. My arm is twisted behind my head, and my leg is kinked under my back. Blood drips down my forehead. I'm paralyzed. Thunder booms and lightning flashes across the sky.

It all makes sense, like connecting dots to form a map. The lake, my brakes, Garrick smothering me with death omens. Someone wants me dead and whoever they are just succeeded.

"Ember," the wind howls. The Grim Reaper appears above me and I know this is it. This is my time to go.

"Close your eyes," he says as he begins to pull his hood down.

My eyelids drift shut, but I catch a glimpse of black hair and dark eyes. "Asher…"

But the dark hair melts away and the eyes hollow out into a skeleton. I wonder if this is what death looks like to everyone, or that in my death I have lost my mind.

"Take it, Ember, or else you won't make it. And I need you to make it… for a little while." He plucks a red rose from the stem, bends down, and tucks it in my hair. "Take the life."

My eyes shut and I listen to my heart fade away. My breath surrenders to the wind and my heart gives its concluding beat. My life leaves my body, like leaves drifting from the trees. And every ounce of pain goes with it.

Suddenly, I don't want to wake up.

Chapter 14

Some people believe that right before death, a person reaches a point where they experience comfort and they see the images of every happy moment that completed their life. I've died twice, and each time all I see is the Reaper. So it that supposed to be my happy moment?

"Wake up." Someone pats my face. "Em, open your freaking eyes. You're scaring me."

My eyes roll open to the grey sky, Raven's sapphire eyes, and a thousand wilting roses surrounding my head and drifting in the air. The angel statue stares down at me as I gradually sit up and rub the dirt from my skin. I twist my arms and stretch my legs.

Raven sighs and leans back to give me breathing room. "Holy shit, Em. What happened?"

Every single tree within a quarter mile radius is dead, dried out, and stripped of their leaves. The grass is charred to a crisp and the dirt is cracked out like desert sand.

Did I do this?

"I have no idea…" I press my hand over my beating heart. "How did you find me?"

She holds up the necklace and points back at the hill. "This was lying on the side of the road up there." She hands it to me and I clip it back on. Then she helps me to my feet.

Her death is as black as the night sky—I can't feel it. But I can feel her life pumping through her veins.

"I was hit by a car… I think." My brain is hazy, but I remember tumbling down the hill. "I'm not sure… Can you just take me home?"

She studies me with uneasiness in her eye. "I think we should take you to a doctor."

I shake my arms, checking for pain. "No doctors. I just want to go home."

She wraps her arm around my lower back. Her death is silent, but her life whispers to me: *Take me, take me, take me.*

It takes a while, but we accomplish the walk back and make it to the top of the hill where the trees are blooming with life again. Her car is parked on the side of the road with the engine running and the driver's door open.

I wiggle from her arms, feeling liberated. "Maybe I should walk home."

"Get in the car," she orders sternly, with tired bags under her eyes. "You need to go back home. There's officially a curfew in affect now that Farrah's body was found."

Maybe the same person who killed her is trying to kill me. I hop in the car and slam the door.

She sits in the driver's seat and clips her seatbelt locked. Then she leans over the console and clips mine. She pulls out onto the road. "I really, really think you should go see a doctor—you look terrible."

"I'm fine." I pull a rose from my hair and run my fingers along the dried out petals, fascinated with its lack of luster. "A car just bumped me a little and I tripped down the hill."

"Yeah, right." She shifts her car and speeds down the highway, the tires squealing. "You don't just trip after a car bumps into you—you had to have been run over."

"I'm not going to the doctor," I say. "So take me home."

She flinches at my hostile tone and doesn't say a word for the rest of the drive.

***

I've calmed down by the time we pull up to my house. It's still early but the sky is bleak with clouds. The lights are on in the living room and my mom's red Sunfire is parked in the driveway.

I unbuckle my seatbelt. "I'm sorry for snapping at you. I don't know what's wrong with me... I just feel so... confused."

Raven presses her lips together and eyes my house. "It's okay. You were still my friend through my little meltdown."

"With Laden?" I brush the dirt off the front of my legs.

She nods slowly. "I'm not ready to talk about what happened yet, but I promise you I had nothing to do with his disappearance. And you have to promise me you'll tell me what happened today, when you're ready."

"You mean with Cameron?" I ask. "Or with the car?"

Her gaze steadies on me; there are bags under her eyes and her olive complexion looks sheet white. "Both."

"Cameron turned out to be a douche bag." I open the car door. "And when I'm ready, I'll try to explain what happened with the car."

She smiles. "I love you, Em. You know that, right?"

"I love you too." And at that moment I mean it.

I climb out of the car and go into the house. My mom is sifting through the bills at the kitchen table with takeout in front of her. She has on her uniform, a checkered dress covered by a white apron, and her hair is pulled up into a bun. I head up the stairs.

"Where have you been?" she asks.

I back down the stairs and step into the kitchen. "I was out at the lake."

Her brown eyes are as huge as silver dollars. "Why are you covered in dirt and scratched?"

"I picked a fight with a rose bush."

"And you lost?"

"No, I think I might have won." I have the dead rose in my hand and I place it on the table.

She sets the papers down and stares at the rose. "Where did you get that?"

"That's what was left over from the fight." I plop down in a chair and grab a fry from the takeout bag.

She picks up the rose, twirls it in her fingers, and dead rose petals float to the table. "You know I never expected your dad to leave."

"Which time?" I chew on the fry. "When he moved out or when he disappeared?"

"Ember, I hope you don't think your dad's coming back." She drops the dead rose on the table. "He's probably dead."

"I know that." I pick up the phone bill from the table, stamped with a bright red *OVERDUE*. "But I won't completely accept it until they find his body."

She collects the trash and tosses it in the garbage. "I never meant to blame Grandma's death on you." She slips on her jacket and ties the waist shut. "I was just upset." She pats my shoulder and sweeps my hair back like how she did when I was a child. "If you ever need to talk about anything, I'm here." I nod, trying not to cry, and she grabs her keys from the counter. "I'll see you in the morning."

After she leaves, I sneak up to the bathroom and check her prescription bottle in the medicine cabinet. She's been taking her meds again, which might explain the uplift in her attitude. On the way to my room, I run into Ian in the hallway.

"You look like crap," he announces, eyeing my dirty clothes. "Ember, that guy didn't... Did he try..."

I shake my head before he can finish. "I tripped down a hill."

He slips on a faded flannel jacket. "Hey, I got someone coming over later tonight, so don't lock up."

"I never lock up," I remind him. "And did you know mom's been taking her meds again?"

He ruffles his hair and pulls on his knitted beanie. "Yeah, I talked to her this morning. She showed up after you left, totally out of it, and I got her to take them."

"What about you?" I pluck a twig out of my hair. "Are you still taking yours?"

"Of course." He rolls his eyes.

"Is that the only drug you're taking?"

He tucks his hands in his pockets. "You know I don't do that crap anymore. Not since... Well, anyway, I'm going to check out for a little bit. And like I said, leave the door unlocked just in case my friend shows up before me." He pauses at the top of the stairway. "Oh yeah, and if I were you, I'd go for the one with the dark hair."

I clutch my bedroom doorknob. "What are you talking about?"

"The guy thing." He starts down the stairs. "I don't like that Cameron guy... He's too... I don't know, cocky or something—definitely not your type."

"You haven't even met Asher yet," I argue with no valid point because I want Asher too.

He shrugs and vanishes down the stairs. Moments later, the front door slams shut. I sigh and open my bedroom door. All I want to do is take a hot shower and wash off today.

"Hey."

The sound of his voice sends my heart soaring. My eyes dart to Asher sitting on my bed, the hood of his jacket pulled over his head, and he's playing with the raven feather. The window is open behind him and the wind gusts in, flapping the edges of the papers and pictures hanging on my walls.

"How did you get in here?" I ask, shutting the door.

He looks up from the feather with hooded eyes. "Your brother let me in."

"So that's what the remark was about," I mumble, then hunt for the right words. "What happened earlier... with Cameron—I shouldn't have done that."

"Done what exactly?" An underlying meaning hints in his words. He sets the feather down on the bed, slides the hood off his head, and rakes his fingers through his hair, leaving wisps in his eyes.

"Do you really want me to tell you?" I slant back against the door and fold my arms.

With his eyes locked on me, he pushes to his feet. "I need to know—it's driving me crazy not knowing." His eyes skim my body. "Especially when you look like that."

I rub the leftover dirt off my arm. "I fell down a hill."

He shakes his head and inches closer, eliminating some of the space between us. "I'm not talking about the dirt all over you."

"Oh." I glance down at the ribbon on my shirt—it's halfway undone. "He took me up to the lake, jumped in the water, and got my necklace out my car at the bottom of the lake."

Surprisingly, he's unfazed and takes another step toward me. "And…"

"And then half the school showed up and I bailed. I started walking down the highway. A car swerved at me and I fell down a hill."

He's a sliver of space from me. "A car *swerved* at you?"

I force the lump down in my throat. "That's how I fell down the hill."

"Did they do it on purpose?" he asks, aghast.

I shrug. "It's hard to say, but maybe."

He shuts his eyes, looking like he might cry. When he opens them back up, his pupils are dilated, only a slender ring of grey showing. He places his hands on the door, trapping me between his arms. "Are you okay?" His eyes investigate my body for wounds, but every one of the cuts and bruises have already healed.

I nod, unable to look away from his eyes. "I already told you I'm a walking miracle."

His gaze flicks to my lips and his voice deepens to a growl. "Did he kiss you?"

"Huh?"

"Cameron. Did he kiss you?"

My stomach somersaults and I lick my cracked lips. "Do you really want to know the answer to that?"

He drags his tongue ring along the edge of his teeth. "I need to know or else it will drive me crazy."

"He kissed my neck," I divulge truthfully.

"That's it?" His pierced eyebrow arches up. "That's the only place he kissed you?"

I nod. "That's the only place he kissed me."

His breathing quickens and his eyes turn animalistic, the small amount of grey evaporating, so there's nothing but pupil left. "Ember, can I kiss you?"

Why does he always ask first? I clutch the front of his shirt and yank him against my lips, delivering him my answer. His lips don't protest and he easily slips his tongue inside my mouth, bringing a sensation of warmth to every portion of my body. He lifts me up and my legs hook around his waist as he carries me to the bed. We fall together and my legs vice-grip around him. I feel alive and invigorated. Nothing exists at the moment but him and me.

My hands find the zipper of his jacket and I start to unzip it. He takes the hint, leaning up enough to shuck off his jacket and throw it across the room. He has a plaid shirt on underneath and I fumble to unbutton it. But he catches my hand and ceases me.

"Are you sure you're okay?" he asks, breathless. "You seem anxious."

I undo another button. "I'm fine."

"But I don't want us to move too fast," he says as I unfasten a button.

I pause, crushed with self-doubt. "You don't want this?" *Don't want me?*

"No, I want more than you're probably ready for." He cups my cheek with his hand. "That's why I think we should slow down."

I blink up at him. "Do you want to slow down?"

He shakes his head and laughs softly. "I'm a guy, aren't I?"

"Then how about I tell you when it's too far." My voice is jagged, but I maintain his gaze.

He slowly unbuttons the rest of his shirt, slips it off, and tosses it next to his jacket. My breath catches at his lean muscles and then at his tattoos. On the front section of his right rib is an angel with black feathers and tears in her eyes. Her black hair flows down her back, hiding her identity, and her feathers are molting. Tattooing his opposing rib is an inscription. I run my fingers along the cursive writing:

Nigredo caped terra et possederunt corpora mortale.

Ignis acquiritur super agros et fames possederunt maria.

Mors vincit iram et Angelos morte. Erat, sed omne sacrificium unum contrarium.

Morte puellae umero uno utrisque coniunctum esset electio salvificem mundum.

Sed non facile ad pugnam.

He covers his body with mine, so every part of us is melted together, and I wrap my arms around him. He kisses me deeply, sucking on my bottom lip, and trailing delicate kisses down my neck. My body conforms to his, steaming with desire. My chest heaves as he unties the ribbon of my shirt. He pauses, waiting to see if I protest. I don't, and he unties it completely. The shirt gives open and his soft lips touch my skin. I shut my eyes and let the beautiful moment swallow me up.

We kiss until our bodies force us to breathe. Asher ties my shirt back up and then puts his own back on. Then we lie in my bed with my head resting in the crook of his arm.

"Ember," he speaks slowly, as if I'm a skittish cat. "You know you can tell me stuff, right? I feel like... I don't know... it feels like you keep things to yourself, like you think that for some reason you can't trust anyone."

My dad's words dance through my head. *Emmy, if there's one thing you need to know about life, it's to never*

ever trust anyone or anything. Life is a freaking mind game and you and I are the pawns.

"I barely know you." I trace patterns on his forearm. "Well, except for your lips. I know those pretty well."

He bites back a smile. "I know…" He looks down and meets my eyes. "But I want you to get to know me and open up. I feel like you have a lot of things bottled up in you."

"So do you. Like your father. You don't like to talk about him. And you never did fully explain why you moved here." I bite down on my tongue. "I'm so sorry. I don't know what my problem is." Head trauma. Death. Dead bodies. Or the fact that I stole the lives of a thousand plants.

His Adam's apple bobs up and down as he swallows hard. "No, it's okay." He slides down so we are at eye level. "We moved here to escape the memory of my dad. Even after he died the painful memories of when he was around still stayed in the house. So my mom and I packed up and moved here to be closer to family."

"I'm sorry." I feel like a bitch. "I shouldn't have forced you to tell me that."

"I wanted to tell you." He tucks a strand of my hair behind my ear. "Because I want you to feel comfortable sharing things with me."

I open my mouth to tell him everything, spill out my heart and soul, but again my dad's words echo in my mind again. "I sometimes feel like life is just one big test to see how long we can survive."

I tuck my head into his chest and squeeze my eyes shut, waiting for him to leave.

"Do you want to hear what my tattoo means?" he asks, his voice soft like a fragile feather.

I'm surprised. I thought he would get mad or think I was insane. "Yeah, I'd love to hear it."

"It's actually a story my father used to tell me all the time." He confines my hand against his chest and his heart beats swiftly against my palm. "Blackness caped the land and possessed the bodies of the mortals. Fire acquired over the fields and famine possessed the oceans. The wrath of death was winning and the Angels of Death suffered. It was the end, but a single sacrifice reversed it all. One beautiful Grim Angel with death in her blood and on her shoulders connected them all, and with a single choice she would save the world. But the fight would not be easy. Death would play with her mind and her life, but Angels would do everything they could to protect her. She would struggle with right and wrong and mess up along the way, but in the end she would have to make the right choice, otherwise Death would win and humans and Angels endure an eternity of suffering."

"But what does that mean…" I start to doze off. "And why were they fighting to begin with… Aren't they both death? Or was it over…" *Souls.* I try to open my lips to ask him if he knows about the story in the book, but aching exhaustion possesses my body.

"It's getting late," Asher whispers. He tenderly kisses the tip of my ear. "I have to go."

My eyelids flutter open. "Okay…"

"I heard your brother come back." He climbs over me. "So you're not home alone."

I nod, barely able to keep my eyes open. "Alright, I'll see you later…"

He chuckles. "I'll see you tomorrow, Ember." He kisses my cheek and seconds later I hear the bedroom door shut. I roll over and fall asleep with the calmness of Asher still lingering in my body.

Chapter 15

I'm woken up to a banging on the front door. They bang and bang and bang. Finally, I throw the blanket off me and climb out of bed. My room is pitch black, and blue and red lights flash outside my window.

"Ian." I stumble into the hall. The last time the cops showed up, Ian had wrecked the car. My mom went easy on him because Alyssa's death was a fresh wound, but he was in the hospital for two days recovering from severe head trauma.

I throw open the front door. Two uniformed officers stand on the front porch. One's short and lumpy and the other tall and bulky. A black and white cop car is parked in the driveway and my neighbors have congregated on their front porches, watching their scene in their pajamas, the red and blue sirens lighting up their burn-her-at-the-stake expressions.

The shorter officer reads a paper attached to a clipboard in his hands. "Are you Ember Rose Edwards?"

My pulse skips a beat. "Yeah, I am."

"And are you the owner of a 1970 Dodge Challenger?"

Oh shit. "Umm…"

"And lying will only get you into more trouble," the officer warns.

"It's mine." There's a crumb in his mustache and I can't stop staring at it. "Or my dad's and mine."

"Your dad's Patrick Edwards?" The tall one asks and I nod. "He's the one who disappeared a few years ago and you were brought in for questioning."

I nod. "Yeah, so?"

He scowls at me and skims the paper with his finger. "It says on here that you're on probation for drug possession."

I bite at my tongue. The drugs weren't mine—they were Ian's. But I took the wrap for it because he'd just suffered a manic episode. "Yeah, I am."

"You're going to need to come with us." He takes off the handcuffs from his belt. "Your car was pulled out of the lake tonight."

"I didn't know it was a crime for your car to be in a lake," I smart-mouth.

He offers me zero tolerance. "No, but it's a little suspicious you never reported it and then it's discovered near a crime scene."

"What?" I stammer. "What crime scene?"

"There was an incident at the lake," the shorter cop explains. "A girl came up missing tonight and we got an anonymous tip that your car could be found at the bottom of the lake at the last spot she was seen."

"That's bull," I say. "I was here at my house all day."

"What about your car?" he asks with a condescending smirk that crinkles the skin around his eyes.

I hesitate. "That's been gone for a week or so."

"Stolen?" he asks and I shake my head. "Then why didn't you report the accident?"

I shrug and lie, "I didn't want my mom to get mad at me."

The cops exchange consequential looks. The shorter one steps off the porch and heads to the cop car.

The taller one says, "I'm Officer McKinley and that's Officer Adams. We're going to need to take you down to the station for questioning. If you'll go easy, we won't use the handcuffs."

I glance around at the ridiculing eyes of my neighbors, planning my escape. I disappeared once, and I can do it again. "Fine. Can I at least get some shoes on?"

He points behind me at a pair of my flip flops. "Those should work."

Asshole. I slip on the flip flops and follow him out. The garage door is open and Ian's car isn't parked inside, which is weird because Asher told me he was home. Raven runs out of her house in her silky pajamas and slippers. She stops at the edge of the driveway.

"What's happening, Ember," she whispers, glancing cautiously at the cops.

"Get your brother and come down to the station in case you have to bail me out," I hiss. "Not Ian and not my mom. I don't want them dealing with this."

She nods with wide eyes. "Okay, we'll meet you at the station."

I duck my head as I climb into the back of the cop car. The last time I was in one it smelled like sweat, smoke, and old meat. It smells just about the same.

The officers climb in and slam the doors. We back onto the road and I spot Cameron climbing out of his Jeep. He smiles and gives me a little wave. Suddenly, I have an idea of who told the cops my car was at the bottom of the lake.

Chapter 16

I wait in the holding room for about an hour, a little cop trick before they try to break me. They forced me to take off all my jewelry and empty out my pockets. I rest my head back and slouched in the chair taking turns watching the clock, staring at the brick walls, and trying to see through the glass.

Finally, Detective Crammer enters. She's wearing a simple black pantsuit and her blonde hair is pulled back in a tight bun. She pulls out a chair across from me, sets a folder on the table, and puts on her glasses.

"Ember Rose Edwards." A conniving grin ranges her thin lips. "So we meet again."

I straighten up in the chair. "So we do."

She eyes my filthy clothes over. "Rough night?"

I stare at her with a vacant expression. "Nope."

She explores the pages in the folder. "Where are your mother and brother tonight?"

"My mother's working at the All Night Diner," I tell her. "And my brother's at a friend's."

"Do you need to call them?" She shuts the folder and overlaps her hands on it. "Someone needs to pick you up when we're done here."

"No, my friend's brother will come pick me up." I cross my arms on the table. "My mom doesn't need to miss work and Ian probably won't answer his phone." I worry she might force me to call, since I'm a minor.

She slips off her square-framed glasses and wipes the lens with the sleeve of her jacket. "Do you know why you were brought in tonight?"

I shrug. "Because my car was found at a crime scene."

"At a crime scene just like your father's and Laden Miller's," she says. "What do you know about Mackenzie Baker?"

"Mackenzie Baker?" Her shocking words throw off my game. "Is she the one that vanished tonight?"

"I'll be asking the questions," she warns. "Now what do you know about her?"

"She's a junior like me, I have a few classes with her, and she's the head cheerleader. That's all I know about her."

"Were you at the party tonight? The one by the lake? A few people said they saw you there."

"I was at the lake before the party started," I answer. "But I left when people started showing up."

She jots what I say on the top of the folder. "And how did you get home?"

"I got a ride from a friend that I called to come pick me up," I tell her and she scribbles that to her list.

"Who did you drive out there with?" She writes a number on the corner of the folder.

"A guy," I say and her eyes elevate to me. "Cameron Logan."

She doesn't seem to recognize the name, but cops are good at playing dumb. "And who is he?"

"He just moved here from New York," I explain. "He's my age and lives down my street."

"Was he part of the reason you left?" She puts her glasses back on.

"Partially," I say with hesitance. "He was flirting with another girl."

She opens the folder and searches through her notes. "What's the girl's name?"

"Mackenzie Baker."

Her head snaps up. "You know lying is only going to get you into more trouble."

"I'm not lying," I gripe. "That's the truth."

She reluctantly returns to her notes and pens down a few more notes. Then she closes the folder and slips off her glasses. "Again, we'll be in touch. I have no doubt about that." She sticks out her hand for me to shake. "For now, I'd say it'd be best for you to stay in town."

My muscles tense as I take her hand. A thick, vile sensation blasts up my arm. *Blood and a thousand petals scattered across the dirt. An angel stands in the center of a mob, stripped of its feathers, and beaten blue. Their face is curtained with a halo of black hair. She steps forward and raises a knife, but a black figure swoops down from the sky and snatches her by the shoulders. She screams as they fly up, up, up and then drops her to the earth.*

I jerk back at the *X* on her wrist. "Who are you?"

She tugs the sleeve of her jacket down and turns for the door. "I'd watch out, Ember," she says, opening the door. "They say insanity is passed down through generations. And your dad was diagnosed with schizophrenia, which can surface at a young age." She slams the door behind her.

It takes every ounce of strength I own not to jump up from the chair, pick the lock on the door, and chase her down. Thirty minutes later they release me. They have no real evidence that I did anything wrong, besides not reporting that my car was missing. I go to collect my things at the window and the big-haired lady with bright blue eye shadow hands me a plastic bag containing my bracelets. She turns her back to the window and I bang on it.

She glances over her shoulder at me, annoyed. "May I help you?"

I hold up a bag and jiggle it in front of the window. "Yeah, I had a necklace in here."

She spins her chair around and stares at the bag skeptically. "One moment please." She rolls to the phone and takes her sweet time hanging up. "That's all that was collected."

Glancing at the bag, I shake my head. "No, I had a necklace with a big maroon jewel."

"Well then it sounds like you'll be able to find it easily when you get home." She huffs out of her chair and walks out the side door.

I dump the bracelets on the counter, fasten them on my wrists, and clasp my silver-winged earrings into my ears. "I know I was wearing my necklace."

Raven and her brother, Todd, are sitting in the waiting room, which only has one other person, an older man eating an egg McMuffin. Raven runs up to give me a hug, but quickly stops herself. She zips up the suede jacket that's over her thin silk pajama set.

Todd is twenty years old and is the spitting male version of Raven. He has spiky blue hair, a lip piercing, and tattoos all over his muscular arms.

"Hey troublemaker." He gives me a hug and I inhale through my nose until it's over. "What the hell did you do this time?"

We push through the glass doors and I bask in my freedom. The sun is awake, the sky a clear blue. Elderly couples stroll up the sidewalk and eat breakfast out on the patios. Pink flyers with Mackenzie's face on them are plastered all over the street posts, doors, and walls of the surrounding buildings.

"Well apparently it's a crime to crash your car into a lake and then not tell anyone." I slide into the backseat of his 1980 Pontiac Firebird with a large eagle painted on the hood.

"Wait? You *wrecked* your dad's Challenger?" He revs up the gas and the engine backfires. "Like it's gone?"

Raven exchanges a look with me and I shake my head. She wants to know what really happened, but I don't want to tell her in front of Todd. The first thing I need to do is talk to Asher. Because I think I'm ready to hear his answers now.

***

Todd takes us to breakfast at Sherry's Diner. It's a seventies themed restaurant where they still allow people to smoke. Our waitress is Betty Lou, a middle-aged woman with big beehive hair, oval glasses, and a white apron over her pink dress.

"Hi y'all," she drawls. "What can I get you?"

Raven and I are sitting side-by-side in the booth across from Todd, reading over the same menu. "Can we have just a second?" Raven asks.

Todd hands Betty Lou his menu and tells her, "I'll have eggs, scrambled, wheat toast, and a ham steak."

Betty Lou jots his order down. "I'll go put this order in and come back and get y'alls after."

Once she's gone, Todd gets up from the table. "I'm going to go use the men's room."

He struts toward the back area of the restaurant and Raven whispers in my ear, "He's screwing the waitress."

I pull a face. *"Betty Lou?"*

She rolls her eyes and points her finger at a slender waitress with fiery red hair standing behind the serving counter. "That one… wait just a second and she'll walk back toward the bathrooms."

We pretend to stare at our menus, but really our attention is on the girl. Her nametag says *Steph*. She's pretty, maybe a few years older than Todd, but other than that she seems like his type. Sure enough, about a minute after Todd vanishes into the bathroom, Steph goes wandering back there.

"How do you know about them?" I ask Raven.

She runs her finger down the menu. "He's been bringing me to either dinner or breakfast here almost every day for the last two weeks and it's like a freaking routine. So are you going to tell me what's up with the police?"

Betty Lou appears at the end of our table and we hurry and give her our orders. She collects the menu, walks behind the counter, and refills the glasses of water for the people at the bar.

"Before I tell you," I say in a hushed voice. "I need you to tell me about that *X* got on your shoulder."

She frowns and unzips her jacket to show me her shoulder blade. "It was just a scratch I got when I was making out with Laden. His stupid car had a wire sticking out of it."

There isn't anything left of the scratch. "Okay, then why were you acting so… happy after he died?"

She puts her jacket back on and flips her bubblegum pink hair out of the collar. "Something really bad happened that night... Laden almost raped me."

My heart literally stops. "What? Why didn't you tell me?"

"Because he disappeared right after it happened and I worried I'd become a suspect." She peeks over her shoulder and then drops her voice. "Besides, you have your own stuff to deal with, like death and your mom and Ian."

"You could have told me," I whisper. "I wouldn't have told anyone. And I can handle more than you think."

"No, *you* think you can handle more." She takes a sip of her water. "But it's okay. I talked to Asher about it and he really helped me understand. And that whole psychotic episode I was having was just my need to deal with what happened."

"When did you talk to Asher?" My voice comes out sharp and I clear my throat. "I'm sorry, I just didn't know you two had been hanging out with each other."

"Calm down." She scoots the utensils out of the way and rests her elbow onto the table. "We're just friends. And I was talking to him about it because he was the one who saved me from getting raped."

"That's... that's not possible," I stammer. "He was saving me that night."

She thrums her finger on her lip. "Well, it was before or after he saved me then."

I shake my head. "There's no way he could have made it to both places in time."

"I'm not sure, Em... maybe you should ask him because all I know is that Laden is a rapist and I don't feel bad that he's gone. And Asher was basically my angel that day."

"Your *angel*? What do you mean by that?"

She quickly looks away. "It's a figure of speech, silly."

"And what about Garrick?" I ask. "Where does he come to play in all this?"

"Oh, he was there that night too," she says staring across the restaurant. "Garrick and Asher both showed up when it happened. Asher knocked Laden off me and then Garrick took me home. I'm not sure what Asher did with Laden, although I have a guess."

"Asher wouldn't kill someone." But I hardly know him, so there isn't much proof behind my statement. "And besides, whoever made Laden disappear also made my dad disappear. And Asher wasn't even around when that happened."

"Maybe it was just one of those freakish coincidences? Or a copycat? And would it matter if Asher did kill Laden?" She focuses her eyes on me. "He had me pinned down with a knife to my throat. I'm pretty sure he was going to kill me."

I speechlessly stutter for words that don't exist. Thankfully Todd drops down in our booth. He pulls a cigarette out of his jacket pocket and pops it between his lips.

"Okay, so what'd I miss?" He lights the cigarette and exhales. "Anything good?"

Raven and I let out a loud breath. "Nope," we both say.

***

Todd makes Raven go home with him to help clean the house, which gives me a little more time to figure out how much I want to tell her. Someone has painted "Murderer" in bright red across our front door. This happened a few times after my dad disappeared, only it was on my car window and it usually happened in the parking lot of the school.

I grab a can of paint remover from the garage. "It's like a freaking witch hunt," I say as I work to scrub it off. In the end, half the paint comes off the door, but it's better paintless than labeled with hate.

As soon as I make it to my room, I find my cell and dial Asher's number. It sends me straight to his voicemail, so I text him.

Me: We need 2 talk.

Asher: Why? What's wrong? R U ok?

Me: I'm fine. I just have some questions.

Asher: Out with my mom running errands. Can I talk to u tomorrow at the dance?

Me: Dance???

Asher: Yeah. The Halloween dance. I thought we could go.

I complete forgot tomorrow was Halloween and that there was a dance at our school. But I'm not really the dancing type.

Me: I guess. But can I meet u there?

Just in case this goes bad, I'll have my own ride home. I need to know what the Anamotti is, if he knows anything about detective Crammer, and what he knows about Angels and Grim Reapers.

Asher: Sure... r u ok?

Me: Yep. I just really need 2 talk to u about something... the thing we talked about the other night. I think I'm ready for the answers. And I have other questions 4 you.

It takes him a second to text back.

Asher: I know. I'll c u at the dance at 7. I'll b the one dressed as the artist ;)

I smile at the message, but then quickly erase it. Please, oh please don't let him be a serial killer. I like him too much. I toss the phone on my bed. It's early and I start to climb into bed to get some rest.

"Ian!" My mom's scream echoes through the house. I trip out of bed and stumble down the hall into her room. Her bed is unmade and her waitress uniform is discarded on the floor. The bathroom door is shut and the knob is covered with blood.

I pad up to the door and ask tentatively, "Mom? Are you in there?"

She sobs from the other side. "Go away… I want Ian."

I jiggle the doorknob. "Mom, unlock the door. Ian's not here right now, but I am."

"No!" She screams. "I don't want you here. You're a killer! You're a killer! You killed your grandma!"

I bang my fist on the door. "Mom, please just open the door up. You're scaring me."

Something bashes against the other side and glass shatters. I run into my room, grab my phone off the dresser, and call Ian on my way back to her bedroom.

He picks up after three rings. Music blares in the background. "Yo, yo, yo. What up?" He's drunk.

"You need to come home," I demand. "*Now*. Mom's having another one of her meltdowns and she only wants to talk to you."

"*What?*" His voice sobers up.

"She locked herself in…" I trail off. The bathroom door is open. "Ian, just get here now. And get someone sober to drive you."

"Okay," he says, frazzled. "I'll be there in ten."

I hang up, toss the phone on the bed, and check inside the bathroom. The white tile is obscured with fragments of glass and the sink and mirror are stained with blood. The shower curtain is torn from the rod and pills scatter the inside of the bathtub.

"Mom." I step back into the bedroom and glance under the bed. "Ian's on his way, and he told me to tell you that it was okay to talk to me." I pad over to the closet door and throw it open. "Mom?"

"I'm not in there." Her chillingly numb voice floats over my shoulder.

I spin around and press my hand against my heart. "You scared me."

She's just outside the doorway with a pair of scissors in her hand. An *X* on her forehead drips blood into her eyes and the entire front of her shirt is drenched in blood. "It's not okay to be around you at all." Her eyes are unemotional, as if she's detached from reality. Blood trickles from her wrists as she raises the scissors above her head. "You're a killer! The cops think so! And Grandma knew, even though she wasn't thinking rationally. But you did it anyway."

I surrender my hands in front of me and slowly back up, seeking the bed for my phone. "Mom, how many of those pills did you take?"

"Enough to numb the pain—he told me I had to." She skulks into the room, then pauses, slanting back as if someone is whispering in her ear. "Yes, I know, but she's not… Okay, I will try." Her soulless gaze locks on me. "Ember, my dear child, why did you ever have to be born? Ian was fine and your father and I were so happy his *disorder* did not pass along to him. But then you arrived and we could see it in your eyes. The way you talked to the air and whispered secrets to the plants while you drained their life away."

"I…" *Does she know about me?* "Mom, what are you talking about?" I reach over the bed for my phone. "And Dad didn't have schizophrenia, everyone just thought he did."

"I'm not talking about schizophrenia!" She shrieks, her face bright red. "I'm talking about a curse passed along to you."

My fingers brush the edge of the phone. "Mom, just calm down—"

She rages forward with the scissors held out in front of her. I leap on the bed and bolt for the bathroom, but she cuts around the bed and sinks the scissors into my chest.

"Mom…" I stare at the scissors pierced deeply into my heart. A river of blood streams out and I gasp for air as I fall onto the bed.

She hovers over me, watching me with expectancy, like she is waiting for something miraculous to happen. "I'm sorry, my sweet baby, but he made me do it. Death is more powerful than the mind."

Blood gurgles up my throat as I yank out the scissors. "Mommy…"

She places her hand over my heart. "Go ahead, take it. I know you can. You did it with your grandma."

Blood seeps out the hole in my chest and runs a river over her hand. I look into her eyes, wondering if it's really her in there or if tonight her mind finally took the final flight.

Thump, thump, thump, thump. My heart sings a song as it dies.

"Take it, Ember," she whispers. "Before it's too late."

My eyes close as my heart sings the last lyric, my veins hollow out, and my lungs shrivel. I sense someone else's presence in the room. Gradually, I open my eyelids. The Grim Reaper looms behind my mother, concealed under his hood. He whispers something in her ear.

"It's time," she tells me with her hand extended. "Please, Emmy. It's time. The grains of sand have expired and my hourglass is empty."

"Take it, Ember," the Grim Reaper tempts. "Take her life."

I feel the thunder of her heart connect with the silence of mine. Her blood mixes in my veins and fills my lungs back up. I gasp for air and open my eyes, watching in horror as her skin wrinkles to a lady twice her age.

"Mommy." I throw her hand off my chest and she collapses to the floor. I hover above her, checking her wrist for a pulse. She looks so old and frail—so gone.

The Reaper watches me from the corner and I throw a shoe at him. "I hate you! You ruined my life!"

"What the hell?"

I glance back at Ian standing right behind me. His eyes are opened wide and are filled with helplessness as he stares at our mother lying dead on the floor.

The Grim Reaper's laugh echoes through my head as he sinks away through the bedroom wall.

"Call a damn ambulance!" I yell at Ian and start CPR on my mom.

He blinks dazedly and takes his phone out of his pocket. Tears pool in my eyes as I pump my mom's chest and breathe for her. I keep going, refusing to stop until the paramedics arrive and take over. But even when they roll her away in the stretcher, she still isn't breathing on her own. And she still looks so old.

They wheel her out into the ambulance and speed off to the hospital with their lights flashing. Ian and I hop in his car and he hands me his jacket. I slip it on and cover up the blood on my shirt. But I can't hide the blood on my hands.

That will be there forever.

Chapter 17

Ian and I return home later that night after my mom was stabilized and heavily sedated. She had taken a high dosage of her medication, plus there were traces of street drugs and alcohol in her system. By the time the doctors got her breathing again, the sudden aging had subsided. But there were a few extra wrinkles around her eyes.

She is under observation and we can't see her until a full mental analysis is ran. We hardly speak and Ian heads straight up to his studio. He doesn't know what really happened, which is good because he can't handle what he does know: that my mom overdosed and that she cut up her forehead and wrists.

"If you need anything," I call out as he trudges up the stairs. "Please come get me."

"Sure," he mutters, slipping off his shoes at the top of the stairs. "I'm just gonna go paint for a while."

I doubt he's going to paint. He'll probably lock himself up in his room and smoke himself into a stupor. As soon as he is upstairs, I collapse on the sofa with my feet kicked up over the back. "All I want to do is sleep forever. Please just let me sleep forever."

A raven zigzags just outside the window, back and forth, back and forth, and then it lands on the windowsill. It spans it small wings and shakes off a few feathers.

"Go away." I throw a couch pillow at the window.

Tucking its wings in, it spins in a circle. I toss another pillow at it. Parting its beak, it caws. I begrudgingly drag myself off the couch and place my hand on the glass. "Why won't you just go away?"

Granting me my wish, it flaps away in the direction of Cameron's house. It's late, so most of the houses are dark, but the light in Cameron's attic is on. I'm possessed by a rage that doesn't belong to me, scorching uncontrollably like a wildfire. As if my feet no longer belong to me, I march out the front door and across the street. The untied shoelaces of my boots drag behind me and blood still stains my shirt and hands.

His Jeep is parked out front and the tires are covered with chunks of mud. I cup my hands around my eyes as I peek through the back window, wondering if I'll find rope and a roll of duct tape, like the kind I saw on Mackenzie in her death omen.

"Find anything interesting?" Cameron's amused voice is startling close.

Slowly, I rotate to face him. He's standing closer than I expect and the heel of my boot slips off the edge of the curb with the shift of my weight.

"Easy there." He catches my arm and balances me onto the curb. He's wearing faded jeans, no shirt, and his skin almost glows beneath the dim trail of moonlight. There is dust in his blonde hair and on his hands.

I wrench my arm free and his dusty handprints mark my skin. "Why did you do it?"

He knows exactly what I'm talking about. "But I didn't do it."

"Yes, you did." I dust the dirt off my arm. "You were the only one who knew the exact location of my car."

"Am I?" He shakes his head and dust flies from his hair. "Because I was under the impression that you didn't get yourself out of that car the night you crashed."

"Who gave you that impression?" I ask. "And why is there dirt in your hair? Have you been digging graves up again, looking for your—" I make air quotes, "'family jewel'?"

"Actually, I ended up finding that in the strangest place." His eyes travel up my body and linger on the hole in my shirt. "And I think I should be the one asking you the questions. Starting with why you look like you just committed murder."

"Tell me, Cameron." I struggle to maintain my composure. "What happen to Mackenzie last night after I left?"

He reaches above my head and sets his hand on the Jeep. "Why? Are you jealous?"

"Jealous that I wasn't the one who got killed?" I back against the door of the Jeep and cross my arms.

"You know, it seems like I'm the only one you have this spitfire attitude toward." He leans over me. "Everyone else I've seen you with, you're nicer than can be. And you were like that with me at first, but now... what happened?"

"You blew me off at the lake," I admit. "And then told the police where my car was, after Mackenzie disappeared."

"I didn't tell the police where your car was," he says. "What was one of the first things I ever told you about me? That I don't lie."

"I think that's the liars' motto."

He bows his head in frustration and his hair tickles my nose. "Ember, Ember, Ember, what am I going to do with you?" He raises his head back up and the sorrow in his eyes is restored. "Is this because I was flirting with Mackenzie, because the only reason I did that was to make you jealous—like how I felt when I showed up at your house and some guy was sleeping in your bed."

"You know what?" I duck under his arm. "I don't even know why I came over here. It must have been a crazy impulse."

"Because you wanted to see if I killed her," he calls out as I storm across the street. I halt and he says, "That's what you think. That I'm a killer, but you're wrong and I can prove it."

I glance over my shoulder. "I'm calling your bluff."

He waves for me to follow him as he strolls backward down the pathway. "Come with me and I'll prove it to you." He enters his house and leaves the front door wide open. A light turns on from inside.

I make my way to the edge of the front path. "Does he really think I'm going to go in there?" I mutter to myself. Then again, it seems I can't die, so what does it matter.

Like a shadow, he transpires in the doorway with the light of the house radiating behind. "Are you coming?"

I shake my head. "Whatever you want to show me, you can show me outside."

He sighs and slinks from the doorway back into the house. Minutes later, a blonde girl pokes her head out.

Ember

"Ember, would you please just get your creepy ass in here," Mackenzie says with a trace of pleading in her tone. "Before someone figures out I'm here."

I glance over my shoulder at the silent houses lining the street. I come to the mind-blowing conclusion that I'm probably losing my mind, like certain poets of the past. Or like a Grim Angel. I plod up the path, past Mackenzie and through the entryway. Cameron shuts the door and we go into a living room with red walls and a brick fireplace. The mantle is ornamented with plastic plants and family photos. Above it is a mirror trimmed with a gold frame. The air smells like cinnamon and apples.

"This isn't how I pictured your house," I remark, sitting down on a striped sofa. Across from the coffee table is a matching sofa, and Cameron and Mackenzie sit down on it. Mackenzie looks like she's wearing Cameron's clothes: an oversized flannel shirt and a pair of boxers. She has leather bands on her wrists and neck, like she's suddenly decided to try a semi-gothic look.

"The cops think I killed you," I tell her. "They brought me down to the station a couple of nights ago for questioning."

"Wow, Killer Girl speaks," she says snidely. "You were so quiet at school I thought you were a mute."

Cameron lays a hand on her bare knee. "Easy, remember she knows you're here now, so play nice."

She crosses her arms and says exasperatedly, "Yeah, but only because you made me let her in. Personally, I don't give a crap if she thinks you're lying or not." Cameron tilts his head at her and she recoils. "I'm sorry. And I'm sorry too, Ember. Look, it's just that... Well, I was having problems at home. And things were just *really* bad and I was telling this to Cameron at the lake and he suggested I disappear for a while and take a break."

"You know everyone is looking for you, right?" I press the severity. "There are flyers all over the town with your face posted on them. This is really messed up."

"Messed up?" She laughs, and then starts to cry. "No, messed up is growing up in a house like I did."

"A lot of people have bad home lives," I pronounce unsympathetically. "It doesn't mean we run away."

"Oh yeah, what's so messed up in your life?" Tears roll down her sun-kissed cheeks and she scratches under the leather band on her neck. "Did your dad use you to close job deals with old perverted men? I just wanted to get the hell away from it for one moment, just breathe. Haven't you ever wanted to just breathe?"

"Every single day of my existence," I whisper.

Cameron catches my eye and raises his eyebrows, seeking my response.

"So what? You just hid her somewhere and then scattered feathers all over the shore and painted it up with an X and an hourglass?" I ask him.

Cameron's eyebrows knit together. "I hid her, but I didn't do the feathers and weird paint thing. Why would we do that?"

"To make her disappearance look like the rest of them."

"As good of an idea as that is, we didn't do that."

"But that's what the detective said." I fall back in the couch with my forehead creased. "Why would she do that?"

"To mess with your head probably, see if you would let something slip." Mackenzie shrugs and rearranges the bands on her wrists. "It's kind of their M.O." When Cameron and I gape at her, she adds, "What? I watch a lot of *Law and Order*, okay?"

I tap my boot on the floor, bubbling with anxious energy. "They think I killed you… and they think I killed Laden."

"No, they don't. They just don't have any other leads." Cameron's eyes journey down my body. "Although, if they saw you now, they'd probably lock you up."

I wrap my arms around myself. "I had an accident."

He points over his shoulder. "Is that why there was an ambulance at your house?"

I focus the interest back on Mackenzie. "So what am I supposed to do? Just pretend I never saw anything and let them keep investigating me?"

"Would you?" she asks, hopeful. "That would be really great, at least until I can figure out somewhere else to live. I'll be eighteen in a few weeks, so I'll be good to move out on my own."

I rub my exhausted eyes. "I don't mean to sound rude, but can't you just tell someone what's going on?"

She laughs, but it's forced. "You don't think I've tried? But my mom always sides with my dad, saying I'm doing it to draw attention to myself. And my dad is a big funder of the Hollows Grove Police Department."

"Is he paying them off?" I ask, flabbergasted, and she gives a subtle nod. I consider the dilemma for a moment, but there isn't much to consider. "Fine, I'll keep my mouth shut, but please try to figure something else out, before they actually arrest me."

"Thank you, Ember," she says gratefully. "And I'm sorry, you know, for treating you so badly in school." She gets up and wraps her arms around me.

My eyes widen and I prepare myself. But her death never announces itself.

She retreats for the doorway, telling Cameron, "I'm going to go lay down, Cam. I'm really tired."

Once she's gone, I say to Cameron, "So it still doesn't explain how the cops found out where my car was."

"That's a question I can't answer for you." He rests his arms on his legs and intersects his fingers. "The only thing I can say is that there has to be someone else who knew where your car was."

Asher. And perhaps the person who was tailgating me that night.

"Did someone save you?" he prods. "Or did you swim out of the car on your own?"

"I have excellent panic reaction skills." I get to my feet. "I should get home. It's late."

He accompanies me to the door, but pushes it closed when I open it. "Can I show you something first, before you go?" His nice guy act is back, like when we first met and had that briefly decent moment in his Jeep.

I go with him upstairs into his room. There's a bed, a dresser in the corner, and a door that extends to a small patio with a camping chair. The walls are black and bare except one, a white accent wall with lines and lines of poetry.

"Are they your words?" I ask, amazed, and he nods. I walk up to the wall and read the poem that centers them all.

"In separate fields of black feathers, the birds fly. Four wings, two hearts, but only one soul. They connect in the middle, but are separated by a thin line of ash. It's what brings them together, yet rips their feathers apart. They can never truly be together as light and dark. Unless one makes the ultimate sacrifice, blows out their candle, and joins the other in the dark."

Cameron watches me with interest. "So what do you think it means?"

"They could never be together," I say. "Unless one died? But why? What makes the other one fly in the land of the dead?"

"That's something you'll have to figure out on your own." He chips a flake of blood off my shirt. "You should know that a poet doesn't like to explain the meaning behind his words."

I bite at my fingernail. "Yeah, I understand that completely. But you should know that, as a poet, I have a desire to understand words."

"You know," he steps closer, "we never got to go to that poetry slam."

"That wasn't my fault," I remind him.

"You're the one that ran away that day." He places a hand on my wrist and tenderly drags it up to my shoulder. "I was trying to make you jealous."

"Cameron," I say with caution, looking at the wall. "You didn't happen to see a black car with really tinted windows up at the lake, did you?"

His fingers discover my collarbone and he traces gentle circles over my skin. "No, why? Did something happen with this car?"

A soundless sensation numbs my mind and I feel myself falling to him. But I shake my head and sigh through it. "I should get going. "

His fingers travel down the front of my body as I turn to leave and he hitches the bottom of my shirt. "You can stay here, if you want. You can sleep in my bed." He raises his hand innocently. "I promise not to touch you, unless you ask."

"Is that the same thing you told Mackenzie?"

"Mackenzie and I are just friends. But I like that you care."

I dither back and forth between him and the door.

"Come on, Ember," he coaxes in that voice that's hard to resist. "Please stay."

I force my willpower to my legs and back away for the door. "I'm sorry, Cameron, but I think you're a little too much for me."

"That's what all the girls say," he jokes, but there is a vast sea of pain in his eyes. He sighs. "Hold on. I'll walk you to the door."

Chapter 18

When I was thirteen, my mom locked me in the attic for an entire day because she believed I killed several of her house plants. It really wasn't that big of a deal, only she didn't let me have anything to drink or eat and there were no bathroom breaks permitted. I walked out of the situation without being too traumatized.

The only thing that bothered me was her belief that I killed the plants on purpose. At the time, it seemed ridiculous; the idea a person could dry out houseplants in less than five minutes. But now I wonder if perhaps I did do it. And if my mom has always known there was something different about me.

I wake up on the couch, with my legs flopped over the back and my head hanging upside down. It's late in the afternoon, the sky tinted a pale pink. Children are laughing outside and someone is throttling a motorcycle.

I lie motionless, with a splitting headache, trying to fall back asleep, not ready to face the day, or find out what Ian's been doing in his studio all night. I heard someone sneak in late last night, but I didn't care enough to go see who. There were muffled voices on the stairway and then footsteps headed into the attic.

Without changing position, I reach for the remote on the coffee table. The front door swings open and someone comes whisking into the house. Their high heels click against the floor. "What the hell happened?" Raven asks. "Why was there an ambulance here yesterday?"

She looks strange upside down, dressed up as an angel with white-feather wings and a silvery-satin dress. Her hair is curled and wound with white ribbon to form a halo on the top of her head.

I sit up and rub my eyes. "Because my mom flipped out and tried to slit her wrists." The words tumble out.

"Ember..." She doesn't have a clue how to react to my honesty. "What can I do to help?"

I drag my butt off the sofa and her glitter-framed eyes widen at the blood all over my shirt. "You can let me go to sleep for a really, really long time. That's all I want to do is sleep."

She gasps. "Why is there dried blood all over you?"

"Because my mom stabbed me with a pair of scissors," I confess.

She pries open the gap in my shirt where the scissors had violently entered. "Em, that's not funny."

"I'm not trying to be funny," I tell her. "She stabbed me with the scissors and then I almost killed her by sucking the life out of her to heal myself."

"You're in shock." She pulls her hands away. "Or did you hit your head?"

"Nothing's wrong with me." I push past her. "I'm going to go up to bed to get some rest. Maybe I'll sleep for an eternity."

She seizes the back of my shirt. "No, you're not. You're going to go to this party and have some fun. Depression runs in your family. And I will not let you sink into that dark hole."

I spin on my heels. "My mom is locked up on suicide watch and I found out that my death omen curse stretches farther than I originally thought. I sucked my mom's life away to help myself survive. I'm not going to a stupid Halloween party."

"You are not going up to your room to write sad poetry about death and pain," she insists. "Your mom's pulled a similar stunt before, when she locked you up in the attic for an entire day after she thought you purposefully killed all the plants."

"No, that was different—she actually killed me this time," I say. But was it her or the Grim Reaper? It seemed like she could hear him and see him.

"I don't care what she did," Raven says with a bossy attitude. "You're going."

"Have you lost your mind?" I annunciate each word. "My. Mom. Tried. To. Kill. Me."

"Are you sure?" She twists the silver chain of her necklace. "Maybe you should think about it really hard."

"I…" I stare at her, watching her eye twitch. "What aren't you telling me?"

"Nothing." She rubs the corner of her eye like she has something stuck in it. "I just think you should go out and have some fun for once."

"I think you should go," Ian intrudes from the bottom of the staircase. He's dressed in jeans and a white T-shirt with red paint smeared on it, along with his face and arms. "In fact, I'll drop you off on my way to my own party."

"You've both lost your minds." I head for the stairs, but he blocks my path. "Move out of my way, Ian. Please."

He shakes his head. "I'm not going to leave you are here by yourself after what just happened. Mom will be fine— you'll be fine. In fact, I got a call from the hospital this morning and they said she's doing really well. Her wounds are healing really quickly and the meds have stabilized her mood. We should be able to see her tomorrow."

I thrum my fingers on the sides of my legs. "I'm still not going."

"Yes, you are," Raven insists.

I shake my head. "I always go with you to every party you've ever asked me to, but not this time."

Ian gently shoves me toward the stairway. "Quit being a baby, go get a damn costume on, and go have some fun for one flippin' night in your life."

"Asher will be there," Raven entices with a waggle of her eyebrows. "He texted me and said to make sure you were still coming, because you wouldn't answer your phone."

Asher. The Anamotti. The *X* on my mom's head. It all rushes back to me.

"Okay, I think I—"

Suddenly the Grim Reaper materializes behind Ian. His head is tipped down as he rises up to the ceiling. He elevates his hand to his face and the sleeve slips down his arm, revealing his human hand.

"He's human," I whisper, unable to move.

He puts his finger to his lips. "Shhh… There's no need to be afraid. The answers are in me," he purrs mellifluously and the sound of his voice is enthralling. "Come with me, Ember. I'm begging you. Never look the other way."

My mind starts to melt to his request, but the touch of Raven's hand on my arm pulls me back.

"Em, get it together," she commands.

I blink the feeling away. "I told you to stay away from me."

His finger shifts to bone and beneath the hood, flames ignite. He swoops for me and I duck to the floor. He hovers above my head, his cape flowing onto my back. He puts his mouth up to my ear and his breath smells like a thousand stolen graves. "I got your mother to kill you, imagine what else I can do. Do not go against my wishes, Ember Rose Edwards. The only answers you need are from me."

I feel him whisk away, a hush of air across my back. When I push back to my feet, he's gone and Raven and Ian are staring at me, their faces frozen in horror.

"Em," Raven speaks tentatively. "Are you okay?"

"Yeah… I think so." But I need to get the hell away from all this madness. I need to breathe.

"Look," she says in her stern tone. "You've been through a lot the last couple of weeks and I don't want you home alone, especially on Halloween—you know how crazy things get sometimes."

"I know… Alright, I'll go." I snag my jacket from the banister and dash vigorously for the door. Against the Reaper's warning, I'm going to Asher for answers. I've been forced by the control of death too much in my life and I think it's time to break free of it.

"Um… Em." Raven steps in front of me. "Don't you think you need to change first?"

I shrug at my bloody and ripped clothes. "I'm sure no one will notice. It's Halloween."

She shoos me toward the stairs. "You may not care, but I already have other plans for you. Big plans. One that will make Asher fall on his knees."

"I'm not really worried about how I look right now or whether or not Asher will fall on his knees," I hinder at the bottom step, disputing. "I'm only going because I need to talk to Asher about something and it's not important if I look hot."

"Just give me like an hour," she pleads, with her hands folded in front of her. "One hour to work my magic and then we're out. Okay?"

***

Two hours later we're still in my room. I'm sitting on my bed, while she lines my eyes heavily with black eyeliner. Then she traces my lips with a deep red lipstick. Every one of her touches brings quietness, not death. Something has changed in her—or maybe in me. I need to test it out, find out if death has finally left me. Or if it's left her somehow.

I try to text Asher while I sit there, to see if I can persuade him to come to my house instead. But he won't answer my text.

"Keep texting him all you want," Raven singsongs. "But he's under strict orders not to let you off the hook for going to this party."

I growl at the phone and shove it aside.

She leans back and admires her handiwork. "I am damn good if I do say so myself." She steps aside so I can look in the mirror. My grey eyes sparkle against the silver and black eyeliner and my lips appear full and plump. She's tucked a rose over my ear and my black hair flows down my back. Around my neck is a choker centered with a rose and a black dress fits against my body. My feet are laced up by a pair of my black boots and black feathered wings span out from my back. Suddenly, I'm kind of excited, like for one night I can pretend to be someone else.

"Isn't it a little weird, though," I say, inspecting myself in the mirror. "I mean, the black feathers... people already think I made Laden disappear and that might set them off more. And then there's the Mackenzie thing..." I haven't shared the truth about that with Raven yet.

"Who gives a shit what they think," she declares, flicking a mascara wand through her eyelashes. "You didn't do anything and if anyone gives you crap, you'll knock them out—bring out the bar-fighting Ember I know."

A black ribbon secures the entire front part of the dress together. "I do like the costume."

"Well, you make one hell of a Grim Angel," she says, clipping the lid onto the eyeliner.

My head snaps in her direction. "Is that what I'm supposed to be? I thought their bones showed through their skin."

She gives me a once-over. "On some they do... the ones that go crazy. But some are as beautiful as the Angels of Death." Her cell phone beeps and she sends a text.

I run my fingers along the soft petals of the rose in my hair. "I thought you said you didn't know much about them."

"After you talked about them, I went back and picked up the books to try and refresh my memory." She reapplies her lipstick in the mirror. "You looked so upset that I couldn't remember anything."

I stroke the tips of my wings. "So what else do you know?"

She bites down on her glossy lip. "A lot, but I want you to prepare yourself for what I discovered." Then she grabs my hand and pulls me out the bedroom door. "They are exceptionally beautiful. So beautiful in fact, that some humans can't actually see their beauty."

I follow her down the stairs. "And what about the insanity part? Is that true? Do they really lose their minds from the burden of death and the Reapers' blood?"

She falters at the front door and realigns her foot into her white satin high-heel. "They can, if they give in to the wrath of death. It's all about good and evil with these things, I guess. At least that's what the book said."

I turn sideways to fit through the doorway. "As in the Grim Reaper? He's the wrath of death, right?"

She stutters at my knowledge. "Yeah, that's the Grim Reaper. The belief is that a Grim Angel is a hybrid of Angel blood, mixed with Reaper blood, mixed with human blood."

We hop into her car and I lean forward because my wings create a hump on my back.

Raven takes her wings off and tosses them into the backseat. "Reapers are considered the bad version of death. They collect the evil souls and they are very powerful. Allegedly the Grim Angel breed was put on Earth to stop some battle between the Angels of Death and the Reapers over who should get which souls... or maybe it was that one of them was stealing souls." She adjusts her mirror and backs onto the street. "The Grim Angel lives on Earth as a human, carrying both the power of heaven and hell in their bloodstream—their bodies hold balance to keep the Angels of Death and the Reapers at the same level, so neither would have more power over the other."

"You make is sound like the Angels of Death are as bad as the Reapers," I say, noting that her version of the story matches up with the one I read in the book. "Aren't angels the good ones?"

"In some ways, yes. They are the ones that collect the good souls, but the book said that they got greedy trying to balance out the soul collection when Reapers started stealing innocent souls." She sighs. "But anyways, I guess Reapers constantly try to trick Grim Angels and mess with their heads so they would surrender to death and join them. It's like a game to them or something, even though technically neither the Reapers nor the Angels are supposed to interfere with their lives."

Her tires screech as she peels onto the highway. The sidewalks are flooded with kids in Halloween costumes carrying bags of candy. The houses are gleaming with purple and orange lights. A girl in an angel costume skips down the sidewalk, holding her mother's hand in front of a house with an eerie mist across the front lawn. Can Angels and Grim Reapers really exist?

I rotate away from the window and slump against the door. "So what happens to the Grim Angels that don't lose their minds? They just live being tortured by death until they die?"

Raven doesn't answer right away. "Basically, I think so."

I'm reminded of Asher's tattoo and the story: One girl with death on her shoulders connected them both, and with a single choice she would save the world. *But the fight would not be easy.* He had to be talking about a Grim Angel.

She reaches into the backseat, swerving her car as she hunts from something. "Here, there's the book." She tosses a book onto my lap and regains control of her car. "It actually doesn't say much more than what I've told you, but I marked the pages if you want to read through it."

"Thanks." I open the book. "And I mean that. You really didn't have to go re-check this out and read it."

She fiddles with the temperature, turning it up then down. "Look Ember, I know I've been a really shitty friend for most of our friendship, especially during the last week or so. But I want to start over—I want to be a better friend."

"You're a good friend." I flip to the page she marked. "And last week's bitchiness is totally acceptable considering… what happened." I pause, one thing still bothering me. "But Raven, can you do me a favor and never call me crazy, even when you're mad?"

She nods with regret. "I'm so sorry. That was such a low blow. And I know you're not crazy."

I'm not so sure anymore. In fact, I'm starting to wonder if a Grim Angel lives inside me.

As we drive over the bridge, we both stop breathing. The road is still stained with the *X* and the median is scuffed from the collision. There is a small spot decorated with flowers and ribbons.

My mind flashes back to the bar fight and the way Asher took down a guy twice his size without even so much as blinking. Could Asher have killed him to protect Raven? But why would he decorate the scene? "What do you think happened to Laden?" I ask. "Do you think he's... Do you think Asher really killed him?"

She clutches onto the steering wheel. "You know what? I really don't want to know what happened to him. If Asher killed him, then so be it."

I clear my throat and distract my thoughts onto the book. "Grim Angels are the most important and most dangerous breed of Angels that have ever existed. They have a direct insight to death..." I read aloud with a shiver. "They have the power to either destroy the human race or save it, depending on where their legions end up lying." I glance up from the pages. "But how can they destroy the human race? That's what I want to know."

She flips the page and taps it with her finger on the title. "I'm not sure, but read this. It's really interesting."

"The Grim Reaper is believed to be the collector of the evil souls. They possess the ability to not only separate one's soul from their body, and guide it to the next world, but they can also trick an individual to render their life over to them." *Oh my God, my mom.* "They like to play tricks on the bodies of the souls they take, leaving them hanging from trees, hiding them—"

She taps the brake so hard it locks up our seatbelts.

"What's wrong?" I ask, unlocking my seat belt.

"What if… what if Asher's a Grim Reaper and you're a Grim Angel?" It's like a light switch has flipped on in her head.

I rapidly shake my head. "There's no way that can be true. Why would you even say that?"

"Ember, think about it. You can see death. If you were a Grim Angel, this could be why," she presses. "And Asher has so much interest in you. And he knew where your car was. What if he told the cops?"

"No. There's no way." But doubts tug at my mind. When I died in the rose garden and I saw the Reaper take off his hood; back at the water, while I was drowning; and I saw the Grim Reaper before suddenly waking up on the shore next to Asher.

I shake the thoughts from my head. I will not jump to conclusions just yet, not until I hear what he has to say. Especially since Asher brings me an indescribable calmness and he has never openly done anything to hurt me. And he's had a lot of chances.

"It says in the book that they like to mess with Grim Angels' heads and try to ruin their lives, make them go crazy, and get them to surrender to the Wrath of Death," she says. "Think about it, Em. What if Asher did something to Laden after he saved me, but only so he could reenact what happened with your dad? What if he has been wiggling his way into your life to fuck with your head?"

"Why are you making these accusations?" I ask. "When just a few seconds ago you were defending Asher."

"Because it's making sense now."

"No, it's not. Nothing is making any sense. At all. My whole life doesn't make sense. It's like I'm always one step away from walking off a cliff."

"Read some more," she urges. "See if there's anything else that might give us some more clues."

I continue in an unsteady voice. "Grim Reapers are also excellent shape shifters, more often than not in the form of snakes, rats, cats, birds, and sometimes humans. Through their abilities, a Grim Reaper has been known to steal many innocent souls with a simple bribe or trick. This was the cause of the first battle between good and evil that lasted nearly a decade." I stop reading.

She reaches over and turns the page. On the top of it is a beautiful angel, with wings as black as the ones I'm wearing and hair as dark as ash. "Keep reading. I think you're getting close."

"An Angel of Death brings a more peaceful death to the individual whose soul they collect. They only collect the souls of the dying innocent and carry the spirit over to the next world. They bring a sense of calm with their touch." *That sounds more like Asher.* "Unlike the Grim Reaper, they wait for death and do not feed off the life of an individual. They are gentle by nature, but passionate in battle." My eyes meet Raven's. "Passionate in battle?"

"It talks about a battle more toward the back." She diverges into the school parking lot, not reducing the speed, and I'm slammed into the door. "But you can read about all this later. Right now, I want you to focus on having fun."

"Yeah… right."

Strobe lights flash in front of the entrance and a shroud of torn sheets hang from the front doors. Hay bales, with skeletons situated on them, border the sidewalk. On the sloped roof of the school, the Grim Reaper stands. It's fake, with yellow eyes, but it sends a chill up my spine.

"Em." Raven's voice brings me back to her. She parks the car next to a group of people dressed up like the Scooby

Doo gang. "I have to tell you something. And it's really important." She texts someone and then tucks the phone into her bra.

"Really." I give her a look. "In your bra?"

Her face drains of humor. "I might need my cell phone."

I bite down on my lip until it bleeds and fills my mouth with the bitter taste of rust. "Raven... do you really believe in this stuff?" I hold up the book. "Grim Reapers, Death Angels, and battles between good and evil? Or are you just showing it to me because I asked about a Grim Angel?"

Her eyes are as soft as they've ever been, and at that moment she is the same friend that slapped Ricky Stewart in the face when he cut off a piece of my hair in kindergarten. "My best friend has been able to see how everyone is going to die since she was four years old. If that shit can exist, why can't this?"

"I think the gift might be gone." I place a hand on her arm. "I can't feel your death anymore."

"Your *curse* isn't gone." She smiles sadly and slips the white-feathered wings onto her back.

"Yeah, but what if it's not a curse?" I maneuver awkwardly out of the car, bending low to get my wings out. "What if I'm... what if this whole time I've been able to do all this stuff because I'm not human?"

"It would still be considered a curse, Em. Death stole your life away from you when you were four." She locks up the doors. "Come on, let's go inside."

The chilled wind blows through our hair as we hike across the parking lot. Raven holds the bottom of her dress down and fiddles with her hair. Inside her bra, the phone rings, and she does a little wiggle from the vibration, but ignores the call. We push through the doors and a puff of mist engulfs us.

"Damn Halloween decorations." Raven coughs and waves her hand in front of her face.

I fan my face and blink my stinging eyes until we break through the mist and into the quad. Up on the stage, a guitarist flares on his instrument's strings. The drummer is shirtless and branded with mythical tattoos. Music bursts through several large speakers lined along the wall. Orange and black streamers are spiraling around columns, and purple and silver ceiling lights flash down on the packed dance floor, where people jump up and down, shouting out the lyrics of the song. There are witches, devils, vampires, Frankensteins, and even a few angels. In the farthest corner, someone is fashioned in a Grim Reaper costume.

"God, I hope there aren't too many of them," I mumble.

Raven tracks the object of my gaze. "Oh Emmy, you don't fear the Reaper, do you?"

I shoot her a blank stare. "Is that supposed to be funny?"

She smiles and hooks arms with me. It's the strangest thing in the world, touching her and not feeling her death. We create a wide path with her wings as we weave around the room, toward the common area, a small room just behind the stage. Heads turn in our direction, but I keep focused on the common room doors.

"Why are we going back here?!" I yell over the music.

She points at the doors decorated with spider webs and an *ENTER AT YOUR OWN RISK* sign. "There's a haunted house back there and Asher just sent me a text that he was walking through it with some friends."

I slam to a stop and she's jerked back.

"Em, what the hell?" She unclasps our arms. "What are you looking at?"

My pulse races as I stare at the door. "I'm not sure I want to go in there."

She rolls her eyes and jerks me forward. "Come on, we'll be fine."

"Why can't I just meet him out here?" I argue.

"Stop being a chicken!" She laughs. "I was only kidding about him being the Reaper."

I begrudgingly follow her into the haunted house. It's dark inside and when the door shuts behind us, it suffocates the music. There are skeletons to greet us at the entrance of a hallway of hay bales. Twinkle lights sparkle the way.

I back away, but Raven pulls me forward. "You are going to have fun tonight whether you like it or not."

Shaking my head, I trudge after her. The skeleton jumps up and shrieks at us as we pass it. Raven speeds up, laughing, and I sneeze from the hay. The farther we go, the more scarce the lights get, until there are none left and we're smothered by blackness.

Someone screams and a warm mist dampens my skin. A recording of a laugh turns on, followed by a deep growl.

"Raven," I hiss. "I want to go back."

Her hand falls from mine and she laughs. "Last one to the end's a rotten egg."

I stumble around in the dark with my hands sprawled out in front of me. "Raven, where are you?"

Behind me a light clicks on, highlighting a graffiti wall. I lower my hands as another light turns on and emphasizes a chain link floor-length gate in front of me. I push through the gate and step into the next section, which is lined wall-to-wall with mirrors. The gate slams shut behind me. I whirl around, threading my fingers through the links, jerking it fiercely.

The gate won't budge, so I walk vigilantly up the slender hall between the mirrored walls. "Raven, please tell me where you are. This isn't funny anymore."

I hear her laugh from somewhere and the lights flash off, then on. A man appears at the end of the hall, with dark hair, kohl-lined eyes, black jeans, and a T-shirt. A giant X brands his forehead.

I squint through the blinking lights that reflect blindingly against the mirrors. "Laden?"

"Hello, Ember." He smiles. "Long time, no see."

I back up quickly, but crash into a solid figure. A thousand deaths pour through me: *pain, terror, falling, drowning, fire, pain, pain, pain.* I buckle forward, but he grasps my arm, rotates it behind my back, and reels me to face him.

Garrick's greasy hair shines in the light and he scratches the X on his eye. "You're not playing the game right, do you know that? You're not answering every question we ask and you're not giving in. It's very disappointing."

"*We,*" I say, hoping to throw him off. "As in the Anamotti."

His face remains stoic. "What? You think that surprised me? The bigger question that I think needs answering is who are the Anamotti? And who leads us?"

"I don't know what you're getting at." I try to wrench my arm away.

His fingernails dig into my skin. "Oh I think you do. It's the perfect crime, you know. Telling the person you're after about the group who is chasing after her, when really you are part of it. Earning her trust, so she'll never see it coming."

"Asher isn't after me." I choke. "He wouldn't do that."

"What, lie?" A sly grin creeps over his face. "Or try to kill you? How do you think he showed up so fast that night at the lake after I ran into you? And how do you think *we* knew you were going to be here tonight?"

I writhe out of his grip and back up, peeking over my shoulder at Laden, who is grinning as blood drips down his forehead and onto the floor. "I'm not an angel. And that's what the Anamotti want, right? Angels?"

"Not just any angel, but a Grim Angel." Garrick matches my steps and slants in, putting his face close to mine. "I think deep down you know what you are. *The* Grim Angel, the one that holds the balance of the Reapers and the Angels of Death. The one that carries death with her all the time. The one that will easily crack and lose the balance with her mind. It's in your blood, you know—the insanity."

He lunges for my throat and I knee him between the legs. His face screws in pain as he crumples to the floor. I dart around him and throw myself against the fence. The metal slices open my palms and forces me to let go. I land on my butt, but scramble to my feet and spin around, ready to protect myself. But Garrick and Laden have vanished.

I give the fence a few more shakes, but a padlock on the other side secures it. It hits me: I've walked into a trap. And honestly, I don't know what waits for me at the end. I take a deep breath and hurry down the hallway of mirrors. There is a fork at the end, and I select the right, tiptoeing quietly. Strands of hay flutter in my hair and send me into a sneezing frenzy.

"Ember," Garrick's voice touches my ear. "Don't breathe."

I take off down the hall, my legs struggling as I tear around the corner. His footsteps barrel after me and his laugh echoes forcefully down the hall.

"Ember," he says. "Come out, come out wherever you are."

As I sprint around a sharp corner, my feet trip over something weighty and solid. My body slams to the floor. I quickly flip over to my back and glance back at what made me fall. A person, face down. I crawl over to them and turn them on their back.

Laden's dead eyes stare at me. His pale decomposing skin is ice-cold and the X is an older wound. He's been dead for a while. I think back to my tree with his body hanging in it, and the one I saw in the library. Is this even real?

Garrick's voice drifts compellingly down the hall. "It's hard to tell, isn't it? What's real and what's not. Tell me Ember, does it ever feel like you're losing your mind?"

I leap to my feet, hop off of Laden, and run. Sweat drips down my skin as I accelerate. The school's side entrance door finally comes into view and I can almost taste my freedom. I reach for the door handle, but a hay bale lands on me like the weight of a bag of bricks. My head smacks the tile and the crack of my bones is stomach-churning.

Garrick squats down in front of me. "Ever heard the term 'Don't Fear the Reaper'? Well, it's a little misleading." He swathes the hood of a cloak over his head. "Because everyone fears death, Ember. Even Death itself." Then he pulls out a knife and cuts an *X* across my forehead.

Chapter 19

I open my eyes to the pieces of the stars and a glimpse of the moon. I attempt to roll onto my stomach, but a rope restrains each of my wrists to a tree and my legs are tied to each other. Out of the corner of my eyes, I spot a fire. Feathers and rose petals halo around my head. The wings are still secured to my back, but are bent to conform to the pressure of my body.

"Hello," I call out tentatively. "Is anyone here?"

A woman with a sharp nose and blonde hair woven in a bun appears in my line of vision. "Hello, Ember. It's so nice of you to join us."

My eyes narrow. "Detective Crammer."

"Feel like you're going crazy yet?" The fire glows in her blue eyes and shadows the area underneath her defined cheekbones, so she looks almost skeletal. "Like you don't know what's real?"

"So you're part of the Anamotti," I say, winding the rope around my wrist to gain more control. "Or are you a Grim Reaper?"

Her thin lips nearly vanish as she smiles. She retrieves a knife from the pocket of her jacket. It's small with a silver handle and a sharp tip. Putting the tip of it to my forehead, she pierces it into my skin and blood rivers out like a leaky faucet. "The Anamotti and the Reapers are one and the same. The Anamotti is just what we go by in the human world to help us stay undetected." She gestures around her like she's a queen and a group of people announce their presence by stepping out of the trees. "All of us are Reapers here. Even you." She smiles wickedly. "Partly anyway."

All of them wear a uniform of black cloaks, but their hoods are off, hanging down their backs and showing me their human form. Some of them are unfamiliar, but I recognize Garrick, who mockingly waves at me and winks.

And the sight of a pink-haired girl bruises my heart. "Raven."

She grins dreamily at me and her sapphire eyes are dazed, like she's drunk. "I'm so sorry, Em. I didn't mean to do it. I just couldn't seem to help myself."

Ember

Madness pricks at my brain. I tug on the ropes until my wrists rupture open and blood spills out all over my hands, the rope, and the dirt.

"Oh relax for Christ's sake." Detective Crammer draws the knife down my cheek and splits open my face. "She's under the spell of the Reaper because, unlike you, she's human and can be possessed by him."

Raven moves forward from the crowd, but Beth thrusts out her hand, barricading her back. "Stay back, you little trollop. You are still to obey my orders."

Raven blinks and steps back. "I'm so sorry."

"Raven," I beg, trying to make eye contact with her. "Don't listen to her. Run away! Now!"

"It's pointless to try to get through to her." Detective Crammer says. "The power of the Reaper is more powerful than anything, which you'll soon learn after we get rid of you."

I raise my chin up and look her in the eye. "You know I can't die, right? So whatever you have planned for me won't work."

She pats the handle of the knife against her palm. "Oh yes, the beauty of being able to suck the life away from the living. It makes it harder to get rid of you, but not impossible." She laughs to herself, throwing her head back and some of the other Reapers join in. "It also makes you more prone to insanity and more likely to surrender to the Reaper blood, just like your father did."

"What do you know about my father?!" Craning my arms, I endeavor to get the trees to break with my strength.

"You don't have super strength." She rolls her eyes and bends down in my face. "In fact, you're fairly close to an ordinary girl, only you're connected with every aspect of death. It's not really a gift, so much as a curse. In fact, if I were you, I'd let me put you out of your misery. All you would have to do is surrender to the Reaper and he would take away the pain of death."

I transitorily stop fighting; erasing the pain, taking away death, rupturing the chains that have sentenced me to a life of solitude. But it would still be death, only in a more powerful form. "No, I won't do it."

"Alright, then. I guess, for the moment, you'll let your Angel blood make your decisions. But I warn you, you'll give in." She snaps her fingers and Garrick shoves Raven forward. Raven trips over her bare feet and falls to her knees. Her white wings are broken, and her dress is torn and stained. There is no life in her eyes and it's terrifying. "If you are not willing to surrender, I'll force you to." She puts the knife to Raven's throat and gently cuts a thin layer of skin. Blood trickles out and Raven winces, but doesn't cry out.

"Wait," I say. "Don't hurt her."

"There's only one way out of this." She makes another slim puncture on Raven's neck.

Death or life. Death or life. What's the difference? "I'll do whatever you want me to. Just let her go."

She makes another small incision along Raven's neck and the other Reapers laugh, pulling their hoods over their heads. "Oh I don't want anything from you. I'm just going to torture her and then you, until you lose your mind and give into your Reaper blood."

I thrash my body and jerk on the ropes. "Leave her alone!" I close my palms and attempt to slide my hands through the rope. The rough material claws at my skin, but I refuse to give up—give in.

Detective Crammer snickers and cuts off a small lock of Raven's pink hair. "Do you know how fun it was to torture you? Kill you time and time again. Make you think you were losing your mind. You have a bendable mind and so do the people closest to you. Most of them are insane—do you know that? And do you want to know why?"

"Because of the pain of my existence."

"No, but it's close. Insanity is a very contagious thing; it's easy to get caught up in it. Those who are close to a Grim Angel start experiencing what they go through and it wears them down, driving them insane themselves. Plus, they are susceptible to the Reaper's torture."

Raven gags on her own blood and clutches at her throat. "Ember, help me."

Detective Crammer grabs a handful of Raven's bubblegum pink hair and moves the knife to Raven's hairline, like she's going to scalp her. My whole body spasms—I can't seem to look away. The circle of Reapers tightens around me and their eyes begin to glow.

"Just give in, Ember" the detective says. "And everything—all of it will be gone."

I stare up at the night sky, thinking about my life. Would everything be better if I was gone? Maybe.

I watch as a black figure swoops down from the sky; I assume it's another Reaper. But black feathers fall from heaven and dust the air with a peaceful feeling.

The creature moves inhumanly fast, just a blur as it clips the ropes on my wrists with its hand and turns me loose. Then it rounds back, swipes up Detective Crammer by the shoulders, and carries her into the sky. Her painful scream pierces the night and Reapers push up from the ground, airborne into the sky.

"Passionate when in battle." I quickly sit up and untie my legs. Then I rush over to Raven, lying face down in the dirt. I gently roll her onto her back. Her eyes are shut and the blood flows out from the open wounds on her neck. "Rav, can you hear me?"

She sucks in a breath and her eyes shoot open. "Oh my God, I think I…"

Tucking my arm underneath hers, I aid her to her feet. "Come on, we have to go before they come back for us."

"Too late," Garrick says, landing just in front of us. His voice is human, but below the hood, a skeletal figure peeks out: sharp cheek bones, empty eyes, a soulless heart. "Ember, there's no use trying. We always win this every time. You wanna know why?"

Raven leans on me. Supporting her weight, I inch us back toward the forest. "Because you mess with the Grim Angel's head until they crack. You don't give up."

He matches my steps toward the forest, his cape like a train on the ground behind him. "Because evil is the one that plays dirty—we are the ones who break the rules." His arms lift to the side of him and he's holding the knife. "Therefore, evil always triumphs."

"Go into the trees," I whisper in Raven's ear, inching her forward. "Now."

She blinks at me, half there, half gone. "I'm not leaving you… They want to kill you."

"No, they want to make me one of them," I say. "They can't kill me."

Reluctantly, she slips out from the support of my arm and hobbles into the shadows of the trees, free from the Reaper's power.

Emptiness chokes up my throat as I march for Garrick with my hands out to the side. "Go ahead, kill me."

He grins and the fire crackles wildly behind him. "You know I can't do that. But I can hurt you." He stabs the knife into my throat, severing my skin and my veins. Blood gurgles out and I clamp my hand over the wound. But the soothing murmur of the trees and the flowers sprouting from the dirt instantly connect with me and gradually stitches it up.

Garrick whistles slowly. "That was faster than… No, you couldn't be…"

I ram my knee into his gut, whirl, and slam my elbow into his face. The contact of bone deadens my elbow, so using my other fist, I punch him in the nose. Bar fight tactic and it works. Garrick goes down like a sack of potatoes.

Whirling away from him, I run for the forest. But he scurries forward on his belly and his fingers wrap around my ankle. I smash the heel of my boot into his face, but he just laughs.

"You can't kill death eternally." His voice is as sharp as the knife in his hands. "It was highly entertaining though, watching you try to sift through my thousands of deaths." I kick him again, but he only laughs harder. "You know, you have a lot more power than you think, you just have no idea how to use it."

I claw at the ground as his hands move up my leg like a tight rope, and a raven lands in front of me. Garrick stabs the knife in my calf and grabs me by the hair as he rises to his feet, pulling me up with him.

"Help me, please," I whisper to the bird. It hops from side to side, like it is thinking. "Please, bird. I have a feeling you can hear me."

Garrick's hands slip from my leg, and dust and black feathers whirlwind around me. The sound of flapping wings sends the raven diving for the woods. Without hesitation, I sprint into the forest. "Raven," I hiss, searching behind trees and near bushes as I cut a path deeper into the forest. The stars flicker between the cracks in the branches that form a canopy over my head. "Raven," I dare call out. "Where are you? It's me, Ember."

I keep walking, knowing where I'm going, but worried Raven doesn't. "Please answer me. I promise no one's going to hurt you anymore."

By the time I step into the cemetery, I worry she might be lost in the trees. I need a phone and some help. I head quickly for the gates.

As usual, the cemetery is quiet, filled with death and the chirps of crickets. The trees cast shadows all over the ground and the fence blocks out most of the street lights. My wings are ripped and my skin is soaked with blood.

I weave through the headstones, careful not to step on them. The wind picks up and the hinges of the gate squeak. I hear a whisper and turn in a circle, skimming the trees as I keep moving for the exit.

When he steps out from behind a colossal tree at the back of the cemetery, a wall crumples inside my body. Dressed in black, he blends with the night. But his hair is as white as a ghost. His long legs are stretched out in front of him as he strides across the grass toward me.

"Well, if it isn't my number one fan," Cameron says and my insides explode with chills.

Against the power of my own, I halt next to the statue of the Grim Reaper. "What are you doing here?"

There's a *swoosh* and suddenly he's standing right in front of me, his eyes dark as coals, his face hauntingly poetic. "Don't pretend you don't like me, Ember." A grin pulls at his lips. "You may pretend like you're not interested in me, but I know you are."

I shut my eyes, constrict my muscles, and attempt to lift my foot off the grass—get it to move me toward the gate again. "What are you doing to me?"

His eyes sear like cinders, on the edge of life, but not quite dead as he circles me with his hands behind his back.

"You are so beautiful. So grown up. So full of life, yet always so full of death."

My legs quiver with the desire to run. "What are you?"

"Perhaps you should be asking me what you are." His long finger traces my cheekbone and a dark hunger flares in his eyes, dying to feed. "You really are amazing, yet you've been blinded by the fear of death and have never noticed all the possibilities in front of you. If you'd just accept it—"

"I won't." I interrupt. "I'm not giving in to Death."

"You shouldn't decide your answer until you understand everything." He takes my hand and helplessly, I follow him to the tree.

My body is no longer my own and I speculate how long my mind will remain mine.

He nestles us down next to the trunk, wraps his arms around me, and leans me back against his chest. He sweeps my hair aside and puts his lips against my ear. "Never having to fear or experience death. Imagine writing about immortality, instead of death like everyone else. You could be the first."

"Walt Whitman and Emily Dickinson already did," I smart off. "And so did Spill Canvas."

"Spill Canvas?" His tone tickles with intrigue.

"It's a band, you asshole." I force out a scream, but it harshly cuts off before it reaches my lips. "Cameron, let me go. Please. If you're a Reaper, I thought you couldn't possess me."

"I'm not supposed to… and I can't possess your mind completely—trust me, I've tried. But I can possess your body." He kisses the tip of my ear and moves his lips down my neck. "You were such a fascinating child. Usually when they sent me to mess with a child's head, it was the most droning time of my existence—which says a lot, because I'm old. But you—you were so full of fire and were determined not to get rid of me. But then you told me to go away, and I had to follow the rules." He sucks on my neck, passionate kisses, and then his breath is hot against my ear. "You know I broke the rules for you. I tried to warn you about your dad, even though I wasn't supposed to. And then you ran away with me... Admit it—that was probably the most fun you've had in your life. You and me hiding in the woods, while I listened to you ramble to yourself, trying to pretend I wasn't there."

"You're *that* Grim Reaper. The one who's tormented me since I was four," I say, enraged.

"But you never did meaningfully tell me to go away, except when your dad made me. But you were just a child and your mind was bendable." He pauses, grazing his hand down my thigh. "I tried to warn you about your dad so you could help him. Do you know that? Do you know how much I love you?"

"You tried to force me to kill my mom," I seethe. "That's not love. And you don't even know me."

"I only did that to your mom to help you," he whispers mellifluously in my ear. "I just want you to quit fighting who you really are. If you'd just give in to the insanity, instead of fighting it, life would be so much easier. And we could be together."

"I almost killed her," I growl. "I stole my mom's life to save my own."

"Don't be ashamed of it. It's in your blood and your dad did it many times. Trust me."

"Do you know where my dad is?" I ask sharply. "The detective—or the Reaper—whoever the hell she is, said he gave in to insanity. Does that mean he's dead? Or is he one of you? I need to know. Please, Cameron. Please tell me."

Ignoring me, he angles my head back and looks deeply into my eyes. "We're perfect for each other. Imagine it, alive in death, writing beautiful words together... And I promise I'll never hurt you," he whispers, slowly laying me on my back. "I just want to help you."

"No one can help me," I say. "Especially..."

He covers my body with his and my words evaporate. I no longer know what I want—what I feel. His hand travels up my shoulders, up the side of my neck, and resides on my cheek, while his other hand explores the bare skin on my hip. "I could help you, if you let me. I could make all that sadness go away." He licks his lip as he presses his body against mine, converging with every part of me. "Let me take it all away forever."

My arms fall helplessly to my sides. *Tell him to get off!*

"Ember," he purrs, sliding his hand through my hair. "Let me in."

My knees fall apart, allowing his body closer, and a moan escapes from my lips. "Cameron, don't."

He tips my chin up. "What if I told you I could take away every ounce of pain you have and would ever feel? Think about it. You could have the perfect life."

I shut my eyes as he kisses my neck and my body arches to his will. "That's not possible. Death is pain. And death exists everywhere. Besides, nothing is perfect..."

"It is possible, all you have to do is say yes." Keeping his body sealed to mine, he finds my hands and pins them above my head, rendering me helpless. "Give me permission." His lips touch my cheek, the corner of my mouth. "Please, give me permission."

My lips part open, and I feel my willpower crumble to dust as I realize it might be easier to give in. "You have permission to do what you—"

"Ember, *don't*." Asher's voice jerks me back to earth. "Don't promise him anything."

A grin spans Cameron's face. "Asher, my dear friend, you're just in time for the feast."

"Get away from her, Cameron." Asher demands. "You have no right to be touching her like that."

"And neither do you." Cameron looks like he's enjoying himself.

I force my gaze sideways to Asher, storming across the cemetery ground with his hands clenched into fists. His face is bruised, his knuckles are scraped raw, and the scar beneath his eyebrow ring is more defined.

"What's... what's." My lips hitch shut.

"Get off of her." He's so close, but still so far away. "Or I swear to God I'll—"

Cameron leaps off me, leaving me paralyzed on the ground, and meets Asher in the middle. "Or you'll what?"

"You've broken rules," Asher growls. "A lot of them."

Wrath thunders in both their eyes and they charge for each other. The sky rumbles and the ground quakes. Like mist rising from a lake, a black cloak forms around Cameron and swallows him up. Asher lets out a derailing screech, springs into the air, and black-feathered wings snap out from his back, sending pieces of his shirt flying. The collision of their bodies is like a train wrecking with another train.

Suddenly, my legs bound back to life and I waste no time jumping to my feet. A tornado of feathers and mist swarm the cemetery as Cameron and Asher move like lightning, moving so quickly my human eye can barely detect them. For a second, I stand stunned underneath the tree. An angel and a Grim Reaper? An *angel* and a *Grim Reaper*?

"Ember!" Raven's voice draws me back to my other problem.

She's back in the shadows of the cemetery, curled up next to the angel statue. I run across the grass toward her, waving for her to run. "Raven, we have to get out of here—" I fall face-first into an open grave. Cold skin touches mine and my insides quiver. I push up and blink down at Mackenzie Baker. Her blonde hair is covered in dirt and red lines track her neck and wrists. It hits me like a shove off a cliff. My mind races back to Cameron's house, the bands on her neck and wrists.

"Oh my God," I breathe. "You were dead the whole time… I can see the dead."

Dirt sprinkles down on me and I flip over to my back. Raven looms above the shallow hole, with blood in her hair, blankness in her eyes, and a handful of dirt in her hand.

"I love you Em, I really do," she says. "But you can't save me anymore. I have to give in."

A shovel of dirt rains down on my head. Shielding my eyes, I struggle to my feet and press my fingertips into the dirt.

"Please don't make this harder than it already is, Em," Raven pleads, with a shovel in her hand. "If you would have just given up back at the fire, I wouldn't have to do this to you. *You* could have saved me from this burden." She scoops up another shovel full of dirt and drops it down on my head. "But now you're going to be buried alive, and remain there until you break."

"Raven." I hurdle onto the side, burrowing my boots into the moist dirt. "Think about what you're doing for just a second. You don't want to do this."

She plucks out a twig from her hair and drops in down into the hole, watching it fall all the way to the bottom. "Of course I don't. What I want is a happy life, with a mother who isn't crazy and a friend who can be near people. What I want is to go back in time and never leave that party with Laden, so I could erase what it felt like when he had me pinned down to the ground… erase the feeling of his filthy hands on me…" she trails off, staring up at the sky.

Extending my arm as far as it will go, I stretch for the edge of the hole. But my feet slip out from under me and I collapse back onto Mackenzie's body. Forcing myself not to lose it, I push off her and stand back against the wall. Gradually, I clumsily climb upward. Finally, I heave myself over the lip and roll onto my back on the grass.

Raven bounds on top of me and pins my arms down to the side. I whip up my knees and vault her off. She slams against the angel statue and lets out a groan. "What's happening to me?"

"Nothing. Just stay here, okay." I pat her shoulder and race through the headstones toward the Reaper and the Angel of Death.

Cameron has Asher restrained on the grass and is clutching at his throat. "Tell me, Angel boy, what has it been like being alone all this time? Apparently pretty bad for you to be breaking the rules."

I squeeze my eyes and stop short of them. "I want you to go away, Cameron." It hurts to say it, like a vine of thorns inside my veins.

Silence enfolds and I crack open my eyelids. Cameron is still on top of Asher, but his hand is hanging lifelessly at his side. "Don't say things you don't mean, Ember Rose," he advises. "Think about the last time you wished me away."

"I want you gone," I demand in a steady voice. "I don't want death haunting me anymore."

"You can't get rid of death, princess," he says sorrowfully. "Death is endless."

It frightens me how much his words match mine. "Then I guess I will outrun it for as long as I can."

Cameron climbs off Asher and dusts the dirt and grass off his hands. He lowers the hood of his cloak, so I'm looking directly at him, not the Reaper. "You know I only did it to bring you to me. I only push so you'll give in to me, not to the others."

My heart thumps in my chest as he stops in front of me. His blonde hair glows palely in the moonlight and sadness caves his eyes, like the first time I saw him.

"Why were you really here that night?" I ask, with a shiver. "When I saw you digging up the grave?"

His fingers twitch, longing to touch me. "I already told you, looking for a family jewel." He gently touches the tip of his finger to the hollow of my neck. "Turns out you had it."

"My grandma's necklace..." I trail off, confused. "Why do you want it?"

He smiles miserably. "And I'm sorry I took it, but I had to. Besides, it wasn't yours to have in the first place. It belongs to my family."

"Then why did my grandma have it?"

"Because she stole it from us."

My eyes widen. "Cameron, tell me—"

He shushes me with his finger across my lips. "I don't want to talk about that right now. I want to talk about you and me."

"There is no you and..." My eyes digress to Asher, lying in the grass, encompassed by black feathers. "Did you kill him?"

"He can't die, princess." Cameron frowns. "Unfortunately."

"Why did you kill Mackenzie? And Laden. And I'm guessing Farrah is probably on the list, too." My legs beg me to run, but my desire to know the truth overpowers them.

"I didn't kill Laden. Asher did," he says. "And Mackenzie and Farrah died from the same human's hand, not mine. And if you listened closely to her story, you probably could figure out the culprit."

"Her *dad*?"

He shrugs. "That's for you to figure out, if you want to. I just collect the souls. And I'll admit, I didn't try to stop Mackenzie's death. I wanted her to suffer for all the times she was rude to you."

His misconstrued logic is a puzzle to me. "That's the craziest thing I've ever heard."

"I know you don't understand." He cups my cheek, emitting both ecstasy and sheer terror through me. "But that day when I saw you in the cemetery, I knew I had to have you and that I would hurt anyone that ever caused you pain."

"Your little *friends*," I point over my shoulder at the forest, "hurt me. Do you know about that?"

"I can't help that without breaking more rules. But it can all be over if you want it to be. All you have to do is agree to be with me—want to be with me. And then I'm allowed to help you."

"And what? Become a Grim Reaper and start collecting souls and killing people?"

"There's more to it than that," he says, his eyes blazing. "More to you than what you realize and you're in for a rough and painful life until you realize that. But it can all be over if you'll just give in to your Reaper blood."

I compress my hands into fists, and will myself to deny his request, even though a small part of me wants it. "I'm telling you to leave, just like I did when I was four."

His face falls and his eyes flash with anger. Lightning zaps across the sky, but I refuse to look away. "Is that what you really want, Ember?"

I swallow the refusal building in my throat and make myself want it. "That's what I want."

He bites down on his lip so hard blood drips down his chin. Then he cups the back of my head and pulls me in for a rough kiss. I taste the blood on his lips, the foul darkness of death, but a flicker of something substantial is hidden deep inside him, like a seed in the center of an apple.

He releases me, breathing fervently. "I'll pay for that one forever." He backs toward the gates, his eyes locked on me. "They'll come for you—the rest of the Reapers. They won't stop until they get you to crack."

"Then I'll tell them to go away, too."

"That won't work on them, sweetheart," he says gravely as he sinks farther into the shadows. "The Anamotti aren't quite as easy-going as me." Then with a swish of his cloak, he alters, sprouting wings and shrinking into a raven. He circles around my head, before disappearing into the night sky.

My body aches to fly away with him, be free, shed my skin, become one with the night.

Asher makes a noise and I rush for him. "Are you okay?" I ask, not daring to touch him.

His shirt is torn from his cuts and bruises cover his beautiful pale chest. His black hair is disheveled, his lip is split open, and his striking wings are crooked, the feathers scarce.

"I'm fine," he assures me with a weak smile.

I crouch down in front of him. "Does it… does it hurt?"

His eyes unite with mine, zealous and hungry. "Nothing could hurt at this moment. You just sent him away."

"I've sent him away before." I brush stray feathers from his arms and then rest my hand in the curve of his shoulder, feeling his warmth. "But he came back."

"I know." His hand finds my hip. "And he'll find a way to keep coming back until you completely surrender to him—they all will."

"What did you do to them?" I ask. "The other Reapers—the Anamotti. Detective Crammer or whoever she is?"

"She's a Reaper—all the Anamotti are. They're the Reapers who have banded together to eliminate the Grim Angels, even though it's forbidden to touch them. And I took care of them, for the moment, but they'll be back."

I note his hands on my hips, wondering if *he's* allowed to touch me. "You mean, until they make me lose my sanity."

He nods, his eyes never parting from me. "That's the point of all this, yes. We are all cursed to this world until you do."

My knees sink to the ground. "Cursed?"

"Our curse to this world," he explains. "It's our punishment for our part in the Battle of Death. The Angels of Death and the Grim Reapers are bound to the Earth by the existence of the Grim Angel. And it's only the Grim Angel that can free one of us back to our homes."

"But aren't the Grim Angels supposed to create balance, so no one can steal souls?" I ask.

"They are, but they will break the balance. The Reapers have been working to weed out every Grim Angel that exists, until there is only one left standing. And that one is the one that will have to pass the test. If they can live their life enduring the Reaper and Angel blood, then the Angels of Death will gain back their power over the souls and be freed from Earth. If they give in to the insanity of the Reapers, then the Reapers gain control over the souls."

"But I thought Reapers collected the evil souls and Angels collected the innocent."

"That's how it used to work," he says, reaching for me, like he wants to touch me, but withdraws his hand back. "But the rules were broken and a bet was made. Now whoever wins, wins all the souls."

"But if Reapers could collect any soul," I glance at the tombstones, "then it would be bad."

"It would probably be worse than you can even imagine." His voice weighs heavily in the air.

"How many are left?" I ask, gripping the grass, fearing the answer. "How many Grim Angels still roam the Earth?"

"I'm not exactly sure. There used to be a lot, but the Reapers have been singling them out and many have died of old age. The longer they exist, the scarcer the Grim Angels bloodline is." He winces as he adjusts his weight. "And the Reapers must know how few there are, because over the last couple years, they've been really determined to hunt them down, even though they're not supposed to."

"That's what I don't get," I say. "If they're not supposed to, then why doesn't someone stop them?"

"It's up to their leader to punish them. Or we could go into battle," he says. "But Michael, my father and the ruler of the Angels of Death, won't allow us to bend any rules under any circumstances."

"You said your dad was bad. And dead." I frown. "And that you moved from New York to get away from him."

"We did," he says, holding back something with a fire in his eyes. He swiftly changes the subject. "You look beautiful like that." He strokes the tip of my fake wing. "When I saw you, I almost had a heart attack. For a second, I thought somehow... you became one of us."

The wind howls violently, flipping my wings in front me and my body off balance. Asher slides his fingers over my hips and hugs me against his chest. I sense the impending goodbye like a death omen waiting for me at his lips. My black hair flaps in thin wisps around our faces. We stare at each other, hearts beating, eyes connected, never desiring to move. The moment is fleeting, like the sound of a weightless laugh, the flash of a lightning bolt, the last breath of the dying.

"You're leaving me, aren't you," I say quietly.

"I broke the rules and now I can't stay. I wasn't supposed to get involved with you—no one is. It's all supposed to be of your own free will, to prove a point." He kisses my lips and I grip onto his shoulders. "But I couldn't help it. When I saw you that night at the party, standing there by yourself, so sad and lost, I knew I had to get to know you. You were the first Grim Angel I met that's ever done that to me."

I hook my arms around his neck and breathe in his comforting scent. "Why were you there at the party?"

"I was collecting someone's soul for Michael." His hands travel down my spine and reside on my lower back. "But I messed up. I let the person live and took someone else's soul instead."

"You were supposed to take Raven's, weren't you?" I arch into his hands. "You let her live and took Laden's soul instead."

"I could see in your eyes when you were talking about her that night that you need her."

"And you killed Laden, because he was trying to rape her."

316

"I wasn't supposed to take his soul or kill him. I just got carried away," he says, and I'm reminded again of what I read in the book: passionate in battle. "And the Anamotti used it to their advantage. They took his body and made it look like your dad's crime scene to mess with your head."

"And you got in trouble for it," I say. "What are they going to do to you?"

"I'm in trouble for a lot of things." He lures my chest against his and kisses me with such heat my skin nearly ignites. I rake my fingers through his soft hair and his hands grip my thighs, his fingertips pressing into my skin, wanting everything, but knowing he can't take anything.

But I need him, like I need air. "Don't go," I plead. "Please stay with me. You're the only one who's ever made me feel at peace. "

The sky rumbles and his eyes travel upward to the dark clouds. His face is masked with pain as the sky begins to drizzle. His long eyelashes flutter against the raindrops. "I have to. Michael doesn't ever let any angel go unpunished. And besides, you have to do this on your own."

They sky booms again like the snap of an elastic band. I feel it break, my freedom.

He guides my ear toward his mouth and drops his voice to a low whisper. "Find out everything you can about Grim Angels and the Battle of Death. Find out what happens with the last Grim Angel standing… There's a part I can't tell you. And Ember, don't trust anyone. *Ever*." His hand slides down my neck, searing hot against my damp skin. "Shut your eyes."

Reluctantly, I close them and cling to him. I hear his wings snap wide and then a delicate flutter as he flaps them. He kisses my forehead, my cheek, my lips, and then like a feather in the wind, he flies away.

When I open my eyes, I'm alone, kneeling in the mud, rain soaking my hair and clothes. I refuse to move; I'll stay here forever in the cemetery with the only peace I have left.

"Oh my God!" Raven screams and I turn around. She's staggering through the mud toward me. "What the hell happened? How did I get here? Em, I'm… I have no idea what's going on or why I'm in a cemetery." She stops just short of me and glances down at her white dress, tattered and marked red with tonight's torture. Her artificial wings are ripped to pieces and her neck is still bleeding a little.

I pick up a piece of Asher's shirt, stand up, and press it to her neck. "We need to get you to a hospital." I drape her arm around my shoulder and lead her toward the gate.

Her death is back; *standing on the ledge and someone begs her to jump, so she does.* Different, but still painful.

"Em, why are there feathers all over the grass?" she asks. "Was it from your costume?"

I make the decision, the thing my dad tried to engrave in my mind since I was young, and what Asher warned me to do—don't trust anyone. "Yeah, Raven, they are from my costume."

We walk together across the cemetery, yet I'm in this alone. A pawn in a game between the Angels of Death and the Grim Reapers—between good and evil.

But which one am I?

As if giving me an answer, sirens sing through the night and blue and red flashes vibrantly across the dark cemetery. Doors shove open and cops hop out of the vehicles.

"Alright," one of them yells with his gun out in front of him as he glides through the gates. "Put your hands up where we can see them."

I obey, knowing I'm in trouble this time. Mackenzie's body is in a grave and the only proof that I didn't kill her flew away with the wind.

Raven sobs into my shirt and clutches onto me. "I want this to all be over. Please make it stop. It's driving me crazy."

I raise my hands in the air, renouncing. "Don't worry. It's almost over."

A swarm of cops bustle through the gates, spotting their flashlights across the grass and tombs, guns and batons in their hands. The one that shouted at me approaches with caution, step by step, never looking away from us. When he reaches me, I let Raven stand on her own.

"Ember Edwards, I should have known," Officer McKinley's expression instantly turns biased as he remembers the night he picked me up from my house, after my car was found in the lake. "There was an anonymous tip that the body of Mackenzie Baker could be found at the Hollows Grove Cemetery."

With my hands up, I shake my head. "I don't know anything about that."

He spotlights the flashlight in Raven's eyes. "What's she on? And why is there blood on her neck? Were you two doing some kind of ritual out here or something?"

"Like a vampire ritual," I joke unenthusiastically.

He narrows his eyes. "You don't need to get smart. This is Halloween—all the crazies are out tonight."

Raven blinks and shields her face with her hand. "We were taking a shortcut to our houses through the woods and I tripped and cut my neck on a branch."

Internally, I sigh. "That's what we were doing, just barely—heading to go find a phone and call the hospital, because neither of us have our phones."

The cop checks underneath the piece of shirt Raven has pressed to her neck and then pulls a revolted face. "That's going to need a few stitches." He sighs. "Come on, follow me."

As we walk for the gates, the cops search the cemetery, by the trees, behind headstones. A female officer, with her hair braided in the back, wanders toward the hole in the ground where Mackenzie's body lays.

"Hey, I think I got something over here," she shouts, with her gun poised in front of her.

A lanky officer, with a bald head, hurries over to the hole. He beams the light down in it and I wait for him to announce he found the body.

"It's just a hole," he calls out. "It's probably some high school prank or new fad, like that grave that was dug up a few weeks ago."

Cameron.

Officer McKinley stops us and shines the light in our eyes. "You two know anything about this?"

Raven and I shake our heads innocently. "Nope."

He zones in on me. "Are you sure that's true?"

I wonder if he's a real cop, or the same kind as Detective Crammer. "Yep, it's true."

He shakes his head, unbelieving. "Well, I'm still going to have to take you in for some questioning. We have to make sure your story adds up."

We head across the grass toward the gates as the rest of the cops keep searching for Mackenzie's body. Although, I have a feeling her body may be gone forever. But who took it is the mystery.

Cameron? Or Asher?

Raven and I climb into the back of the cop car, each on our separate side, divided by lies, secrets, and distrust. As the policeman drives with his lights flashing, I watch the cemetery disappear from my view, feeling the trail of death follow me.

Epilogue

I wake up to a bright sunny day, shining through my bedroom window. My cheek is resting on an open book, and my sweaty skin sticks to the pages. I stayed up all last night reading through pages about angels and death, searching for answers and a way to bring an Angel of Death back to Earth.

I climb out of bed and get dressed in a ratty T-shirt and some cutoffs. The house is as quiet as a cemetery. My mom is in a drug treatment facility trying to recover from her addiction and when she gets back I have to decide how to ask her about Grandma and the necklace without putting stress on her.

Raven is on vacation with her mom, who got released from the same facility my mom's at the day after the Reapers tried to destroy us. And Ian spends most of his time locked away in the attic. His muse disappeared for a little while, and when I asked Ian about it, he told me it was none of my business. But I heard her—or him—sneak in last night.

My life is lonely, but I prefer it that way for the moment. Being around people hurts just as bad, if not worse, now that I know what I am—know that my insanity can wear on them.

I wander to the computer and click it on. I've been working on trying to track down the author of the book Raven has. His name is August Millard, unless it's his pen name. I found an email address for a writer with the same name, but if it's not the same guy, he'll probably think I'm nuts. Or maybe he'll think I'm crazy either way; perhaps he's a writer of words, not a believer of them.

I check my inbox, but it's empty.

What if I told you I could take away every ounce of pain you have and would ever feel?" I could make all that sadness go away." So I sink into the couch and flip through the channels, searching through the news, looking for headlines about a body being found. But the news isn't on until later, so I shut the TV off. I clean the house to distract myself. I turn up "Holding onto You" by Story of the Year and block everything out. I scrub every room downstairs and then move upstairs.

After I'm finished, I drag the garbage can out to the curb. The sun is setting behind the mountains and the sky is splashed with neon pinks and oranges. Leaves flutter down and, from across the street, Ms. Courtenay is rearranging her sprinklers.

She glances up as she drags the hose across her yard. I politely wave and her gaze darts down at the lawn, like I don't exist. She's afraid of me still, just like everyone else in the town is. Laden and Mackenzie are still considered missing persons, but I know they're dead.

My eyes travel down the street to a two-story house with unmaintained grass and a *For Sale* sign in the yard. I have no idea what happened to Cameron's parents, or if they were really his parents. But every time I look at the house, I feel a pull toward it—toward him. Sometimes, I think about asking him to come back. It's out of sheer insanity—I know that, and that's what helps me keep my lips closed.

However, if I knew how to bring Asher back I would. I tried a few times, murmuring to the wind for him to come to me. "Asher, where are you," I whisper.

The wind is my only answer.

"Hey, stranger." Todd, Raven's brother, walks down the driveway and picks up the newspaper. He's wearing ratty jeans, a black T-shirt with holes in it, and his blue hair is sticking up like he just woke up. "Thinking about buying a house?"

"Huh?" I collect the mail from the mailbox.

He smiles. "I saw you staring at that *For Sale* sign like you were about ready to rip it out of the lawn."

I align the envelopes against the palm of my hand as I walk to the edge of the thin strip of lawn that separates our houses. "Do you know anything about where they went?"

He shakes his head and glances at Cameron's vacant house, with dust in the windows and a dried lawn out in front. "I'm not sure. But it's weird, right? How they moved in and then a few weeks later the house went up for sale."

I shrug. "You know how it is. A lot of people can't take Hollows Grove. Like your sister."

"Yeah, she seems worse about it now with the," he makes a line across his neck, "with the scar on her neck. She's taking that one hard."

"She just needs to give it time to heal," I say, but deep down I know it will never fully heal. After everything settled down, Raven started to remember things she did— horrible things that she won't always share with me.

He wraps the newspaper in his hand and nods his head at a car on the street. "You think they're ever going to give up whatever it is they're looking for?"

I turn around and give the cops in the patrol car a small wave. They pretend not see me and eat their lunch.

"I don't think so," I say.

"But why are they so fixated on our neighborhood?"

326

I glance down at Cameron's house, at a short frail person with a pointy nose, standing near the mailbox. "I'm not sure… maybe they think someone here knows where Mackenzie is."

"Her family seems really determined to find her," he remarks, holding up the newspaper. There is a picture of Mackenzie's face on the front page under the headline: *Have You Seen Our Daughter?*

I watch the man at Cameron's distractedly, trying to figure out where I've seen him before. "Yeah, well maybe they should start looking closer at her family." It clicks. That's Cameron's uncle, Gregory—the one that was digging up the grave for him the night I first saw Cameron.

"Ember," Todd says. "Are you okay?"

I quickly force my eyes off Gregory and change the topic. "So when will Raven be coming back?"

He backs down the driveway toward the front porch. "Didn't she call you?" he asks and I shake my head. "Oh… well, she got back late last night. I thought she went over to your house when she got here."

"No… I haven't seen her since she left..." It's like a jigsaw puzzle coming together: Raven is Ian's muse. And I don't like it because it means Raven was spending a lot of private time with Ian while she was possessed by the Reapers.

"Well, don't take it too personally. She's been acting like a total mental case, mom says, drawing weird pictures of hourglasses and having conversations with herself."

"Is she home right now?" I hurry for their front door.

He shakes his head. "Nah, she went out shopping or something."

Without saying goodbye, I sprint into my house and up to the attic door. I hammer my fist on it, but Ian doesn't answer, so I shove the door open. "Ian, are you in here?"

The lights are on and System of a Down's "Lonely Day" is playing from the surround sound speakers. Canvas and sketches cover the walls, paint dyes the wood floor, and the oval window is covered by a sheet. It smells like sage and something stronger... something I've smelt many times in Ian's studio.

"Dammit." I pick up the butt, squish the tip against the edge of the windowsill, and throw it in a cup of water balanced on a stool. I turn to leave but notice a large canvas in the corner, covered with a black sheet. I tug it off, letting it float to the floor.

It's a picture of Raven. She's lying in the middle of a snowy field, wearing a black cape over her head. Blood drips from her mouth and the corners of her eyes. Grasped in her hand is an empty hourglass and underneath her body is a bright red *X*. On the bottom corner of the drawing, bleeding in red, it says: *Alyssa, please forgive me.*

"What the fuck is this? She's not... No, she couldn't be..." Shaking my head, I walk swiftly to Ian's room and bang on the door. "Ian, open up the door. I know you're in there!" I bang louder. "I can smell the smoke coming through the door."

I jiggle the knob and rattle the door. "Ian, open up the door. You're worrying me."

I run back into my room and grab a bobby pin. I crouch down in front of Ian's door and work the pin until I hear it click. I push the door open and smoke blows in my face. I cough and then let out a frustrated sigh. Ian is sprawled on the bed, in his pajama bottoms and a ratty T-shirt, clutching a photo.

Fanning the smoke from my face, I pad over to his bed. Without even looking, I know it's a photo of Alyssa. Even with his eyes shut, his torture and guilt is written all over his face.

Cameron's words reply in my mind: *What if I told you I could take away every ounce of pain you have and would ever feel?*

I take the photo from his hand and flip it over. *Death made me do it, Alyssa, and I'm sorry. But now I have to move on to the next angel.*

The next angel? He can't be talking about... No, Ian could not have killed her. I struggle not to rip the photo into pieces. Setting it down on the dresser, I give Ian a soft shake. "Wake up, Ian. We need to talk."

But he's passed out, stoned out of his mind. I run back to my room to get my phone. I need to talk to Raven and find out if she's still here, or if the Reapers have gotten a hold of her again. But when I enter my room, something feels off, like the air is unbalanced.

The window is open and a black feather is ruffled on my bed. I pick it up and my gaze lands on the wall, where the ink of a fresh poem is drying.

In separate fields of black feathers, the birds fly.

Four wings, two hearts, but only one soul.

They connect in the middle, but are separated by a thin line of ash.

It's what brings them together, yet rips their feathers apart.

They can never truly be together as light and dark.

Unless one makes the ultimate sacrifice.

Blows out their candle, and joins the other in the dark.

It's the poem that I read on Cameron's wall, but three extra lines have been added.

Or if the other dares to fly across the line and steal the other's light

And force them to cross over the line and join the darkness of life.

I'm not gone, princess. I will come back for you until you give in.

—Cameron

I blink as the ink bleeds down the wall. I back away from it and fall on my bed with the faint echo of Cameron's laugh filling up my unstable head.

It's starting again—the games, the tricks, the battle for me to surrender. And, like everything in life, I'm not sure how it will all end. Or when my sanity will fly away into the sky, just like a raven.

Jessica Sorensen lives with her husband and three kids in the snowy mountains of Wyoming, where she spends most of her time reading, writing, and hanging out with her family.

Other books by Jessica Sorensen:
The Fallen Star (Fallen Star Series, Book 1)
The Underworld (Fallen Star Series, Book 2)
The Vision (Fallen Star Series, Book 3)
The Promise (Fallen Star Series, Book 4)

The Lost Soul (Fallen Souls Series, Book 1)

Darkness Falls (Darkness Falls Series, Book 1)
Darkness Breaks (Darkness Falls Series, Book 2) Available May 23, 2012

Connect with me online:
http://jessicasorensensblog.blogspot.com/
http://www.facebook.com/pages/Jessica-Sorensen/165335743524509
https://twitter.com/#!/jessFallenStar